2
]4

∂
]4

]4

A WOMAN OF IRON

A WOMAN
OF IRON

Sheila Holland

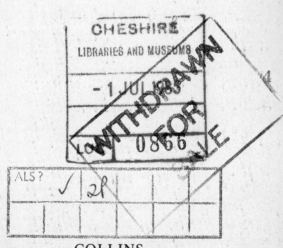

COLLINS
8 Grafton Street London W1

William Collins Sons & Co Ltd.
London · Glasgow · Sydney · Auckland
Toronto · Johannesburg

ISBN 0 00 222914-5

Originally published as THE TILTHAMMER by Sheila Lancaster
by Hodder & Stoughton in 1980

Copyright © 1980 by Sheila Lancaster

Made and printed in Great Britain by
Robert Hartnoll Ltd., Bodmin

One

HANNAH AWOKE, AS she did each morning, to the clack of feet. In summer the dark sky would be curdling slowly with threads of milky white, and the first uncertain chorus of the birds would begin the clearing light, their voices tremulous, as though every morning began for them with the fear that the sun would never rise. In winter, the pitch dark canopy lay everywhere upon the ironworks; the birds slept on their perches in the surrounding trees and only woke when the dawn shift arrived and broke the midnight spell with orange flares of fire and tramping feet. This morning when she opened her eyes, yawning reluctantly, a white mist of late spring crept shiveringly over the narrow sill into the low-roofed room in which the female servants slept.

Disentangling herself from the bedlinen she crept to the window and stared down through the narrow dormer at the men as they tramped past. Most of them looked half asleep, their shoulders drooping with weariness. Work began at five in summer, at six in winter. Today they counted it summer, since the light made it just possible to see. Before the sun was up the furnace would be fully charged and working full blast, the water-wheel turning to blow air blasts through the fire, the white-hot stream of molten iron pouring forth into the sanded rows of moulds which the men called the pigs, since they looked for all the world like a row of piglets waiting for swill.

She glanced across the mud yard at the brick-cased buildings of the works, their shape dark against the lightening sky, narrowing as they rose from their bulky foundations. Shield Mill was thirty years old. The date of its building had been cut into one stone lintel above the furnace house. It had replaced the old casting-works, run by the present ironmaster's father.

The Shields had made iron for generations. The earliest of them had run a bloomery, with hand-driven bellows, casting small amounts of iron which only sufficed to keep himself and his family. Now the master of Shield Mill employed a work force of thirty men and their children, had built them houses and paid for their children to attend a school for two years before they commenced work.

Some of the dark figures passing below were the boys in their rent shirts and grimy breeches, their tousled heads roughly dampened with cold water to wake them. Watching them, Hannah thought of her mistress, in her clean, lavender-scented nightgown, sleeping the sleep of the just in fresh linen sheets on a feather mattress, and her teeth came together with a snap.

In church on Sundays she stared at the careful division of the pews; the richly decorous clothing of the gentry, and the pathetic attempts by the poor to disguise their poverty – and she felt the stirring of a doubt which she would never speak aloud. A merciful Deity who looked down in satisfaction upon such inequalities seemed to her beyond belief.

Her eye was suddenly caught and held by a man who walked alone, his shoulders back, his black head held erect, as if he studied the slowly lightening sky. He strode out, his powerful muscled body passing slower men without effort. They ducked their heads as he passed, mumbling a greeting deferentially.

"Morning, Master Colby," she heard, and saw him turn his head and nod in curt recognition.

"Misty morning . . ."

"It'll clear."

He glanced up as if commanding the sky to obey and his eye met her own.

He walks as if he owned the earth, she thought angrily. How could Henry Shield be so blind? In the four years he had been working there, Joss Colby had acquired more and more power; prising the old manager, Mr. Lynn, from his position

6

within two years, taking his place, as cool as a cucumber, and proving so invaluable to the ironmaster that he was now openly his right-hand man.

Joss Colby stared at her as he walked past and she stared back defiantly, unconscious for the moment of her tumbled brown hair, bare shoulders and the rough blue petticoat she wore.

She had overheard the ironmaster talking to his wife a week ago. "He's clever, shrewd and knows the trade backwards. I want to keep him if I can. He gets more work out of the men than old Lynn did. He's worth twice what I pay him, and he works with a will."

One day, Hannah thought grimly, Henry Shield will learn a lesson from Joss Colby that he will never forget. He is a cuckoo in the nest. He will devour everything.

As Joss disappeared she turned away and splashed her sleep-flushed face with cold water, dried it roughly and dressed in her short-sleeved grey cotton gown. Dragging a comb through her hair she tucked the strands under her white cap, squared her shoulders to face the new day and bent over the bed to wake the other sleepers.

It was her first task of the day.

"Is it fine?" asked Nancy, sitting up, her eyes stuck with sleep, her bright yellow hair in disarray.

"Misty."

Nancy groaned and would have turned over to sleep again, but Mrs. Poley clicked her tongue at her. "Get up, do, Nancy girl . . ."

The attic was divided by a short landing. The men slept on the right. The women on the left. Hannah banged on the men's door with a clenched fist and heard them stir, grumbling. It was always hard to get up in cold weather.

Shield House was divided down the centre – the front half inhabited by the family, the back by the servants. While the front stairs were open and spacious, with graceful, curved banisters of highly polished oak, the stair treads glossed enough to see one's face in them, the back stairs were steep and narrow, closed in with wood so that the family should neither see nor hear the servants as they went up and down, and it was easy to trip on the steep flight in the half-light of dawn or twilight.

The servants were not allowed to use the front stairs unless they were ordered to do so by the mistress. It was cause for punishment merely to be seen on them unless excused.

Pausing on the landing halfway down, Hannah listened to the tranquil silence which lay over the front of the house. Only the slow heartbeat of the clock in the hall broke that silence, the walnut long cased clock which had been made in Birmingham on the occasion of Master Shield's marriage, the swing of its pendulum sonorous. The family were all fast asleep and would remain so for hours while the servants worked downstairs.

She trod down the second flight of stairs to the kitchen, lifted the latch quietly and went into the room to make up the fire. By the time the others straggled down the kettle on the iron chain over the fire was singing busily. Mrs. Poley took the key which hung around her plump waist and unlocked the tea caddy which stood on the shelf above the hearth. She spooned dark leaves into a fat-bellied pot while Hannah stirred the pot of oatmeal which made such a satisfying start to the day.

Seated around the table the servants muttered grace then ate with bent heads, their spoons scraping their bowls. Abel had his face in his bowl, scooping up the meal greedily, with the childish satisfaction of a two-year-old. His mother sighed, watching him.

Mrs. Poley was a broad, plump woman of fifty whose husband had died in an accident at the works sixteen years ago. Her hair had turned snow white that day. She had run to the works and seen her husband's twisted, torn body before the men could stop her. The shock of it had brought on the birth of her child two months early. It had not breathed when it was first born. The midwife had slapped it into life, but as he grew Abel proved to be a simpleton. He was slow-witted, worked in fits and starts, cleaning the boots, fetching and carrying, his bodily strength far outweighing his mind.

Hannah found it both pathetic and displeasing to look at him. The coarse, heavy outlines of his face were inhabited by a child's mind. He laughed for no reason, often stood and stared in mindless vacuity, yet he was kind and gentle, loving animals, eager to please the adults around him whom he feared. Joe, the gardener, had a heavy hand and used it when Abel irritated him. He sat beside the boy, a stooped man of fifty with dull eyes who spent his drinking hours at the Black Bull in the village and seemed half alive outside the alehouse.

There were two other maids besides Hannah. Nancy was seventeen, with a rounded body already formed in womanhood and shallow blue eyes which could be cheerful or spiteful according to her mood. Born to one of the ironworkers, Nancy had been a woman since she was thirteen. She thought and talked of men with avid excitement whenever Mrs. Poley was not in earshot. Peg was the eldest of the girls – a dissenter, she was forced to attend the village church by their mistress, but she read the Bible each night before she went to bed. Her dark, sober eyes rarely smiled. She was neat and clean and calm. She spoke of hellfire with the only sign of enthusiasm she ever betrayed. In her twenties, Peg had no mind to marry. When Nancy tried to whisper her knowing little jokes about men to Peg she got short shrift.

The meal over, they all rose. Nancy cleared the table. Hannah was handed the large wooden yoke and swinging buckets, Mrs. Poley sighing as she nodded to her. Nancy giggled at the sight, and the cook turned her face towards her.

"Hush, you girl," she said sternly. "Get on with your work. When you've washed the crocks, do the parlour. I want to see my face in the grate, mind . . ."

Her shoulders bent, Hannah stepped out through the back door into the grey dawn. The empty buckets swung lightly on their chains. The yoke weighed down her bones. She walked round the side of the house to where the well stood, unhitched the yoke and lowered the bucket into the water, her nostrils inhaling the damp odour of the ferns which sprouted from the green-encrusted sides of the well. The brick walls were slimed with moss. Once she had drawn up a toad in the bucket and watched with a shudder as it sprang away, the strong back legs crooked for motion.

The ironworks stood in the flat, green countryside a few miles from Birmingham, surrounded on one side by fields and on the other by thinning woods which had once, according to Mrs. Poley, been dense and thickly set with oak and elm and hazel. The charcoal-burners had decimated the trees. Their little hovels were set in among the timber, damp, dripping little caves beneath the spreading boughs, and the evidence of their presence was always visible, the wreaths of smoke curling up from among the canopied branches. Hannah had never set eyes upon the great house in which the squire lived, a good two miles away, but she had heard talk of it and was fascinated by the gossip of the elegance and wealth of the Arandall family who owned the best part of the land for miles. Henry Shield cursed them whenever he spoke their name. The price they demanded for their charcoal was, he said, excessive. He could remember, not so long ago, when it had been half what it was now, yet the charcoal-burners got little more for it from the landowner than they had in earlier times. "It all goes into the Arandall pockets, every last groat, feeds their fat mares and puts silk on their backs. Bloodsuckers! They know they have us by the throat."

Hannah bent to peer down the well. "Got you!" Two hands seized her by the waist, bending her backward. She gave a cry of alarm, then twisted to see her assailant, laughing as she recognised him.

"Jabey, you fool!"

Jabey Stock grinned at her. They had known each other all their lives, born in adjacent cottages. A few years older, he had been her protector against occasional spite from other children. In torn shirt and ragged breeches, his body showed through the rents in his clothes, his skin grimed with dust and dirt which would in time become imprinted as it had with the older men. The skin of old ironworkers had a rusty tinge from years of working in dirt. Jabey's rough mop of carroty hair shone in the sudden shaft of the rising sun. His kind eyes were brown, doglike, filled with warmth. He would never be a handsome man but he had character in his face, and his body was sturdy with youth and health.

She twisted herself in his grip, her body agile, and he pulled her upward until she sat upright again, settling her dislodged cap. "I might have lost my cap down the well," she scolded. "Then I should have got a whipping."

He looked down at the yoke resting against the brickwork. "Why are you carrying t'water?" he asked, frowning. "Abe's work, that is, not a girl's . . ."

"The mistress ordered it," she said expressionlessly. "I broke a glass when I served the master wine. I must pay for it and carry the water for a week. It served instead of a whipping." She would rather have had a whipping. Mrs. Poley never laid it on hard, and it was over soon enough. The full buckets were heavy as she carried them back to the house and her shoulders ached all day after it.

He gave her a quick look, then away. "It isn't right," he said. "Master shouldn't allow it."

"A quiet life is all he wants," she said scornfully.

"You're thinner than ever," Jabey said, his jaw obstinate. "The bitch drives you hard."

"She believes in the Bible," Hannah said drily.

Jabey stared.

"The sins of the fathers are to be visited on the children," Hannah told him with a little smile.

He gave a muffled grunt of laughter. Their eyes met and her eyes glinted vividly, turning bright green, giving her face a beauty she herself had never seen.

He helped her draw up the water. "Let me carry it," he urged, but she shook her head.

"If the mistress saw you, she'd have me beaten."

Jabey gritted his teeth but said nothing. Water flying from the full buckets, she walked heavily back to the house, her skirts getting splashed, dark marks laid upon the dust. Some of the yard had been cobbled for heavier wear, the wagons in winter had turned the place into a morass of mud and ruts deep enough to drown a child in heavy rain.

The house faced south across the green fields towards

Birmingham, its back towards the ironworks, its front door opening into a neat garden of lawns, hedges, herb and vegetable patches set about with fruit trees. Each square inch was expected to bear fruit, to function and provide food. Joe grew a few sweet william, carnations, roses, but he despised them and only did so at the command of Mistress Shield.

A spiral of blue smoke rose from the chimneys into the fast-brightening sky. The sun glinted on tiles and windows. The odour of simmering lamb broth came to their nostrils. Heavily eked out with lentils and barley the bones of a lamb carcase had been used these three days to provide broth. The fat skimmed carefully each morning, it was reheated with fresh vegetables to fill their stomachs at noon. Mrs. Poley was an excellent manager and a good cook. The servants might work hard but they ate well.

The back door opened as they arrived. The ironmaster came out, eying them. A man of forty, squat, broad, his hair thinning above his stubbled face, Henry Shield's eyes, the same clear hazel as Hannah's, held grim irritation.

"Get back to your work, Stock," he grunted, a thumb brought through his leather belt. "I don't pay you to flitter around my yards."

Jabey touched his forelock, mumbling, and ran off, grateful not to be fined. There were fines for everything – absence, lateness, idling. The men veered between gloomy acceptance of them and a stubborn argument with the works' clerk each payday.

Hannah waited for Master Shield to move out of her way. He stared at her bent head, at the heavy buckets dragging down her shoulders.

"Why are you carrying the water? That's Abel's job."

She lifted her head and the sunlight gleamed on the rich red-brown hair showing beneath her cap. A glint of cold rebellion shot at him from the hazel eyes. "Mistress ordered it," she reminded flatly.

"God damn it, I'd forgot." His heavy face struggled with anger and shame, red colour in his cheeks. Hannah watched, used to seeing that look on his face. His brother had been her father, although the relationship was never openly admitted. Her mother, Bess Noble, had been the daughter of the village schoolmaster. Growing up into a beautiful, sensual girl Bess had been seduced by Francis Shield when she was eighteen. Francis had been generous to her and to his child but his death of a fever had shattered their lives. "What will become of us?" Bess had wailed to Henry Shield.

Six months later, she had become Henry's mistress, but although the affair had been a common-sense solution, it had also been the natural mating of one animal with another; warm-blooded, spontaneous, happy. For years they were deeply contented with each other.

Mary Shield, Henry's wife, came to hate Bess Noble with a chill and bitter feeling which Hannah suspected to have been the only real feeling of her life. Mary was cold by nature, her eyes constantly discontented, her original prettiness worn down by acidity. She showed little affection even for her own child, Caroline.

Bess Noble died when Hannah was twelve. Mary Shield came without warning to the house and took the child away with her. Hannah was put to work in the kitchen. It was not long before she understood that her uncle's wife had brought her there to revenge herself upon Bess Noble's child.

Hannah was given all the most tedious, back-breaking jobs to do. She scrubbed the floors, sanded them, polished pewter, cleaned grates, made fires. Rising with eyes gummed together from lack of sleep, she fell into bed late at night almost too exhausted to sleep. If she met the mistress as she worked she was given a look which conveyed hatred too deep for words. She was whipped for every small offence and often for none at all.

Things had grown easier as time went by since even Mrs. Shield's hatred was not impervious to time. The beatings diminished and if Hannah kept out of her way, Mrs. Shield did not seek her out, but if the girl was unfortunate enough to catch her eye, Mrs. Shield looked at her in that cold hatred which could make Hannah's hair rise on the back of her neck.

Henry Shield had stood by and let all this happen. After

Bess's death he had been too unhappy to take note of what his wife was doing, and when he did realise Hannah's position, he backed away from open conflict with his wife, preferring to pretend ignorance.

His eyes slid away from hers now. He muttered something under his breath and strode away while she looked after him with contempt. He was too frightened of his wife's temper to interfere. Turning, she moved slowly into the house.

She worked in the kitchen later that morning helping Mrs. Poley with the preparation of the noon meal, then flew to the dining room to lay the table, deftly placing cutlery and glass, so busy that she walked straight into Joss Colby before she realised he had come into the room.

Gasping, she looked up. His hands had grasped her shoulders and he looked down at her, his eyes a grey so pale as to be silver in some lights, glinting like the moon on hidden water.

He raised his thin brows, mockery in his face, as it often was when he looked at her. "Where's Miss Caroline?"

"Upstairs," she said, not muting the flat tone of her voice, not bothering to disguise her dislike and distrust of him. She never had and they were both aware of it.

"Upstairs, *sir*," said Joss softly.

She didn't answer, her face sharp with rebellion.

"Sir," he repeated, his hands tightening on her shoulders, shaking her slightly, making her aware of his enormous physical strength. His body had a compact power, forceful, clenched to show mastery. Of a poor background he revealed by every movement, every look of those eyes, his fierce determination.

His black hair was cut to his coat collar, the thick strands neatly brushed back into a queue, but with such vitality that she felt if she touched one hair she would feel as though lightning had streaked along her nerves. He wore plain, simply cut clothes. His shirts were always spotlessly clean. When he worked in the forge he took them off and like the men worked bare-chested. She looked at the broad shoulders, deep chest and strong, muscular thighs, and her hazel eyes turned a bright green with hatred.

14

She had felt like this towards Joss Colby since the first day she set eyes on him.

"Sir is for gentlemen," she said now, knowing what she risked, daring him to repeat her words to Mrs. Shield.

His jawline hardened. A strange, bright look came into the silvery eyes. She was defying him openly on ground they both knew he would die to defend. Joss was fiercely aware of his origins, determined to rise above them. He had a cold brain behind that handsome face. It gave him satisfaction to command respect from the servants in the Shield household.

There had been hidden warfare between him and Hannah for a long time. Although her uncle was too much the coward to protect her from his wife, she remembered his kindness to her as a small girl, she remembered his love for her mother, and she cared that nothing should hurt him. Joss Colby threatened Henry Shield, whether the ironmaster recognised it or not.

"I could have you whipped for that," Joss said between his teeth. His eyes narrowed on her vivid, defiant face. "Watch your tongue, you little slut, or I'll make you sorry."

Hannah's eyes flashed. Joss watched the brilliant colour come into her face as she grew angrier. Her hair had the polished sheen of mahogany, a brown deeply gleaming to a dark red in sunlight. She would never be described as pretty. Her features had too much strength for that, her bones shaping her facial structure powerfully; her nose finely cut and strong, her cheeks tilted, her jawline firm and matching the wide, high forehead with its promise of intelligence. Her mouth was far too wide, the upper lip finely shaped, the lower full and passionate to the point of sensuality. It was a face which would grow into a sort of beauty as she aged but now it was still the face of a very young woman not yet fully formed in maturity; a girl of nineteen.

Joss Colby seemed to find it fascinating to watch. He smiled as she glared up at him.

"Sir," he prompted again, as though deliberately prolonging the struggle between them.

There was a rustle of skirts on the stairs, the sound of

15

Caroline's flute-like, excited voice. Joss dropped his hands from Hannah's shoulders and moved away from her quickly. She turned and got on with her work. She should have finished it long ago. Mrs. Shield would hate to see her in the room when she came into it.

Caroline came into the room with her mother, gave a soft cry of pleasure at the sight of Joss. "Oh, Joss! I had forgot you were to dine with us."

"Forgot?" he asked, bending to kiss her hands, his strong body graceful as he bowed his back. "For shame! I'm cut to the quick."

"Oh," Caroline said, appalled, taking him seriously. "I am sorry, Joss."

Mrs. Shield was staring past them at Hannah, her eyes sharp as she watched the slim, high-breasted figure in the grey cotton dress. Hannah trod quickly, hoping to avoid the usual confrontation, her eyes averted.

"Why have you not finished this before?" Mrs. Shield's voice was icy.

Hannah curtsied, head lowered. "Beg pardon, Ma'am."

Her voice was humble, her manner decorous. Constant whipping had taught her to make it so and even the derisive gleam of Joss Colby's eyes as he watched could not force her to risk a whipping by any overt insolence to her mistress. Even more than she disliked the pain of those whippings, Hannah detested the humiliation of being forced to bear them.

"Hurry yourself, you lazy slut!"

Hannah hurried, but as she did she met those silvery eyes and burned with rage at seeing the deliberate enjoyment with which he watched her. He liked seeing her forced to cringe before Mrs. Shield and he meant her to know it.

Joss Colby knew all there was to know of her position in this house. Every tiny piece of gossip came to his ears and he sifted it through the fine mesh of that cold brain, weighing it for use. He knew exactly what she had risked when she let herself speak to him with such open hostility and she knew that he meant to leave her in suspense about what he would do, how he would react.

Why in God's name had she gone out of her way to defy him? She scurried from the dining room like a white mouse and started to work in the over-heated kitchen, sweating freely, her sleeves rolled to her shoulders, her bodice limply sticking to her body.

Why am I such a fool? she asked herself. Haven't I learnt yet to hold my tongue? If he repeated her insolence to Mrs. Shield she would receive a savage punishment – and Joss knew it.

It would give him great satisfaction to punish her for the way she had spoken to him. At times she thought that she, of all the people at Shield Mill, knew Joss Colby as he truly was – the rest saw only a charming, darkly handsome figure with a smile which could charm the birds from the trees.

It was a piece of mummery which he knew very well how to present. Once as a child Bess and Henry Shield had taken Hannah to see a conjurer in Birmingham. She had stared in dazzled delight as the man threw brightly coloured balls into the air, keeping them moving there until one by one they vanished and she never saw where they went. Joss had that ability to charm and deceive.

He had never bothered to pull that mask over his face for her. Her place in the household made her too insignificant for him to trouble, she supposed, although she had seen him turn his charming smile on Nancy and even on poor, stuttering Abel. To her, however, from the first day they met he had shown brutal harshness.

She could remember as clearly as if it were yesterday her first sight of him.

She had been on her knees, scrubbing the hall floor, her back and head aching. She had been beaten twice already that day. Hearing footsteps she had crouched, fearing another whipping, but he had walked past her, ignoring her.

A young man in a clean white shirt of poor cloth, and leather breeches, his lean waist pulled in by a leather belt, he had taken no note of her at all. She sensed that she was invisible to him, a poor slut in a sacking apron, scrubbing on her knees, a matter of indifference.

She had watched him as he glanced in at the parlour, the sunlight on his thick black hair, his eyes roving over the high-polished furniture, the blue Dutch china and leather-bound books, the gloss of prosperity making the room bright. Joss had stuck his thumbs through his belt, his head cocked to one side, whistling under his breath.

She had seen his mouth curl sardonically, the grey eyes harden, and suddenly as if his head were made of transparent crystal she had read his thoughts so clearly she had almost cried out. Joss had been looking into a future invisible to everyone but himself. There had been chill, ruthless certainty in that face. Coolly confident, he had looked round the room and possessed it.

It had not struck her then how strange it was that she should have been able to read his mind. Later she had decided that he had not put up his usual guard, thinking of himself alone, despising her too much to hide his thoughts. His true self had shown in his face until Henry Shield came hurrying up and Joss turned, pulling charm over that acquisitive face.

She had watched him from a distance and seen his plans solidify. He was clever, he worked hard, he had sufficient education to learn from books what he could not learn by experience. The old manager had been slack and inefficient. Once Joss had ousted him, he took his place and Henry Shield began to leave the daily running of the mill to Joss.

Their production had increased in leaps and bounds since Joss took over. He cut corners ruthlessly, seeing flaws and improving on them, his mind quick and agile. He drove hard bargains with their customers and he got the best out of their workmen. They feared him, less for his enormous physical strength, as for his cold eyes and icy tongue. Joss whipped them to work with that tongue and if one of them dared to step out of line, he had that powerful body to contend with, since Joss would take off his shirt and beat to a pulp any man who challenged him.

When Caroline returned from her school Hannah saw Joss move in on her like a snake on a trapped bird, the silvery eyes fixing the girl until she quivered helplessly, intoxicated by his

18

smile into desiring the fate he intended for her. Hannah had seen the first glimmering of Joss's intention as Caroline stepped down from the cart which had brought her home.

Caroline had tossed her bright curls and Joss's eyes had narrowed in chill inspection. She had looked at him, wide-eyed, as he bowed to her. Henry Shield had looked on complacently, seeming oblivious to the ambitions of his young manager. He was prepared to let his daughter wed Joss since he wanted to bind the young man to him but Hannah suspected that once Joss was Caroline's husband he would take the mill into his own hands completely and Henry Shield would be thrown to one side like useless dross. Was her uncle blind not to see the extent of Joss's ambition?

Hannah carried the tureen carefully into the dining room, her eyes lowered. Peg moved like a well-trained ghost behind the chairs, her hands deft and accustomed, her face blank. Henry Shield leaned over to Joss, thumping his hand flat on the table, making the glasses leap and ring.

"Charcoal is cheap. We know it works. This new coal-fired process is uncertain."

"It's been used for years," Joss said coolly, undeterred by his master's flushed irritation. "They've been using it for glass and other metals. It's readily at hand and cheap. We're running out of forests, Master. Coal's the coming fuel. Charcoal has priced itself out of our reach."

"We've enough customers," Henry Shield muttered, shaking his head. "We make a good-enough profit."

"We have more customers than we can make iron," Joss said. "Why waste chances? We should expand. Make more iron. Make it cheaper. That is what using coke would mean."

"The mill is big enough for me," Henry Shield snapped.

But not for Joss, Hannah thought, glancing at him shrewdly. He turned his dark head and the silvery eyes met her own. They stared at each other, then he turned back to Henry Shield and said in a sharp voice, "If we do not, others will. There is room for us to expand now. We should take it. Either we grow or we diminish. Customers who have to wait will go elsewhere, and each one we lose now means a drop in

19

future income. Coke is being used more and more widely, and by our rivals. We must not be left behind."

"Damn you, boy, don't thrust your opinions down my throat," Henry Shield said with a sour look. "I'm still master of this place, remember."

Hannah glanced at them through her long lashes as she and Peg quietly moved around the table, serving broth. Joss leaned back in his chair, listening to Henry Shield's angry retort, but he was watching her as she approached, and something in his eyes made her tense.

She leant forward to ladle some broth into his bowl while he watched her. Suddenly his glass was swept off the table and splintered into pieces on the floor between his feet.

She stared back in horror, her hands shaking as she gripped the tureen.

"Clumsy little fool," Joss said in pretended rage, standing. "Look what you have done!"

Whiteness flowed up her face as she looked at Mrs. Shield. The older woman leapt to her feet, her lips crooked with suppressed spite. "She has done it again! She is obstinate in her wickedness. Twice in a week! Master Shield, this must be deliberate. Glass is not cheap. Can we afford to have it smashed daily? She must be whipped, whipped soundly."

Henry Shield sighed and muttered glumly. "Get out, girl."

Hannah fled, tears pricking her eyes. Behind her she heard Joss say softly, "Mrs. Poley will lay on gently, Master. She never whips the girl hard."

He had spoken deliberately for Mrs. Shield's ears and the woman spat out angrily as she listened.

"Joss, you shall whip her. She must be taught a lesson and you are right, Mrs. Poley is over gentle with the slut."

Henry Shield slumped over his broth. "Let us finish our meal, for God's sake. It was an accident."

Hannah closed the door into the kitchen shivering. When Peg came into the room a moment later she looked gravely at her. "Hannah, that was clumsy of you! When will you learn?"

"What? What?" Nancy burst out, dying of curiosity.

"Get on with your work," Mrs. Poley snapped, looking at Hannah with dismay. "What's afoot?"

Peg told her and the cook groaned. "Oh, Hannah . . . twice in a week? Why d'you give her chances to have you whipped?"

Hannah saw no point in reply. They would not believe that Joss Colby had done it deliberately. He fooled them as much as he fooled everyone else.

When the meal was ended Hannah stood at bay in the kitchen, feeling like a hunted animal, a cold fear making her skin clammy. Joss came into the room, with his cool, steady tread, and although she did not look up she knew when he entered. Mrs. Shield was at his heels. She uttered with a bite, "Give Mr. Colby the cane, Mrs. Poley."

The cook looked at him in surprise, frowned, but reluctantly gave him the cane. Hannah stood unmoving, staring at the floor.

The other servants clustered in a little knot, watching.

Joss watched her, flexing the cane in his long hands. She knew that he was waiting for her to look at him and would not lift her head.

"Six strokes," Mrs. Shield said and a little gasp came from the servants.

Joss strode over to her, put a hand under her chin and forced her head up roughly. The hazel eyes were a bright fierce green. His features were set, but his eyes leapt as though he were excited, and she saw a line of faint, glistening perspiration along his upper lip.

"Beg my pardon, Hannah, and I am sure Mrs. Shield will be content with a humble, contrite apology," he said in tones so gentle, so soft that the servants all sighed, smiling.

Only Hannah could see his eyes and she stared into them, her face defiant.

"It does you credit, Joss," Mrs. Shield said. "But she must be whipped! And mind, make her smart! I've no doubt she broke the glass deliberately."

Joss smiled down into Hannah's eyes, the mocking expression invisible to those behind them. Aloud he sighed. "Then I see I must do as you bid, Mrs. Shield," he said.

Hypocrite, liar, she thought and her eyes spoke to him, the sweep of her long lashes filled with contempt.

He spun her round, pushing her against the wall, his hands cruel on her shoulders. "Open your dress," he said.

She bent her head, lifting her hands slowly, and he waited, the cane tapping on his palm the only sound she could hear. The servants had frozen in a tableau. Mrs. Shield was breathing thickly, her hands clenched at her sides.

When Hannah's hands dropped to her side, Joss leaned forward and wrenched the gown down over her shoulders, laying her slender back bare, the pale skin glimmering in the afternoon sunlight.

She heard Joss breathing behind her and tensed herself for the blow. It came and despite her fortitude she winced as it struck her body. She bit her lips until blood sprang out on them, clenching herself to withstand the pain. She was held erect only by pride. She thought of how she hated him, how she would love someone to whip him as he was whipping her.

He took his time, pausing between each blow, as if waiting for some sign from her. She could not see his face but she was aware of his emotions. He was waiting for her to collapse but she would not break under the blows.

Henry Shield roared suddenly, "God in Heaven, stop it! Is a twopenny glass worth this?" His heavy face was white with self-contempt, his eyes fierce.

His wife turned on him. "The little slut must be punished. Or do you want her to be a whore like her mother?"

Henry Shield's face flushed darkly. He opened his mouth to spit back rage then, remembering the listening servants, grasped his wife's arm between angry fingers and dragged her from the room.

Hannah pulled her gown up around her shoulders and began to move. She saw everything through a red mist. Moving like an old woman she felt her way along the wall. Joss Colby stood still, watching her, the cane held in one hand.

When she fell forward into the red mist he reached her before any of the servants had moved. Lifting her body into his arms, he carried her out of the kitchen into the wellyard. Hannah came out of her faint when ice-cold water stung on the stripes across her shoulders. She gave a low moan and looked into his face.

She was half-lying across his lap while he sat on the wall. He held her with one arm and stared at her, the sweat still glistening on lip and forehead, his mouth implacable.

"You stupid little bitch," he said through his teeth. "Why wait so long before you gave in? Why play the heroine for me? All you had to do was beg my pardon."

"I'd die before I begged at your hands," she whispered in bitter, thready defiance.

The cruelty deepened in his face. "Make me angry with you, Hannah, and I'll break you."

"You may try," she said, somehow finding the strength to smile contemptuously.

There was a strange silence while they stared at each other, their faces close together.

"Your back is covered in weals," he said, laying a hand on her.

She closed her eyes to hide the pain that brief touch caused. Her head swam. She clutched at his chest to steady herself, her fingers curled in his shirt.

Abruptly he pulled her gown lower. She tried to pull it up again and he said, "Be still!" through his teeth.

His eyes moved over the high, rounded breasts and Hannah's face grew hot, yet there was no insolent familiarity in his face, only the coolly curious look of one who is discovering unknown territory and mentally recording what he sees.

"How much did I hurt you?" he asked, idly touching one of her breasts with a cool fingertip which flicked across the small, pink nipple and made her shudder. His hand fell away. He shot her a narrowed look.

"Do you care? You hurt me because you wanted to! You enjoyed it."

"Did you, Hannah?" he asked, watching her fixedly, a bead of perspiration rolling down his temple.

"I'm a bastard by birth, Joss Colby. You're one from

23

choice." Her angry face blazed in a transient beauty and he watched it with an almost satisfied expression.

"You'll call me sir in future, though, Hannah. You'll call me sir now." He bent a smile on her, his face sardonic.

"You could beat me until your arm dropped off – I'd never call you sir."

She pushed his hands away, jerking up her bodice, pulling herself out of his grasp before she got down from the well and walked away, holding herself stiffly against the pain from her striped back. Joss Colby watched her without moving, a curious smile on his face.

Two

SUMMER SWEPT LIKE a flooding tide over the green land which islanded the smoke and grime of the ironworks. Those who lived and worked among that foul air could not be blind or indifferent to the beauty which nature, with renewing freshness revived in the flat fields and woods. On Sundays when they walked to church, Hannah could almost feel the beating of the sap in the trees which lined their route, and her fingers, in winter so sore with chilblains and rough skin, tingled with new life.

They were able to discard their thick winter clothing, to go without shawls and mittens, walking light and free in the sunlit lanes.

In the meadows the cows moved with their stolid tread among pollen-heavy grasses, turning the earth into baked mud, criss-crossed with cloven marks. Blue-black flies rose in buzzing hordes where they clustered at gate and stream. The cherry orchard at the crossroads by the church began to drop its bridal white in browning drifts of snow, the delicate petals freckled like old paper.

The stark ditches which, in winter were full of withered sedge, drowned in a burgeoning of new green and spawned frogs in great numbers. The skeletal trees which had etched the horizon so short a time ago with black, curving branches, began once more to give the landscape a wild flourish, their leaves so plentiful and bright that Hannah looked at them with delight, feeling as though they were a triumphal fanfare for life itself.

Her own misery lightened with the season. It was hard to be

unhappy when the sun shone and the earth offered such beauty to the eye.

They went to church in procession, like charity children, walking two abreast, their demeanour decorous, only daring to whisper to one another for fear the mistress heard them as she walked at the head of their train.

Peg, whose religious dissent was profound, dared not refuse to attend the service for fear of losing her place, but her lowered eyes and unsmiling mouth were grim.

Birmingham had been on the parliament side in the unforgotten civil war. The smiths had beaten out many swords for the parliamentary army, refusing stubbornly to do a like service for the king, so that eventually Prince Rupert had come down on them like an avenging angel to punish them for their insolent refusal. Birmingham had burned. Many of the smiths had been whipped or killed. The army had deliberately sought out those most intransigent of swordsmiths, destroying their houses and their workshops, but if they had imagined that such treatment would alter the attitudes of those who were left, they were much mistaken.

Birmingham smouldered darkly in the ashes and the voice of dissent which had been loud there before, grew stronger than ever. The freedom which the lack of guilds had bestowed on them had branched out in all directions, like a root snaking underground in unimpeded haste. Little chapels sprang like wayside weeds. Men sought God in other ways than that established by law and custom. The 'glorious revolution' of 1688, only a lifetime away to Hannah, had been greeted with joy by the strongly protestant men of Birmingham. The civil freedoms which the lack of a charter had encouraged were breeding grounds for a religious freedom of conscience.

Peg was a typical product of her time and place. Hannah had never entered into discussion of religion with her. She knew that Peg's simple, stark religion, based as it was on the revealed word of God in the Bible, was meaningless to her. She used her eyes, her ears, her brain and she saw the layered structure of society around her, questioning it with every beat of her heart.

Why were some men born in hovels to spend a life in toil for bread, while others were born in the lap of luxury? It seemed grossly unjust to her, and if God existed, could he approve such an injustice? If he did, why then, he was no God she was willing to worship. If he did not, why did he permit such inequalities?

On Sundays, therefore, she sat in her pew and let the service wash over her head. It gave her, at least, a time of quiet reflection when no bullying hand or voice nudged at her back. Her mind was more intent on the faces of her fellow worshippers than on the words the minister intoned so nasally. She sat and stared at him as he leant on the pulpit, his florid face unctuous. In some lights he was a good man. The Reverend Thomas Martial, aged forty, his bones well-pouched in solid flesh, his eyes like gooseberries, their pale green sheen buried in fat white lids. He had a wife whose round, dumpling face and cheerful manner was popular in the parish, and five children who wore stout shoes and pretty clothes and had their lessons from their papa. Hannah had heard much good of him. He visited the sick and poor, which was more than some of his cloth did, he took broth and comforts to widows and the aged. He had never been known to tamper with any of his female flock. No words of scandal had ever touched his name. Yes, she thought. In some ways he was what the world called a good man. But his table was as richly laid as that of the squire himself, he rode to hounds at every opportunity, he drank rich red port after dinner and stumbled as he went to bed. And listening to his smooth, bland words was like having gruel poured over one's head. He raised no spirit of comfort or hope in those who listened. He might as well have recited his tables.

If that was the best of God's servants, what manner of god was he?

Her eye wandered to where Joss Colby sat nearby, his straight lean back in best woollen cloth, close-woven, stout, the colour of pewter. Above his crisp white shirt his black head was neatly combed into a queue tied with a black satin bow. Unlike the Arandalls, who wore powdered wigs, the lower classes wore their own hair, bearing with the threat of lice which the gentry dreaded so much that they shaved their heads to avoid them. Joss glanced up and their eyes met briefly. He gave her a strange little smile and looked away again.

Her eyes moved to the high-sided pew in which the Arandalls sat. Only their wigs could be seen, but she knew the order in which they sat by heart. First came Sir Matthew, then his wife, her carefully curled head beneath a stylish hat, with their sons following them and then their daughters. A prolific, fertile family, the Arandalls. They had bred ten children of which only two had died in childhood, an achievement to be envied when so many children of the poor died young. They arrived last and left first, walking the aisle with heads held high and proud, aloof faces, never acknowledging the curtsies and bows on either side, the envious, respectful obeisances of their inferiors.

When the service ended Hannah watched them pass, hearing the silken swish of the women's skirts, the click of their little heels on the stone floor. Usually they had all climbed back into their carriage and were gone before she emerged from the church, but today two of them had lingered to speak to the vicar. A groom in a neat, clean livery was walking their horses to and fro before the church. The carriage bearing the Arandall arms had gone. Mistress Shield made a careful curtsy to the two young men as she passed, lingering to hope for a smile in return. They nodded aside to her for one second, their faces blank, and Hannah suppressed a smile. It gave her pleasure to see her tormentor snubbed so ruthlessly, as it might delight a mouse to see a cat kicked.

Even so small a gesture of acknowledgment, however, enchanted Mistress Shield, who hurried on with her husband, talking to him with excitement, so that her decorous train of servants scurried after her like children.

Hannah came last, averting her eyes from the Arandall men, holding her eyes to the front. She heard them laughing as they turned from the vicar and came after her towards the narrow gate, their voices strange in her ears, drawling and

28

light, their accent different from that to which she was accustomed. The flat, nasal tones of Birmingham and its environs was ugly, she suddenly discovered, listening to them. How beautifully modulated were their tones. Why did they speak so differently?

As she stepped towards the gate the young men stepped around her to pass her and colour burnt in her cheeks. How dare they behave as if she were of no account, pushing her aside to go first? She stood still, muttering, "Damn your loutish manners . . ."

One of them, the taller of the two, looked round and laughed, his eyes indifferently flicking over the girl in her drab grey cotton.

The other, younger and slighter, looked and then halted. His eyes were a bright blue, she discovered, filled with laughter. He stood aside, bowing, making a graceful dancing gesture. "Make way for the lady, James . . ."

"You fool, Andrew," the other replied, but he laughed too, and stood on the other side of the gate and made a similar bow.

Hannah knew they mocked her. Drawing herself up she walked through them, her brown head held high, neither looking to left nor right. When she had passed into the lane she heard them follow her, laughing loudly. She walked quickly to join up with her fellows. Someone came up beside her and looking round she met Joss Colby's narrowed, speculative eyes.

"That temper of yours will get you into serious trouble one day," he said.

"They pushed me from their path as though I were an insect," she erupted. "I have no doubt they would have trod on me if it had amused them. Who are they, anyway? What use are they in the world? They are like the lilies of the field. They toil not neither do they spin, yet God knows they consume plenty."

He laughed. "Hot-headed little wench, aren't you? The Arandalls are lords of the manor, Hannah, and they have inherited the earth. The Bible says the meek shall do so, but

29

we know different, don't we? It is the strong who inherit the earth; the lions and their jackals."

"Which are you?" she asked him contemptuously. "More jackal than lion, Joss Colby."

"Both can bite," he said, shrugging, indifferent to her scorn. "While the ironmaster refuses to buy coal and coke it for smelting, we are bound to the Arandalls. We need their charcoal and they know it. The day will come, though, when we do not, and then we'll see who shall be master."

She saw Caroline glancing around to find him and said bitingly, "Your chain is being tugged, Joss Colby. Best run after your mistress before she grows jealous."

He gave her a hard grin. "Watch that tongue of yours, Hannah. You'll provoke me too far one day." Then he walked away to join Caroline and she walked along in the rear, inhaling the fragrance of the hedges on either side of the deep-sunken lane.

Bindweed twined around the hawthorn stakes, the white trumpets delicately veined with pink. She picked one flower carefully, playing the old childhood game of 'Granny-pop-out-of-bed' with it, making the white trumpet leap from the green sheath which held it. Young children loved to watch, amazed by the magic way in which the words seemed to make the trick happen, staring as the flower, like an old lady in a white nightgown, floated through the air.

Dawdling, she was far behind the others now, and with a grimace gathered herself together to run after them, when from the far side of the hedge a black horse leapt across her path, the crooked legs almost catching her head as the animal sailed past her.

With a startled, angry cry she jumped backwards, tumbling into the ditch, off balance. A second horse followed the first, soaring over her head. She saw both animals reined in, heard whooping laughter, and two faces staring down at her with dancing eyes, cock-a-hoop with triumph and mockery.

The Arandalls, she thought sourly.

"A hedge-drab, Andy," said the older, his tone drawlingly insolent. "She sprawls invitingly for you . . . at her, boy!"

30

The other laughed and Hannah's fury made her suddenly reckless. "God damn your insolence," she screamed at them. "You'd call yourselves gentlemen? And ride me down as if I were a strayed dog? I'd have you put in the stocks and pelted with rotting eggs if I had my way . . ."

They stared as if a sheep had suddenly opened its jaws and spoken. The older laughed even more loudly, one hand casually laid on his hip. "You see, Andy, what comes of educating the poor? They learn to talk and bore us to death."

Fumbling in his breeches, he flung a coin towards Hannah. "Here, you little scold, buy yourself a muzzle!" He turned, laughing loudly, and rode away down the lane in the direction of Arandall House, and Hannah cursed him with a fluency she had never suspected she possessed.

Struggling to mount from the ditch, bitterly aware of muddy hems, saturated shoes and stockings, she found the other Arandall sliding from his horse. He hoisted her easily to the path and she gave him an angry stare, brushing down her skirts. She would be whipped for her condition when she reached the ironworks.

"We had no notion you were behind the hedge, you know, you're so small we did not see you before we jumped."

She gave the young man a cold glance. He was as slenderly built as a girl, his fresh pink-and-white complexion and powdered hair making him look effeminate to her.

He smiled suddenly. "You look hard enough, Miss. What do you see?"

"A very pretty young man," she said and her tone was no compliment.

He flushed at that and she turned to walk away, but he caught his horse's reins and fell in beside her, leading it.

"What's your name?"

She raised her shoulder in a faint shrug and did not turn to look at him.

"Come, what's your name?" he repeated a little sullenly.

She gave no answer, walking faster.

"I'll walk with you every foot of the way until I get an answer," he said.

31

"Why should you?"

He looked as if *he* did not have an answer. "If I go home there's a heavy dinner to sit through," he said, as though that were answer enough. "My father will stuff his face until he is bright red, my brothers will swill wine and argue, my mother will have her martyred look, and when my father's done he'll sit and snore in the library until supper time, being Sunday. He uses the library for one purpose only – for sleeping, as though it were an annexe to his bedchamber."

"What would you do in the library?" she asked, curious. What did young gentlemen do with their days? She had often wondered. They had no useful tasks to occupy them. They had no bread to earn. What could they find to do all day?

"Read," he said, half laughing, half groaning. He gave her a teasing little glance. "Can you read, child?"

"As well as you, I've no doubt," she snapped, stung. "Though I've precious little time when I can open a book."

He stared at her, taken aback. "Do you like books?"

"If I had any," she said, pinching her lips.

"The Bible and common prayer book, I suppose," he said, sneering. "And books of sermons."

"Poetry," she said, half to herself, remembering the two old brown leather books of verse which had once been her favourite reading. Her grandfather had liked to see her with them on her lap. He would read them with her, his quiet voice eloquent with meaning. She could still smell the strange, musty scent of their browned pages, the thick black hooks of the lettering springing to her mind. She had read them over and over, the sweet, disturbing words echoing in her mind. After her grandfather's death she had gone to his house to ask if she might have them, but the new tenants had smiled and said, "Oh, those? We used them to kindle fires. There's the bindings somewhere," and she had gone away, cursing in her heart.

"Poetry?" Andrew Arandall turned his powdered head to stare at her, his pink bow mouth curved in amusement. "Say me some. What country rhymes do you know, child?"

The lilting drawl irritated her. Patronising puppy, she

32

thought, closing her eyes the better to recall the words of her favourite of the poems. She and her grandfather had read it often.

> "When I consider how my light is spent
> E're half my days, in this dark world and wide,
> And that one Talent, which is death to hide
> Lodg'd with me useless . . ."

Breaking off, forgetting the rest, she glared at her companion, who was gaping at her in apparent stupefaction, his blue eyes dazed.

"Milton," he said, thunderstruck. "Milton, by God! I never thought to hear him quoted outside Cambridge."

It was her turn to be puzzled. "Cambridge?"

"The university," he said. "I've just come down. My father wishes me to take a living." As if she were suddenly another being entirely, his voice and manner had suffered a sea-change. He spoke to her without patronage, as an equal, his face sober. "Damn me if I will! Bury myself in a country parsonage and play at tending a brutish flock? I'd rather eat dry bread all my years."

"You a parson?" Her eyes ran down his slight, elegant, pretty form and she laughed. "Your father has a sense of humour."

"None," he grimaced. "He means it. James is for the army when Papa can persuade him to take up a commission. Even Papa cannot pretend he could make a parson of James, so the family living is reserved for me, rot them. The fellow over at Arrow Greensted is old and when he dies they mean the place for me."

"What would you live on if you refuse?" she asked practically, fascinated by the revelation that even the great Arandalls were not as free as they seemed.

"Sharp child," he groaned. "God knows. I've a small inheritance from my great-aunt Hatty, but it would not keep me in coals."

"Then you must work," she said, seeing no hardship in the prospect. "You are educated. You could teach."

33

He broke out in laughter, eyeing her with dancing blue eyes. "Me? A pedagogue?"

She stared.

"Schoolmaster, child," he explained.

"My grandfather was one," she said in quick offence, seeing his amusement.

His face sobered, reading the pride in her face. "Was he? Oh, ho, so that's how you come to know Milton?"

"Yes," she said, "my grandfather taught at the village school."

Andrew Arandall's eyes swivelled to her face in acute interest. "Then you must be . . ." He broke off the interested remark, flushing.

Hannah's cheeks burnt. "Must be what?" she asked fiercely. "What must I be, Mr. Arandall?"

"Very proud of him, I'm sure," he said in embarrassment.

She halted and glared at him, her hazel eyes a vivid flashing green. "My mother was no fool!" she said. "I'm not ashamed of her. She used what God gave her." Andrew Arandall's eyes grew round like blue marbles in his pretty face.

She had shocked him rigid, she thought, and was angrily glad at the thought; but then she saw him smile at her with a sweetness which was surprising in one of his family.

"My father always says your grandfather bred her as a rod for his own back," he said. "He was a dissenter, your grandfather, you know: why he liked Milton, no doubt. He was one of those stiff old puritans, a marvellously wordy old fellow, throwing in Latin and Greek by handfuls, like an apothecary weighing purges. Birmingham is full of men like your grandfather. My father says if a man preaches freedom to his children he cannot squawk when they take him at his word." He grinned. "As you may suppose, one thing my father never preached any of us was freedom. Hunting, drinking, wenching . . . but never freedom."

His words had given her a new view of her family. During her years at Shield House she had not given a thought to her own background and the roots from which she had sprung,

34

seeing herself outside any framework, isolated, unique. Now she looked back along the line of mother and grandfather, and her eyes were opened strangely. Was she then, like Peg, a product of her time and place? There was a strengthening comfort about having sprung from recognisable roots. It gave to her cold, barren world a new reassurance.

She looked at Andrew Arandall eagerly. "You met my grandfather?"

"As a boy. I barely noted him, to be frank, except to grin secretly at his way of mumbling Latin. Boys are crude animals. I've heard a good deal about him, though. My father's a great gossip. He's for ever droning on about the scandals in the district." Then he flushed again and looked at her ruefully. "I beg your pardon."

Hannah saw that she was part of one of the scandals which had rocked the neighbourhood, and no doubt it had created quite a stir when her puritan-bred mother took first one Shield and then another for lover. How had her grandfather taken that? Hannah could only remember his gentleness, his reserve, the blue-veined knots on his hands and the way his breathing thickened if he walked too fast.

Watching the Arandalls from the backwater of Shield House, she had never imagined that one of them might know of her existence, that the facts of her birth and life might form part of a conversation in the squire's house. The world, it seemed, was smaller than she had imagined. The almighty, powerful Arandalls on their tall horses in their silk coats and powdered wigs were human beings after all.

For a while she walked in silence, absorbing what she had heard, and Andrew Arandall, fancying he had offended her, asked politely, "Have you been to the theatre?"

She looked at him then as if he were mad, her gaze pitying. "Of course not."

"No, of course not," he said, grimacing. "I'd forgot. With your puritan family I should have known. You should, you know. They're doing the old tragedy of *Othello* in Birmingham soon. Cut about as if by barber-surgeons, no doubt, since it is billed with a comedy and music, but there will be some of the

35

poor bleeding carcase left, enough to fire the mind which is not totally dead."

Totally at sea, she stared at him, and he groaned, seeing her bewilderment. "So Shakespeare did not figure in your strange little education? Only Milton? Well, read him. If you like Milton, you'll enjoy Shakespeare."

"I've no time for reading," she said bitterly, as though it were an accusation. "And no books."

He looked horrified. "No books? That must be remedied. I'll bring you a Shakespeare from the library. We've several."

Hannah looked astonished. The offer was so casually made, so staggering. Her eyes glowed as bright as bottle glass, her hands wrung together as if she prayed. "Do you mean it?" To have books again, to have somewhere into which she could escape, a world of freedom and beauty from which she could not be evicted brutally! It was like seeing the sun come up after a storm.

"You're a strange child," he said, his face pleased and amused. "I've known girls show less enthusiasm offered a string of pearls!"

How could he know how she felt? He would go back to Arandall House and walk into a room filled with books of which he was master. The hunger and thirst with which she contemplated the possibility of having even one book would be foreign to this light-speaking, light-minded man, she thought contemptuously.

They came into view of Shield House and Hannah suddenly paled, realising with a rush of horror what might be awaiting her. A whipping would be too light a punishment. She guessed what epithets would be flung at her when Mrs. Shield realised she had wandered along the lanes alone with a gentleman, and an Arandall at that.

Andrew Arandall looked round and stared in astonishment, seeing her white face and aghast look.

"What is it?"

"I shall be turned off for this," she said hoarsely.

His brows jerked together. "I'd forgot . . . what do you do at the Shield house?"

36

"I am kitchen maid."

"A strange sort of kitchen maid," he said, smiling. "Ours scuttle about like cockroaches in the nether regions of the house."

Her eyes flashed contempt at him. "Did you ever look at one?"

"No and I should never dare, having met you," he said, his eyes filled with laughter. "I've forgot your name, child. What is it?"

"Hannah," she said.

"A good puritan name!" His eyes teased her. "Well, Hannah, let us put our heads together and think of an excuse for you." He glanced at the house with a queer little smile. "I have it! That pretty daughter of the ironmaster's . . . What's her name?"

"Caroline? What of her?"

"My mother said the other day that we should see something of her now she's back from school . . . a warm man, Master Shield, and useful to my family. A few little attentions would do no harm. I'll tell your mistress I've come to invite Miss Caroline to tea." His blue eyes were mischievous. "That should soften her, don't you think?"

He was well aware that Mistress Shield was so hungry for attention from the Arandalls that all thought of everything else would be pushed from her mind if one of that family called to offer a social invitation to Caroline. Hannah nodded, though sickened by the contempt which his behaviour showed to the Shield family. How he must despise them!

They reached the yard and he tied his horse to a post. Hannah would have fled into the house but he caught her hand and held it firmly, smiling at her.

"Please . . ." she muttered, scarlet and shaking.

"Silly chit, do you not see? I've kept you with my eager questions about Miss Caroline! That is our excuse?" He grinned. "Come, Hannah, you shall take me in . . ."

She wriggled to free her hand but he held it deliberately, amused at her anxiety. As they turned to walk to the front of the house, the back door opened and Joss Colby stepped out.

His face was a hard mask as he glanced at the linked hands and then up at Hannah. Andrew Arandall released her and gave him a quick bow. "Colby, ain't it?" His voice drawled, cool patronage in it. "How d'ye do? We met when you came up to the house a few months back."

Joss eyes him with impassive speculation. "I remember," he said, as though he conferred a favour in doing so. Hannah was amused by Andrew Arandall's look of surprised offence. He had mistaken his man if he thought he could patronise Joss and get away with it.

Mrs. Shield appeared in the doorway, taut with suppressed excitement and fury. "So, you're back, you little . . ." Her words tailed off as Andrew Arandall stepped forward, making a low bow.

"Oh, Mr. Arandall . . ." She was incredulous, off balance.

He smiled, taking her hand to kiss it with a pretty gesture which made her flutter and grow pink. "Mistress Shield, Ma'am . . . I beg your pardon for detaining one of your serving wenches, but d'ye see, I could not quite recall which lane led here and my mama most particularly wished me to call today, so I asked this gel to guide me."

"Oh, I . . . indeed . . . of course." Mrs. Shield was inarticulate with puzzlement and fascination.

"A small matter," he said, smiling at her. "My mama had seen Miss Caroline in church and wondered if she would be able to take tea with us some time soon . . . perhaps tomorrow?"

Mrs. Shield's hand was at her scrawny throat. "Oh," she gaped, and had no more to say, her mouth opening and shutting.

"We'll send the carriage for her," Andrew Arandall said. "At three, Ma'am?" He bowed again and turned to his horse. "I shall do myself the pleasure of escorting Miss Caroline, Ma'am, if I may." He swung up to his saddle, bowed and rode away.

Completely forgetting Hannah, Mrs. Shield tottered away with a face full of blazing excitement, and Hannah moved towards the door. Joss stepped into her path.

38

She looked up at him tensely.

"Why did young Arandall spin that web of lies?" he asked curtly.

She lifted her chin, on her guard against his probing eyes. "I don't understand you."

"Don't lie to me," he said. "He had no notion of inviting Caroline anywhere when he was at the church. He and that brother of his were larking about outside and gave Mrs. Shield a put-down when she spoke to them. You were half an hour walking along the lane. What were you at, the two of you, to take so long?" His eyes ran down her muddy, wet skirts and narrowed, taking on a strange silvery shine. "Did he tumble you in the ditch, Hannah?"

Her colour flared and the hazel eyes turned a rebellious green. "He walked beside me and talked about Miss Caroline," she said.

"Do you take me for a fool? If he was hunting females, it was you he was after."

"Me?" She laughed. "What would a gentleman see in me?"

He moved closer, putting a cruel vice around her throat, his fingers biting. "To some men you would be a challenge they could not pass by," he said thickly.

Flushing deeply, she pulled away and ran into the house, slamming the door after her. Mrs. Poley looked at her with angry reproach. "Hannah, Hannah, where've you been this time? Mistress is fair seething, like a pot of maggots . . . she'll whip you sure as there's a Heaven above."

"Where've you been, Han?" Nancy burst out, giggling. "Have you been with Jabey?"

"Hush you," Mrs. Poley snapped. "Or I'll wash your mouth out, girl! Hannah, where have you been?"

"I tripped in a puddle and Master Arandall came along and asked me to show him the way here," she said with blithe disregard of the truth. "He came to ask Miss Caroline to tea!"

The uproar which followed was deafening. They all wanted to know what Arandall she meant and what he had said and how he had looked. She spun them a tall story which they

39

swallowed without question, and in the middle of it was told to go to the parlour where she found her mistress seated in a high-backed chair, her feet on an embroidered footstool.

"What did Master Arandall say to you, girl?" she demanded, and for once her voice held none of the usual hatred. Her eager curiosity was too strong for her to recall to whom she spoke.

Hannah fed her the same fairy story with which she had regaled the servants, and Mistress Shield and Caroline listened, open-mouthed.

"You say Master Arandall asked you many questions about my daughter?" Mistress Shield was quivering delightedly.

"Oh, yes, indeed, Ma'am," Hannah gushed, wide-eyed and innocent. "Whether I dressed her hair and if her curls were natural, whether she had a sweetheart or was free of all entanglements . . . whether she played an instrument . . . whether she had her own horse . . .?"

"You say he asked if she had a suitor?" Mrs. Shield asked huskily. "What did you say, Hannah?"

Hannah lied softly. "I said she had several, Ma'am . . . but none she had accepted as far as I knew."

Mistress Shield's breath caught in her throat. "You may go, girl," she said with stately kindness.

Hannah curtsied and withdrew and as she closed the door heard Caroline burst out huskily, "But I am betrothed to Joss, Mama . . ."

"Not at all," Mistress Shield said flatly. "He has asked to marry you and we have been considering it . . . there's no formal betrothal yet."

"But, Mama . . ."

"Be quiet, Caroline. I am thinking . . . what can you wear? Oh, mercy, what can you wear? You haven't a thing I shall not be ashamed to see you in tomorrow . . ."

Hannah walked quietly down the corridor. A little smile played around her mouth. Fate had placed Andrew Arandall in her path and brought this about . . . the Shields would cast Joss Colby off without a scruple if they thought there was the remotest chance their daughter might catch the eye of Andrew

Arandall. It was ironic and she could have leapt and danced with delight.

The bell rang violently and she went back to the room. "Peg," Mrs. Shield cried wildly. "Fetch Peg . . . she must alter one of my daughter's dresses before tomorrow!"

Peg went running in and the whole house seemed to go mad as the servants were sent scurrying hither and thither to make sure that when Caroline set off the next day at three o'clock she would be as fine as any lady in the land.

"A betrothal may be broken easily enough," Mrs. Poley said. "And what is a Joss Colby compared to an Arandall?"

"I could tell you," muttered Nancy, winking at Hannah, her eyes avid as she thought of Joss.

"Joss Colby is in train to have his nose put out of joint," Mrs. Poley said. "Perhaps then he will not sniff at us . . . what is he, after all, but a jumped up shopkeeper's brat grown too big for his breeches?"

Hannah looked down at her busy hands, clamping the hot iron down on one of the master's shirts. A cold shiver ran down her back. What would Joss do now? She knew him too well to imagine that he would accept defeat. She shivered. Joss would not stand idly by and see his plans wrecked by the intrusion of Andrew Arandall. They were all blind if they thought he would. They did not see the looming dark shadow he cast already over the ironworks.

Nancy sidled up to her and whispered, "What's he like, young Arandall, Han?"

"A pretty young man in a blue coat and silver buttons," she said lightly.

"Did he kiss you? Did he, Han? Did he fondle and whisper sweet words?" Nancy was shrill with her questions, wriggling excitedly.

Hannah looked at her with mild contempt. "Of course not, Nancy. He's a gentleman."

Nancy shrieked, nudging her. "Oh, a gentleman, is he? And do you think they are better than other men? Oh, Han, you're so silly . . ."

It is not I who am silly, Hannah thought, watching the

pretty, knowing, sly face beneath the bright curls, but then Nancy was what God and man had made her. Especially man, Hannah thought wryly, and smiled, spitting on the iron to test its heat.

"Why're you smiling?" Nancy demanded. "Come, tell me . . . what did he do to you? He kissed you, I'll swear that . . . never tell me he did not . . ."

"Then I won't," Hannah said calmly. "If you will refuse to believe me, believe what you choose!"

Joss Colby came into the kitchen in his black thigh-boots and leather riding jacket, his head bare and damp from the rain sleeting down outside. "I'm riding into the village," he said. "Any messages, Mrs. Poley?"

She bustled to fetch a receipt she wanted him to take to her friend, Mistress Cowell, at the third cottage past the church, and Joss turned his dark head to stare at Hannah, who ironed with bent head and a stiffly held body.

Nancy tossed her yellow head, her eyes saucy. "Have you heard of Hannah's adventure, Joss? There's a gentleman after her, kissing and fondling in the lane, and whispering promises . . . she must be careful, mustn't she? A girl of her birth has always to be careful."

Hannah's temper soared into black rage. She threw down the iron and slapped Nancy across her slyly smiling face. Nancy stared at her for an astonished second before bursting into shrieking tears and running out, her apron over her head.

Very flushed, Hannah went back to her iron, and Joss's fingers clamped down on her wrist, halting her.

"So he did nothing to you, did he? You lying little whore," he said through his teeth. "You spilled it out to her, did you? Boasting of your conquests? You blind little fool, he'll ruin you and leave you the way your mother was left with a swollen belly and nothing but shame."

She lifted her head and looked at him, her eyes brilliant with anger. "Nancy wrought that tale from her own foul imagination. I told her nothing. There is nothing to tell."

Mrs. Poley came back and Joss turned abruptly, took the folded receipt and went out without a glance at Hannah. She ironed until her arm ached and her back groaned with fatigue and she wondered what Joss was planning as he rode through the fine rain to the village. He had been very angry, his face savage, as he spoke to her. Joss scented the threat to his plans which Andrew Arandall presented.

Three

JOSS COLBY'S FATHER had been a blacksmith, one of the many free smiths of Birmingham, his tiny workshop merely a hovel of wood put up by himself beside his little cottage. Joss as a boy of five had worked under his father's heavy, unrelenting hand; running around the foul den in a shirt rent to show his dirty little arms, sweat running in smudged rivers down his thin body. He had been knocked from one side of the smithy to the other at times, head ringing, blood smeared on his face.

Joe Colby had a bitter temper and a bodily strength which was not spared to his children. He preached the word of God on Sunday, a Bible in his brawny hand, thumping his fist upon it to smite home the words. Joss would watch with glittering eyes as that great fist was brought down. Joe Colby did not speak of love or mercy. He thundered of justice and right, he called down hellfire upon the unrighteous and the sinners who defied the godly, by which he meant himself.

His wife, Elizabeth, was a pale, wiry woman with dark eyes and hair. Her meekness to her husband had been learnt through years of bodily oppression. Joe Colby's heavy body needed her, and he saw it as her bounden duty to submit to his need. "Rib of man's flesh," he would shout as he smote his Bible. "Woman was created for man and like the animals must do his bidding." Twelve children came of Joe Colby's need of Elizabeth. Eight of them died.

Elizabeth had wept over them all, despite her husband's injunction to be joyful that God called them to his bosom. Joss watched her shadowed face, her shivering misery, and his

44

hatred of his father burnt higher and higher as he grew towards early manhood.

He was, in his own eyes, a man at twelve. He had had his first woman, a Birmingham Saturday-flier, the name given derisively to women who on a Saturday wandered the streets in search of men with money to pay for pleasure. Many of these women were respectable housewives for the rest of the week. Joss never even asked the name of the woman he clumsily coupled with one Saturday night in a dark alley behind the Black Swan. She seemed amused by his inexperience but she was kind enough and took only the sixpence she had first demanded as evidence of his ability to pay, refusing the second sixpence she might have insisted upon.

Blooded, Joss never paid again. He found it easy to get women when he needed them. His father, catching him with a girl in the alley behind the smithy, took his belt to him, just before his fourteenth birthday. Joss was a large, powerful youth by then, however, and he managed to get the belt from his father and lay it about his shoulders in the struggle between them.

His mother ran sobbing to part them. Joss was out of control by the time she arrived. As his arm thrashed down upon his father he thought of the many times he had suffered at the older man's hands. He remembered his short-lived brothers and sisters. He remembered most clearly of all the nights he had woken to hear his mother whimper, "No, Joe, please, no . . ." Blood seemed to fill his eyes. His arm rose and fell while he heard the echoes of his father's thick grunting and the rise and fall of his body as he asserted his rights over his wife's flesh.

"Joss, no!" His mother's scream broke in upon the nightmare in his head he faltered, dazed, and looked at her. His father slumped to the ground. Elizabeth knelt beside him, weeping. Joss flung down the belt and walked away, trembling.

Joe Colby was never to be the same man again. Joss had done him no physical harm which was not cured in a week but he had broken something in the older man's spirit which never recovered. Joe Colby shrank as Joss broadened and grew tall. A year later, Joe died and Joss watched with a savage incomprehension as his mother wept for the man who had made her life hell throughout Joss's childhood. Under his father's brutal hand Joss had learnt to endure, to hate, to survive what seemed unendurable, and he found his mother's capacity for forgiveness beyond belief.

All the tenderness of which Joss was capable had gone to her from his earliest years. His hatred for his father was inextricably bound up with a resentment for the way his mother had suffered and Joss could not understand how she could mourn for Joe Colby.

After the burial, it became clear that the family were penniless. The smithy and house were rented from an absentee landlord whose agent drove them out within a month. Joe's brother, Thomas, took them into his home. A bachelor with a temper as choleric as that of the dead man, he set Joss to work as an apprentice in his ironmonger's shop. Joss worked out his five years grudgingly. His uncle paid him starvation wages and resented every mouthful of food the family consumed. Only Joss's broad shoulders and fierce look kept the old man from beating him as Joe had done.

Joss had no intention of becoming a shopkeeper, although he worked hard and learnt all he could about iron, listening with fascination to the talk of those who came to the shop to buy or sell. His early acquaintance with the metal had left him with an indelible passion for it, the nature and texture of it engrossing him, so that he was always eager to know more of the secrets of working with iron.

Beneath his brusque harsh manner, Joss hid a concern for his mother and two younger brothers which was expressed in practical ways but rarely in words or open affection. It angered him to see his mother wearily waiting on his uncle after a long, hard day spent in cleaning and washing. It made him grind his teeth to see the old man cuff one of the boys for some trivial offence. Joss laid out some of his own few pence to have his brothers taught to read and count. He bought his mother little gifts – a ribbon from a pedlar, an orange from a Christmas fair, but dropped them into her lap with a scowl which forbad her to thank him. Joss despised weakness and shrank from letting his fondness for his mother be seen. Love was a word Joss Colby refused to admit into his mind.

It was in the shop that Joss met Henry Shield. The ironmaster supplied them from his forge. Thomas Colby often tried to get Shield to lower his prices by complaining of the quality of workmanship or the strength of the iron. Listening irritably to the old man, Henry Shield one day caught Joss grinning and looked at him sharply, ready to be angry. Joss winked at him behind his uncle's back. Henry Shield's face changed. He gave the young man an answering wink which Thomas Colby did not notice.

The two men had struck up a quick friendship. Henry Shield enjoyed lingering in the growing town, drinking with Joss in city taverns, talking iron, hearing the gossip which the other ironmasters brought to the shop. On a more personal level, he soon learnt that Joss knew all the prettier whores of the town. Joss took him along to do business with some of them. Henry Shield found a new enjoyment in sharing a girl and discussing her afterwards. He began to confide the details of his private life to Joss and so Joss learnt all there was to know about the Shield household long before he ever arrived.

When his apprenticeship ended, Henry Shield offered him a place at his ironworks. His uncle was more than willing to let him go. He would have had to pay Joss better wages now that he was trained, and he preferred to take on Joss's younger brother, Ben, a biddable boy, willing to jump when Thomas barked.

For Joss it had been bliss to get out of the cramped little rooms above the shop, to sleep alone for the first time in his life. Never again would he have two younger brothers squashed up against him in a narrow bed, never again would he hear his mother sob in her sleep or whimper, "No, Joe, please . . ."

He had missed the life of Birmingham at first. A town-bred boy, he was accustomed to streets and alleys in which to prowl and find amusement, but he soon found himself new pleasures. There were always girls eager to please Joss Colby. He had browsed among them at first like a young colt let free in a field of sweet spring grass. The village girls sighed and quivered as he turned his eyes upon them.

They seemed prettier, fresher, than town girls. Their skin had a bright colour and their bodies smelled of hay. Birmingham girls were always demanding payment for their favours; a buckle for their shoes, a ribbon for their hair. Country girls laughed and gave without asking any return.

Joss was hoarding every penny he could scrape together. He was fiercely determined to buy his mother out of the slavery in which his uncle kept her. She refused to live in the squalid little rooms he rented at the ironworks and Joss knew she preferred the town life. He meant to rent or buy a little house in Birmingham so that she could live like a lady. Elizabeth laughed when he told her so and shook her head at him. "A lady? Me? Joss, you fool!" She dared to put a hand on his broad shoulder, smiling. "Save your pennies for yourself when you wed, lad."

Joss had known he would not need money when he wed. Early on in his friendship with Henry Shield his plan had come to him. He shrugged at his mother, his face expressionless. His mother would be disturbed if he broached his plans to her. Joss might despise her belief in love but he would not argue the toss with her. He said no more but he went on saving, watching the little pile of money grow eagerly. Elizabeth seemed to him to grow more frail with every year that passed. Joss watched Mistress Shield sewing at her embroidery frame, her neatly shod feet on a footstool, while Hannah scurried around laden with work, and he hungered for the day when his mother should sit just so, waited on rather than waiting, in silk gowns and not shabby cotton. At times he woke in the night, sweating, crying out hoarsely, having dreamt that Elizabeth had died. One of the spurs driving him on to climb out of his poverty was a need to make amends to his mother for all that life had done to her.

The first day at the ironworks he had seen Hannah and

guessed who she was, remembering Henry Shield's drunken regrets over the way his wife treated her. Legs apart while he stared around the parlour, conscious of a hungry determination to possess such fine things, he had known the girl was staring at him. He had never looked her way, imagining his mother seated in that room, dressed in silk and never lifting a finger from dawn to dusk.

As he rode later along the deep-banked village lane, he stared at the spring sky, remembering the moment when his involvement with Hannah had really begun. She has been whipped for some small offence. Joss had watched her small, white face and felt a pang of pain in his own body, as though it had been himself who had felt the cane slash his flesh.

Her helpless defiance touched some spring in him, aroused so deep, so profound an emotion, that Joss was shaken to his roots.

He told himself his reaction was merely because her position in that house reminded him of his mother. He told himself it was folly, wasted pity. He told himself not to be a fool.

He had laid his plans long before, listening to Henry Shield and seeing the possibilities which lay open to him. Life in Birmingham had taught him to fight for what he wanted. The weak went to the wall. The strong trampled over their bodies to reach survival, and Joss meant to be a survivor.

Iron was needed more every day. Joss meant to grow with the trade, to reach out for power and wealth. An unaltering resolve had urged him on since childhood, the fierce desire to wrench life into the shape he required of it. Clever, shrewd, ruthless, he knew when to act and when to wait. From the moment when he snatched the belt from his father, he had counted himself a man; and in all that time he had been shaping his own future, a future which should carry his mother, his brothers and his little sister out of grim poverty and into a safe haven.

He felt from the first that Hannah threatened that future. His plans could not include her. She stood in his path like a hedge rose, covered in thorns, driving them deep into him as

49

he tried to struggle past, yet bearing such delicate, sweet-scented flowers that he could not suppress the hunger they aroused in him, even though he knew the consequences.

Why did she make him feel as he did? She was no beauty, he thought impatiently. Her face was filled with spitting defiance whenever they met. Joss knew she did not like him. She never hid it.

Caroline was not merely prettier. She was a biddable girl with a sweet temper. Joss would find it no hardship to bed her. She was the necessary hinge on which his plans hung. He had known at sight that she was his to take – it had been so easy.

Too easy, he thought, his teeth meeting with a snap. He had planned for everything but himself. Every time he set eyes on Hannah he felt an emotion he could not fight or under-stand. He hated her for the threat she unwittingly offered his plans, yet she was plainly unaware of his feelings.

Joss had once asked his mother irritably how she could pretend to weep for a man like his father, and she had looked at him almost sadly, as though the question betrayed some-thing in him which worried her. "I loved him, Joss."

"Loved him!" Joss's eyes had flared with incredulous derision. "Loved *him*?" His deep, angry laughter had made his mother sigh.

"One day you will love someone, Joss."

"I'm damned if I will be such a fool," he had snarled. He saw his mother's softness as weakness, an abandonment of self-respect, and as he grew older and discovered his own power over women he learnt to despise the whole sex. They yielded so easily. He charmed them with a smile and soon realised he could have what he desired from them without needing to exert force. The easier they were, the more he despised them. The more he despised them, the harder they pursued him.

Joss did not imagine he loved Hannah. Love was a trap into which he did not mean to fall. The dangerous excitement she aroused in him came, he told himself, because her angry, contemptuous stare was a challenge he found irresistible. The

ease of his other conquests did not satisfy him. There was no
real triumph to be had from battles won before they started.
Hannah's dislike of him, the icy coldness of her eyes, dared all
his threatened reprisals and the struggle between them had
long turned into a fiercely fought duel which engrossed Joss to
the point of obsession. He had whipped her after her last
defiant stand because of a nagging need to make her give in to
him, and her stubborn refusal to do so had merely intensified
the way he felt.

What had happened between her and young Arandall? Had
the puppy kissed her? Fondled her? Joss's hands clenched on
the reins and his mount jerked, startled. There was suddenly
sweat on Joss's forehead. He could not even contemplate the
thought of another man's hands on her.

Only a short time ago he had talked to Hannah about her
mother, hoping to sow seed in her mind which might flower
for himself in the future. Twisting and turning like an animal
in a trap he had sought for a way in which he could have her
without destroying both their lives and had seen that he might
persuade her into her mother's road.

Placed as she was, her life offered nothing but misery. The
enmity of Mistress Shield would mark her as time went by. It
enraged Joss to listen and watch as Hannah was nagged and
clawed by the woman. Yet Hannah showed no sign of defeat
as he knew to his cost. He did not understand, himself, why
he was torn between contrary impulses when he saw her – the
desire to force her to her knees and the desire to protect her.
The more she defied him, the more he felt driven to hurt her,
and yet it gave him satisfaction to meet the cold glare of her
eyes. She was like molten iron, he thought. Red-hot yet
supple, flowing sweetly yet cooling to an unbreakable
strength. Joss loved to watch the iron gush forth into the
prepared beds. From his earliest years iron had fascinated
him.

He looked up at the dripping sky. Rib of man's flesh, his
father had called woman. Bitterly Joss admitted to himself
that Hannah was part of himself, bone of his body. Until she
was welded to him indissolubly, flesh of his flesh, engulfing

him, he would be a partial man, incomplete. I need her, he thought, and there was no softness in him, only a fierce straining for completion, a bitter, burning hunger.

Lady Arandall sat in a high-backed chair in her drawing room, her small feet on a tapestried stool, sewing languidly at her embroidery frame. She looked up at the rain running down the windows. From the library came the thick sound of snoring. Her daughter, Charlotte, was playing a tinkling air upon the harpsichord, the white curls of her wig nodding. A short-nosed pug snorted on the carpet beside the fire, lifting its head as sparks flew out from the half-consumed log from which flames licked slowly. Lady Arandall sighed, her face bored.

Charlotte rose, curtsied and drifted from the room. The fire sank slowly and Lady Arandall rang her tiny hand bell, watching as a young footman trod silently into the room.

She watched him as he attended to the fire. He was, she thought, a pretty boy, his strong calves filling out his stockings in a charming fashion. Turning, he bowed, and she stretched out her small foot.

Without a flicker of expression the footman knelt and removed her red shoe. She watched his bent head as he pressed and stroked her foot. They had been her greatest pride in her girlhood, those tiny feet. Men had drunk toasts to them in London. She had married at sixteen, borne child after child, her body ploughed nightly by a dull bore she resented. Now she was in her forties, although her enamelled face bore no evidence to that, and she felt she had wasted her prime.

"A little higher," she murmured.

The young man's hands obediently slid up to her ankle, moved out of view under her full hooped skirts. She lay back, inwardly purring like a sleek cat.

The footman's wig had slipped slightly. Lady Arandall giggled and he looked up, flushing. He rose, leaning over her, and kissed her hard on her smiling, painted mouth. Her lips opened and her tongue slid inside his mouth, wriggling like a snake. He lay on her touching the round white breasts rising from her low gown while they kissed.

The door opened and the footman was up in a second, his wig put straight, his red face averted as he moved solemnly from the room. Andrew, mouth crooked, felt like kicking him on his way, but it was not the first time he had found his mother amusing herself with one of the footmen. He looked at her with irritated distaste. She smiled sweetly at him.

"Where have you been, Andrew? La, that fire is so hot! I am quite parched. Pour me some madeira."

Andrew obeyed, his eyes hard. It was shameful to find one's mother being pleasured by a damned servant, he thought, but it could be useful. "Mama, that's a damned pretty little girl, the ironmaster's daughter. It would be an obliging courtesy to have her to tea, don't you think? He makes us so much money, Mama, and they would take it kindly of us to show her some favour."

His mother sleepily surveyed him as she sipped her wine. "Chasing the girl, Andy? It could make trouble. Old Shield is a hard man."

Andrew leaned on the ironwork hearth, grinning lazily at his mother.

"He cannot make iron without charcoal, Mama."

She picked up her fan and moved it slowly, her cherry-red lips full where the footman had bruised them. "All the same, Andy, do you seriously ask me to entertain the chit in my own house? A manufacturer's brat?"

Andrew held her eyes. "We all take our pleasures where we find them, Mama."

Her face stiffened. She stared, then laughed lightly. "Lud, boy, as you please then, but do not blame me if your father makes a furore over it."

He shrugged and walked to the door. "Shall I send James to you?" he asked softly as he left.

Lady Arandall shut her fan with a furious click of bone. She stared like a cat into the fire, biting her lower lip. Her husband's snoring droned into her ears.

Andrew went into the library softly. His father lay back, the

53

handkerchief rising and falling over his face. Very quietly Andrew found the book he sought and went out again. As he closed the door he saw James slip into the drawing room. He grimaced and shrugged.

The long case clock in the great hall swung solemnly to and fro and filled the lower house with its portentous sound. Below stairs the servants squabbled and worked in the dark kitchen. A small girl hunched on a stool worked solidly at the great copper pan in which the soup was heated. In the upper rooms the family passed Sunday as they always did, amusing themselves as best they could, scattered throughout the house.

In his bedroom, Andrew looked out at the thin, falling rain with melancholy eyes, and thought of Cambridge, envisaging the narrow streets crowded with young men, the spires and towers above the winding, weedy river, the wet roofs and cloudy glass of the chambers he had shared with friends. Boredom settled on him like grey dust.

He thought of Hannah and his face lightened. A strange mating, that, between her puritan-bred mother and the ironmaster's brother. Strange mating, stranger consequence. There was something in her face, a brightness and individuality, which was unforgettable. Pretty? No, he thought. Not that. Never that. When she smiled, though, she had a fleeting beauty. It came and went like sunshine on a winter day. It was bred in her eyes, born of her spirit rather than her flesh, yet it was revealed in her flesh, as sickness might be, leaving its stamp for all to see.

When she spoke Milton's words Andrew had felt as though she peeled away some mask which had deceived him into thinking of her as he thought of everyone else he met. The words had bared her mind. He had felt a strange echo in himself.

He had used sensuality as a disguise when he spoke to his mother because that was the only language she understood, but Andrew felt no sensuality towards Hannah. Her mind spoke to his mind. It was too rare an occurrence for him to risk losing sight of her. Most people bored him. His family were stupid loutish fools. He was sickened by their rutting mentality, their greed for food and drink, their inability to rise above the pleasures of their bodies.

One reason why he felt no interest in a career in the Church of England was his innate distaste for the whole ethos exemplified by their local vicar. Andrew, educated in traditional lip-service to the protestant religion, had a fierce puritanic dislike of everything second-rate, a hatred of compromise and pretence. At Cambridge he had once or twice been tempted by the fire and ritual of the Catholic Church but his upbringing had held him back. Secretly he had drunk the health of 'the king over the water', yearned for the Jacobite cause which stood for everything to which his family were opposed.

He had written poetry since he was fifteen, keeping it from the eyes of his family, who would scoff at him if they read any of it. While his brothers hunted, drank and womanised, he held aloof. None of the young ladies produced from local families well-bred enough to mate with an Arandall, had pleased him. They bored him. They irritated him.

He opened the volume of Shakespeare which he had brought from the library. Strange stuff, he thought, but potent, leaving unforgettable echoes in the mind.

Hannah would like it. He felt sure of that.

Caroline's visit to the Arandalls lasted precisely one hour. Lady Arandall extended a limp hand to her, surveying her from beneath her thick white lids as if she were a strange animal brought into the house.

By great good fortune none of the male members of the family, bar Andrew, were present. They had ridden off after a light luncheon to view the preserved game birds with one of the keepers. The sky was a pale washed blue. The sun straggled over copse and stream like a fugitive, giving an elusive light to the flat landscape.

The Arandall girls sat up around the table, faces blankly well-bred. Caroline in her finery looked pathetically out of place. Andrew handed her fingers of thin bread and butter, pressed ratafia biscuits upon her. Lady Arandall languidly asked her how her mother and father did and without waiting for a reply said: "Fine weather, ain't it? Will you take more tay?"

Caroline, flushed and on the point of tears, looked helplessly at Andrew. He smiled and pressed her hand under cover of the table. His mother shot him a maliciously amused look, perfectly aware of his movements.

Tea over, the silent girls passed from the room in their pretty, simple gowns, the full skirts brushing the carpet. Andrew rose and Caroline anxiously rose with him, trembling. Andrew bowed to his mother and Caroline sketched a shaky curtsy.

Lady Arandall laughed to herself, then went up to her bedroom. She rang the bell and lay down upon the embroidered coverlet on the four-poster. James came in and closed the door. Lady Arandall's painted red mouth smiled across the room. He knelt upon the bed and unfastened her garments. In her tight-laced corset she lay laughing at him as he wrestled with his own clothes. He pitched her white wig to the floor and pushed back her petticoat skirts. Angrily, brutally, he took his revenge for the mockery she showed him. He used her body violently, as though she were one of the kitchen wenches with whom he sometimes shared a bed. Lady Arandall gasped enjoyably, her shaven head glistening with sweat. That night she would passively permit her husband's brief joyless mounting, but James was giving her pleasures she had never known with Sir Matthew. She dug her fingers into his broad, muscled back and her eyes gleamed with pleasure. James grinned down at her like a dog, his eyes blank. He despised and disliked her for permitting him to do these things to her. He felt he triumphed over her by showing her crude brutality. Lady Arandall could read his mind without difficulty and her smile was malicious. James was only the last of a long line of strong young men servants who had served her in this room and she knew exactly how to read his thoughts and emotions.

"A pity you're such a clumsy oaf," she sighed as he at last lay still on her. "With a little experience you could learn to give me some pleasure."

His skin reddened. He gritted his teeth. When he had dressed sullenly and gone, Lady Arandall lay there, sprawled in elegant dishevelment, and laughed.

Her eyes narrowed. How had Andrew passed the last hour? she wondered. As enjoyably as herself, no doubt. The girl was, as he had said, pretty. Beddable, no doubt. Shy, unmannered and tongue-tied, though. Still, between the sheets that would make no matter. Andrew would not be desiring conversation with her.

She heard her husband's lumbering approach on the wooden treads and got up. He came into the room as she was brushing her hair before the mirror. Eyeing her unclothed state, he said thickly, "Changing your gown, m'dear?" He put his arms around her and kissed her bare white shoulder. "Still the prettiest girl in the county," he mumbled. Lady Arandall, sighing, allowed him to pull her on to the bed.

He looked at her unsuspiciously as he entered her. "Ah, ready for me, my love?" His heavy jowled face smiled down at her. He had never once admitted the notion that his wife might be unfaithful to him. She had borne him so many children. She was so pretty, even now, her enamelled pink and white skin smooth and gleaming. Sir Matthew had no idea that her heavy paint hid deep smallpox marks. The white lead filled the pits left by an early brush with the disease. Some people were beginning to protest that painting with lead could disfigure, poison, even kill, but most women ignored such unfounded complaints. The smooth white complexion which paint gave a woman was too much admired for anyone with vanity to be prepared to risk losing admirers by forsaking her paintbox.

Andrew was listening to Caroline's nervous prattle with a mixture of boredom and compassion. She had a sweet little face, he thought, watching her eyes shining and her face lighting up as she spoke of Joss Colby. She meant Andrew to understand that she loved Joss. Her parents might desire her to encourage the squire's son, but Caroline was too deeply in love to think of anyone but Joss.

Andrew escorted her back to the ironworks and Mistress Shield received him with over-obsequious courtesy, giving her daughter a look which ordered her to be encouraging to the squire's son. Andrew caught the look which passed between them and was not sure he found it altogether flattering that Caroline should prefer Joss Colby to himself. She had made her passion plain to him, in her shy, simple way, and he marvelled that a female should look twice at the son of a blacksmith.

"I should like to look round your works, Mistress Shield," Andrew drawled, sipping his wine with hidden distaste. Lord, where did they get such stuff? he thought.

"Of course," Mistress Shield smiled eagerly. "Run and fetch Mr. Colby, girl," she told Hannah, her face changing as she looked at her. Andrew caught that look, too, and decided he did not care for Mistress Shield.

Hannah ran to the yard, hearing the regular thud-thud of the tilthammer as she drew nearer. A half-naked, sweating figure staggered out of the sheds, blinking at the daylight like a mole. He was a great muscular creature with red hair and arms like knotted wood. Lifting a stone jar to his mouth he thirstily swallowed, his arm muscles rippling. The men could only work in the terrible heat for a while before they came out into the air to breathe and drink to replace the sweat they lost as they hammered. Grinning at Hannah, he dived back inside, the hellish glare of the fire, the thunder of the tilthammer engulfing him.

Hannah stood at the open door and called Joss, her quiet voice swallowed up by the crash of the hammer. The men's figures moved in the darkness like the denizens of hell, their skins flushed red by the fire, their bodies glistening with sweat.

Jabey came out, wheeling a barrow of iron. He grinned. "Han, what are you doing here?"

His face was grimed, his eyes rimmed with white perspiration. She laughed. "You look like a blackamoor."

He rested the barrow and made threatening gestures with his black hands. "Careful, or I'll make you as black as myself!" His palms slid down her face, smearing dust on her skin. "There, that'll teach you to make fun of me."

She laughed at him again, her eyes bright. "I shall have to wash it off now or I shall get another whipping!"

"You look the way you did when we were small and played in the lane," Jabey sighed, staring down at her, his hands now resting on her slender waist.

They looked at each other sadly, two young creatures trapped in a bitter existence, the sunlight warm on their faces, picking out stray gleams of gold in Hannah's hair, turning Jabey's head to flame.

Jabey bent his head to kiss her gently and was suddenly lifted away from her as lightly as if he were a toy and flung across the shed to land in a crumpled heap against the wall, gasping. The men hammering looked round, shouting comments, laughing. Hannah looked up into Joss's face in shock. His lips were drawn back from his teeth in an animal snarl. A heat and uneasiness flooded her under his stare.

"I'll have no bitches slinking round my works," he snapped, fury sparking in his eyes.

She had never seen him at work before. The kitchen women were forbidden to set foot in the sheds since their presence distracted the men. Joss wore no shirt – none of them did in that awful heat – and his bare chest, like theirs, was flushed by fire and rough with thick, black hair which grew in a wedge down the centre of his body.

The strength of that naked, muscled frame, filled with peasant vitality, made her feel strangely weak. His head was aggressively set on that powerful neck, his black hair ruffled back from the hard lines of his face, his broad shoulders rippling as he set his arms akimbo, his long sinewy hands on his hips.

The hammering went on behind them. Men ran from bench to fire, carrying metal in great iron tongs, beating it into the shape they wanted while sparks flew from the hot metal as it cooled and bent.

Little Tam Riggs ran up, sweat streaming down his skinny body. "I've done the floor, M'ster. Shall I fetch more water?"

Joss threw him an impatient look. "Aye."

Hannah watched the boy's bright eyes in that foul mask. Tam worshipped Joss, followed him like a dog, eager to please him. Silly child, she thought, watching him run off.

Jabey stumbled towards them, coughing. "T'wasn't Hannah's fault, Master Colby," he began and Joss cut him short with a glare.

"Get back to work."

Jabey began to speak again and Joss took a step towards him, menace in his face. Jabey turned away, hands clenched at his sides. Joss looked at Hannah, a peculiar smile on his mouth.

"You're wanted at the house," she said sharply.

"When you bring me a message, you'll call me sir," he said softly, deliberately provoking her, his eyes very bright.

Her eyes flicked downward and she was stubbornly silent. He took her arm and pushed her toward the house. "I could break your scrawny little neck with one blow," he muttered, as if the thought gave him deep pleasure.

"Do it, then," Hannah spat out. "D'you think I'd care? You'd be doing me a kindness to take me out of this."

He stopped to look down at her. "That's it, pity yourself. My God, Hannah, life's what we make it. You've a brain in that head. Use it. Why kick against what you cannot change? Take life in both hands and bend it or bear with what you've got to accept."

"Easy for you to talk! Would you be so smug in my place?"

"I'd not stop in it," he said, his smile harsh. "Neither man nor woman, god nor devil, should treat me the way they treat you."

"I shan't bear it," Hannah said below her breath. "I'll get out of it some day."

Joss gave her a quick, penetrating look his brows dark. "How?" He glanced over his shoulder at the forge, the

60

bones of his face taut. "By marrying Stock? You'd exchange one slavery for another. Stock can barely feed those he keeps now. He'd give you a parcel of brats and an empty belly." His voice lowered, grew deep and hurried. "Your mother had more sense. She knew the way of the world. We all take ourselves to market, Hannah, and sell as high as we can. Don't sell yourself cheap. Wait for a better offer than Stock can give you."

Something in the way he watched her made Hannah shiver, her eyes widening in shock. Looking away, she said nervously: "They're waiting for you at the house."

Joss grimaced and strode away while she came slowly after him. She went into the kitchen to start peeling the vegetables. Through the window she saw Joss and Andrew walking towards the yards. Little Tam came slowly into sight, laden with a bucket in each hand, walking carefully so as not to spill a drop. Joss glanced towards him, smiling as he watched the child's intent face.

One of the wagons suddenly rolled away from the wall, the iron wheels grating. Joss looked at it sharply then yelled. "Tam! Out of the way!"

Tam looked round, startled.

"The brake's gone," Joss roared, leaping forward as he shouted. Tam was too stunned to move, his head turned over his thin shoulder to stare in horror at the wagon as it thundered down on him.

"Oh, God," Hannah moaned, dropping her knife and Mrs. Poley ran to the window exclaiming, "What's amiss, Hannah?"

A second before the wagon hit the frozen figure of the child, Joss reached him and took him in a violent swoop out of the wagon's path. They rolled together over and over on the dusty cobbles while Andrew Arandall stared.

Hannah and Mrs. Poley ran out. Men poured from the sheds. Joss got up, dragging Tam with him, a hand at his neck, shaking the child like a terrier with a rat. "You stupid little dolt! Were you mazed? You heard me warn you. Why didn't you run?"

White-faced, blood on his temples from the fall, Tam stammered back, "Sorry, Joss."

"Sorry? I'll tan your hide for you." Becoming aware of the audience outside the works, Joss swung and bellowed at them. "Get back to work. Who asked you to stop?" They turned and shuffled away while he watched them, brushing dust from his breeches. "Wagoner!" A brawny man in a torn shirt came slowly forward. Joss eyed him angrily. "You nearly killed that child. I want all the wagons looked at now, today. Get that brake mended. You'll be fined for this, I promise you."

The man knuckled silently and vanished. The wagon had crashed into the hedge just outside the works. Hannah watched him running to it and then turned to Joss. "Poor child, he looks sick," she said, glancing down at Tam's white face.

"Sick? I'll make him sick. I'll teach him to heed me when I give an order. I'll whip him until he can't sit down."

"You dare to lay one hand on him!" Hannah flared.

Joss's black head swung. His eyes were brilliant with anger. "Are you threatening me, Miss?" he asked softly.

"I deserve a whipping, Miss," Tam whispered shakily, tugging at her skirt.

They both looked down at him. Tam's eyes pleaded with Hannah not to argue with Joss. His spine was rigid. His hands clenched. Joss gave a short laugh and tousled the boy's hair roughly. "Get back to work, you lazy little scoundrel. Next time I give an order, jump to it."

"Yes, Master Colby," Tam gabbled, running off.

Joss looked sharply at Hannah. "In the past five years three men have been killed by runaway wagons in this yard!"

"There was still no need to bawl at the child."

"He has to learn to obey me without question. He nearly lost his life because he didn't jump when I said jump."

"He's not a dog!"

"He has to learn to act like one," Joss said fiercely. "All the men obey me without thinking. In the works a split second can make the difference between life and death and there can only be one voice to shout the order. That voice is mine.

There'd be confusion in there if I didn't keep them all on a tight rein." He took her arm in a vice-like grip, staring at her. "Don't ever question my authority in front of my men again or I'll teach you as I've taught them."

Andrew strolled up, a lace handkerchief in his hand. "You saved that boy's life, Colby. The bravest thing I've ever seen."

Joss released Hannah and gave Andrew a dry glance. "All in a day's work, Master Arandall." Somehow the sardonic voice managed to make the words an insult and Andrew flushed.

"I thought you would both be crushed to death," he said, still trying to be polite.

Joss showed him his teeth in a grimace which passed for a smile. "I've no intention of getting killed for a slow-witted little dolt like that," he said, turning on his heel and striding towards the sheds.

"What a strange, rude fellow he is," Andrew murmured to Hannah, staring after him. "Brave enough to save a life and yet so uncaring of what he's done."

Joss turned. "D'you want to see the works or not, Master Arandall?" he shouted, his eyes fixed angrily on Hannah as Andrew stood beside her.

Andrew Arandall became a regular visitor to the house over the next weeks. Mistress Shield was intensely excited by his attentions to her daughter and managed to persuade her husband to take her to Birmingham to buy material so that she could have new gowns made for Caroline. Their absence altered the whole atmosphere of the house. Mrs. Poley gave the servants an afternoon free while she walked down to visit her friend in the village. Peg took her Bible into the fields. Nancy sought earthly comfort with one of the men. Hannah sneaked into the parlour to look at the unread books left lying around for show by Mistress Shield. While she was turning the pages, Joss walked into the room and stared at her.

"What are you doing?"

She put the book behind her back. He stepped closer and held her with one arm while the other forced the book out of her hand.

"Can you read, Hannah?" His brows lifted, his silvery eyes mocking her.

She refused to answer, her eyes defying him. That strange look came into his face. His eyes slide down to stare at her mouth. She felt the flesh of her lips burning as though he touched them.

He moved closer, one arm still around her waist, and she could hear him breathing quickly, roughly.

His eyes lifted after a long moment and met her startled, shaken stare.

Thick silence lay between them. Hannah did not know what was wrong with her, what was happening. Some unknown, bewildering feeling was throbbing in her veins.

She saw his teeth sink into his lower lip. Blood spurted in a line across the pink skin.

"Get out," he said hoarsely.

She could not move. Her feet felt rooted. She stared at him, trembling.

His face went white. The hard bones of his face clenched. There were flames in his eyes and she could not drag her gaze from him. Fear came into her face, the fear of the rabbit under the eye of the snake.

Caroline's light step broke in upon their mutual absorption. Joss pivoted, shuddering like a man woken from sleep. Hannah ran from the room into the kitchen and out into the clean, fresh air.

"Oh, Joss," Caroline moaned, running into his arms, totally unaware that Hannah had ever been in the room. She clung to him, a dry sob at the back of her throat.

He forced himself to smile, the movement of his mouth stiff. "What is it, my sweet?" He patted her shoulders automatically, but his mind was leaping with other images. He was almost sick with hunger and he felt drained, as though the struggle he had just had with himself had left him empty.

Caroline poured out all her anxiety. She told him of her mother's eagerness to encourage Andrew Arandall. She whimpered that the squire's son was coming to visit her again soon, that her parents were buying new stuff with which to make fashionable gowns for her to wear while she entertained her new admirer. "I am afraid, Joss," she sobbed. "They mean to refuse us permission to marry now!"

Joss was listening intently now and he was furiously angry with himself, with Hannah, with the Shields. While he had been trapped in a bitter lusting for a bastard servant, he might have lost his chance of a bright future. He looked over Caroline's bright head, his face shuttered.

"Joss?" she whispered miserably. "Joss, you do still love me? You will not let this happen? I love you, Joss. I could not bear to marry Master Arandall."

Joss had risen above his hunger for Hannah. He was thinking coolly. He looked down at Caroline and he smiled. "My dearest," he said. "My own love, it would be cruel of them to part us now."

He kissed her gently, softly, and she wound her slim arms around his neck. When he pulled her down on to the sofa she went willingly. He bent over her, kissing her. Her eyes closed and she moaned under his mouth. Joss looked round the room with appreciation. Until he came to this house for the first time he had never been in such a fine room. He thought of the bed in which he had slept with his brothers, the sheets alive with fleas and bedbugs. His first sight of this room had bred in him a desire for all that it implied of success. It was the place he would have chosen, he thought drily, to make certain of Caroline.

She was trembling in his arms. He ran his hands through her fine, light hair, his mouth now moving down her exposed throat until she was half dazed, groaning. He had never been so bold before. When he pulled her down with him among the cushions she struggled, gasping anxiously. "No, Joss!"

"My shy, sweet little love," he murmured in her ear. His hands touched her bodice. She shivered. He began to kiss her again and she kissed him back eagerly. His hands unlaced her, fondling the soft white skin which now lay exposed to his wandering fingers. Caroline was beset by contradictory emotions. Her head fell back weakly. She was whimpering. He thought of Hannah's fierce defiance and a faint sigh came from

65

him, then he forced himself to bend his mind to the girl again, caressing her expertly, waiting with an experienced mind to feel the moment when her body grew responsive enough to be beyond her control.

She was not the first virgin he had taken. He had learnt to read the signs. Caroline was still frightened, still stiff. He stroked and fondled her seductively, whispering love words, kissing her captive mouth.

When at last he pushed back her skirts she clutched weakly at them, muttering a denial, but her voice held no confidence. He could sense that she was already passive, waiting for him, some part of her mind having already submitted. She lay under him like a trapped rabbit waiting for the death blow of the poacher's strong hand.

Joss was very gentle, yet there was inevitably pain, and she gave a sharp cry which he muffled with his hand, looking at the door with wary apprehension, since it was no part of his plan to have them discovered. He needed to have made sure of the girl. Her father would not try to get out of their bargain once Caroline had lost her virginity.

She tried to push him away, her hands trembling. She was terrified, her desire for him lost in the pain. Joss removed his fingers from their gag on her mouth and kissed her softly. He lay very still, resuming the soothing movements of his hands. Gradually Caroline softened again. He moved, delicately arousing her. Her slim thighs trembled and she put her arms tightly around his neck, whispering, "I love you, I love you."

Joss looked at her through narrowed eyes and smiled. With a plunge which made her cry out again he began to thrust deeply into her, holding her down as she struggled, ignoring her cries of hurt, her begging. He might have no other chance to leave her with a child in her womb. He needed to be certain. This was no casual mating. He was seizing his future.

The thought made him eager. Powerful with a desire which was impersonal towards the girl herself, he used her body mercilessly now. Caroline stared up at his set face, shaking. "Joss, Joss," she cried suddenly and the words trailed away into a pathetic, high whimpering as her body writhed into orgasm. Joss shot his seed deeply into her, indifferent to the body he was using, only convulsed with a sensation of triumph in this moment. Caroline heard his deep groans as she lay still herself and tenderness lit her small face.

"My dearest Joss," she murmured, stroking his black head. "My sweet love." She pressed him against her body, cradling him. Now that the pain had subsided she was weakly grateful to him, adoring him.

She felt reborn, a woman now, no longer a child. His cries of fierce satisfaction had convinced her that he loved her as she loved him and she was given courage by the belief.

Only later as they sat demurely on the sofa did she look at him nervously. "Joss, what if I have a child?"

"We'll be wed before anyone suspects it," he told her, and there was the faintest echo of irony in his voice, the half-hooded gleam of his eyes sardonic as they glanced around the room.

Caroline sensed his distance from her and frowned. What was he thinking about?

He caught her puzzled look and at once he smiled, all charm. "Trust me, Caroline."

"I do," she said eagerly, leaning to kiss his cheek. "I was frightened to begin with but now I shall be brave, Joss."

He looked at her bright, pretty little face with an irritation which he concealed. Why was she such a dull fool? A soft, chattering little creature, half child, her brains summer-like, a mere covering over her mind. Strip away her babble of gowns and dancing and homely gossip and she was completely stupid. She had no interest in anything outside her home. She knew nothing but pleasure and her daily round of tasks. What sort of life would he have with her? Would she grow into just such a woman as her damned mother? The idea made him shudder.

He made himself remember how much depended on her. He had to wed her if his future was to flower as he planned.

Joss left her and walked through the yard to the works. Jabey was wheeling rods to the wagons waiting to be loaded. Hannah sat on the well wall, eating a withered apple from the

67

apple loft, the last of the autumn's fruit. Joss glanced her way and saw the sunlight glint on her dark red-brown hair, giving it a metallic brightness. She threw the core from her, the movement lifting her high breasts in a graceful curve, then waved to Jabey, smiling. Joss cursed silently, turning away. The price of ambition wrenched at him like hot pincers.

Four

CAROLINE SHIELD HAD been suffering morning sickness for three days, sneaking out to rinse her own washbowl before a servant saw it, hiding her condition as best she could, with a sick-beating heart and a sense of dread. She dared not confide in her mother. Mary Shield would be violent when she knew that her daughter was expecting Joss Colby's child. Andrew Arandall had aroused such hopes in the Shields that if it all came to nothing through Caroline's own misbehaviour she knew that she would pay dearly. Her parents had spoiled her from infancy, petting and indulging her, but she had seen enough of her mother's treatment of Hannah to have a dim inkling of what might befall her if Mary Shield ever became really angry.

In the grey dawn light she stole out of her room with her bowl, teeth chattering with fright. If she could only get down to the kitchen to empty it without being caught by one of the servants!

She was in the kitchen when a pang caught her. Heaving, she leaned over the slop bucket. Hannah found her like this and the two girls stared at each other for a few seconds before either spoke.

They had rarely, indeed, spoken alone before. Caroline kept strictly to her own side of the house. When she spoke to Hannah it was briefly and shyly. But now Caroline was white and shadowed around the eyes.

"Are you ill?" Hannah forgot to speak humbly. Concerned, she stared at the girl, searching the drawn countenance.

Caroline did not know what made her answer truthfully. Instinct drew the words out of her. "I am carrying Joss's child." When the sentence ended her mouth stayed open in alarm and incredulity. Why had she said it? She looked beseechingly at Hannah, putting out a clammy hand to clutch at her. "Do not tell, do not tell!" Tears welled up in her eyes and rolled down her face. "Please, Hannah!"

Hannah looked at her in shock and anger, although why she should feel either she did not know, for what else had she expected of Joss Colby but that he should make certain of Caroline in the only way he could, having had his way as she well knew with so many other of the local girls. Already his dark head and strong features could be seen on little faces in the neighbourhood. He had never had to pay for his adventures. He had chosen girls whose families had no means to strike back at him. One girl had been wed off hurriedly before her condition was obvious. Another had run away to Birmingham after the birth of her child. The third worked at the inn, serving in the noisy bar, a cheerful slattern, turning a deaf ear to the comment of her neighbours. Oh, Joss had known precisely how to accomplish his ends, sure of his own fertility, intending hers.

"Does he know?" she asked, forgetting entirely to speak with the soft voice of the servant.

Caroline was too deep in misery to care. She looked at Hannah with the terrified eyes of a child. "No," she whispered, panic in her voice. "When he does . . ." She broke off, swallowing, her fingers digging into Hannah's arm.

Hannah was puzzled. Why did the girl look so afraid? Joss would marry her. He would jump at the chance. Was she so stupid that she did not know that?

"My mother," Caroline gasped, and the terror in her eyes made it all clear to Hannah.

She sighed. Of course, she thought! Mary Shield would want blood for this! It was not of Joss that Caroline was so frightened, it was of her own mother. Childlike, she wanted to delay the moment when the truth became known. Looking at her slight body in the white nightgown, Hannah tried to guess how far her pregnancy had advanced. If she was throwing up in the mornings it must be early days yet, she thought.

Taking the washbowl from the girl she rinsed it and threw

the foul water into the overnight slop bucket. "I'll empty this now," she said, lifting it. Caroline waited in the kitchen until Hannah returned. The other servants had not stirred yet. The men were still passing on their way to the yards. Hannah filled the kettle and set it over the fire. She talked as she worked. "You must tell Joss at once. He will see your father. Let Joss arrange it all. It will come best from him. Your mother need never know at all if your father agrees to keep it from her."

Caroline put her slender little arms around her body, hugging herself. "Papa will be angry."

Hannah shrugged, stirring the meal in the pot. "It must be done. Better sooner than later."

Biting her lip, Caroline whispered, "Master Arandall . . ."

Hannah's face was blank as she looked back at the girl. Caroline paused and went on tremulously, "My mother wishes me to marry Master Arandall, not Joss! He . . ." Again she broke off, shivering.

Hannah did not need to be told any of that. She understood the situation completely. How could she tell Caroline that Andrew Arandall was amusing himself? He had no intention of matching with the daughter of an ironmaster. He was bored with his home, weary of a pointless existence, a man with intelligence and wit amusing himself with a little adventure. Her face tightened. Men were all the same, brothers under the skin, whatever their class, questing like animals for satisfaction without considering what harm they did to others.

Andrew had been visiting Shield House for nigh on two months now. He came almost daily. Everyone took his visits to be on Caroline's behalf alone, but Hannah knew perfectly well that he came as much to see her. They met secretly in the spinney beyond the works. Andrew would wait for hours until she was able to slip out for a few moments. He lay on the grass reading, apparently content to hang about like a lovesick boy, yet an eavesdropper would find nothing loverlike about their talk. Andrew sat with his hands laced around his knees, telling her of Cambridge or the towns of Italy he had visited on his tour of the continent. He never once touched her. They talked almost like two men. No one had ever talked to

Hannah as Andrew did. Had he so much as looked at her with amorous intent she would have stopped meeting him, but their relationship was of a kind and quality she found deeply satisfying.

Although the thought had never been put into words, it was the relationship of teacher and pupil. Andrew discovered that he had a genius for teaching. He loved to watch her mind flowering under the influence of his own. He was eager to hear her reactions to the books he lent her. His eyes glowed when she became excited by the new ideas, knowledge, poetry he was revealing to her. They argued over the views of philosophers, ancient and modern. They read Plato together, and Hannah was illuminated with delight by the beauty of the language and the calm sanity of the thought. Andrew was half shocked, half excited by her revolutionary ideas of religion, her cynicism, her shrewdness. Hannah was scathing about Andrew's romantic view of the Jacobites, his tug towards the Catholic Church. "Popery, superstition, humbug," she told him and he earnestly argued with her in defence of some aspects of it.

He looked on her as a sculptor looks at an unhewn block of marble from which he may release the beauty he has dreamt about. Hannah had been imprisoned in the Shield household, her mind essentially neglected, her spirit raw. Andrew's talk and the books he lent her were giving her wings, lifting her from servitude, showing her a world she had never known existed.

They rarely spoke of Caroline, but once or twice Hannah had seen them together when they did not see her. She knew that Andrew's light teasing manner to the other girl concealed patronage, contempt, a not unkind indifference. Andrew was not the sort of man to willingly hurt another human being, but he was selfish enough to use Caroline without understanding or caring what effect his frequent visits might have on her. He could not fail to be aware that the Shields were delighted with his attentions to her, but he was capable of using that pleasure for his own purposes.

Hannah felt anger stir within her. Andrew had no business

to behave as he had done! How dared he manipulate Caroline as though she were a puppet without feelings?

Caroline was sobbing drily, her slender body shivering in the cold kitchen. "We are blood kin," she whispered, looking at Hannah in a weak pleading fashion. "Help me, Hannah."

Hannah felt pity for her, seeing how useless she was at fending for herself, knowing that she must help her if she could, just as she would never be able to walk away from a rabbit trapped in a poacher's snare in the woods. Pity was an emotion she could have well done without, she thought, her mouth twisting.

Who had ever felt pity for her in this house? Except the servants, whose case was little better than her own? Caroline had never been actively unkind to her but she had never reached out a pitying hand in the past. She had turned away when she saw Hannah beaten. She had been silent when Mistress Shield screamed abuse at her.

Hannah despised herself for feeling pity and concern for Caroline now. A strong man like Joss Colby was free of the tangling web of pity, taking without mercy what he desired, lacking no shame in his fierce pursuit of ambition. The strong must not pity the weak, any more than the lion pities its prey. It was the way of nature.

Yet I do feel pity for her, she thought wryly. I must be weak, myself. Perhaps all victims pity each other. Perhaps we sense a common bond and it is ourselves we pity, ourselves we have to help?

She smiled at Caroline and the other girl blinked, seeing for the first time the brilliance of those eyes when they were filled, as they were now, with light and strength.

"Don't weep or you will have red eyes. Go back to your room now. The others will be down in a moment. I hear them moving about. Don't fret. I'll think of a way to help you."

Caroline trembled and impulsively flung an arm around her, kissing her cheek, then ran out, her long nightgown flaring around her. Hannah stood there with a surprised hand to her cheek. It was the first time she had ever received a kiss in this house.

She saw to the breakfast. The kitchen filled up. They muttered their prayer and set to eating their bowls of meal. Abel was laughing to himself and when his mother looked sternly at him murmured: "A spider ate a fly. A spider ate a fly." Mrs. Poley frowned. "Abel!" His mouth turned down. Water slid from the corner of it. He looked as though he had been beaten. A tear trickled from one eye. "Poor fly," he said. Hannah gave him some more of the thick oatmeal and he smiled happily at her, distracted. Mrs. Poley sighed.

It was rare for Abel to find such things amusing. Normally the sight of a spider eating a fly would have disturbed him. His mind was becoming more and more cloudy, Hannah thought. Poor boy.

Abel stood turning the meat spit later, watching the juices spurt red from the crisping skin. Hannah saw his finger rub along the meat and watched him lick it afterwards. His mother cuffed his head.

He turned on her like a dog, teeth bared, growling. Mrs. Poley stepped back, aghast. The other servants ceased their work and stared. Joe muttered in his throat. "Aye, aye, I knew t'would come . . ."

Mrs. Poley sent Abel to carry in the wood and he slunk off. Nancy looked sideways at her. "Dangerous, it is, having him around. I'll be afeared to sleep in my bed." Mrs. Poley slapped her, white-faced and drawn, then went on kneading the bread she was shaping for the tins.

Hannah was on her knees cleaning the brass around the fire, the rhythmic movement swaying her whole body, when a pair of boots halted just within her view. She looked up from them to Joss's dark face.

"The family are still abed," she said shortly.

His hand shot out and lifted her to her feet. Her head came to his broad shoulders. Joss put a hand into the fine brown hair, entangling his fingers in it deliberately, tugging it, hurting her. Their eyes met silently.

Hannah made up her mind in that instant. "Caroline is breeding," she said in clipped tones.

His hand stiffened. The strong dark face was blank. She

74

watched him and saw the glitter of triumph in his eyes.

While Andrew Arandall was calling on Caroline daily, the Shields had more or less forbidden Joss the house. They had made it plain that he was no longer a welcome suitor. Joss's lips curled back and his white teeth showed straight and strong.

He laughed. Then he bent his head and fiercely, brutally kissed Hannah's mouth. His arms came round her and he crushed her against his body. She was unprepared, completely taken by surprise. Once or twice, Jabey had kissed her gently, but the savagery of Joss's kiss had no resemblance to a loving caress. She lay limply in his arms, neither responding nor fighting, too dazed to think of either.

He was hurting her and enjoying it, raping her mouth hungrily, in an invasion which forced her head back upon his arm, one hand moving down her body, fondling the warm soft curve of it.

At last he lifted his head, breathing thickly. Hannah was white. Blood showed upon her lip where he had forced it back upon her teeth. Joss stared at her, his eyes leaping.

Coming to life, she put her hands upon his chest and shoved him away. He went, an arrogant smile on his mouth.

"Save that for Caroline," Hannah bit out. "You sicken me!"

His face took on a raw, scraped tightness, the heated excitement leaving his eyes.

"What are you going to do about Caroline?" Hannah asked him. "Her mother will half kill her for this – you must speak to her father and get him to break the news."

"What business is it of yours?" Joss's face was hard with anger now, all the elation gone from it.

"Caroline asked me for help. Poor stupid little bitch, she's trapped, just as you planned, Joss Colby."

"I used no force. She wanted me. Her mother may fancy Andrew Arandall as a son-in-law but Caroline wants me. If she's trapped, it is a trap she walked into of her own accord."

Hannah could not dispute that. Andrew was handsome in

75

his pretty fashion but Joss Colby's physical vitality and powerful body dominated the women towards whom he looked and blotted out other men as effectively as a storm-cloud obliterates sunshine.

Joss smiled, seeing the admission in her face. He put out a finger and brushed it along her lip, then showed her the smear of blood he had wiped away before, holding her eyes, he sensuously ran his tongue along his finger, licking her blood.

Red rushed up her face. Until today their long hostility had seemed neuter to her: an awareness of personality, a clash of loyalties. She had only seen Joss as a threat to her uncle, her interest in him fuelled by her suspicions of him. She had believed Joss's aggression towards her to be based on his knowledge that she, of all the members of the household, saw his motives and his plans quite clearly.

Now she became aware of a force within Joss which brooded upon her. Without a word he made it clear to her and under those fixed, intent eyes she could not evade the knowledge which was thrust upon her.

Joss wanted her.

She had never been aware of herself as a woman until this moment. Unawakened, she had walked free of the physical lures which so excited Nancy, impatient of the other girl's sly sensuality.

Dry-mouthed, she ran her tongue over her lips and his eyes followed the movement.

"Have I silenced that tongue of yours at last?" He gave her a look of barbed mockery. "Are you frightened, Hannah?"

"I'm not one of your women, Joss Colby, and I never will be," she threw back, but she was trembling, and his eyes told her he knew it.

"Oh, yes," he said softly. "You will, Hannah."

"I'd see you in hell first!"

A fugitive gleam of humour crossed his face. "If you were there with me, it would not be hell."

She gasped. She had imagined his desire for her to be a sudden thing, a passing fancy, and the deep husky words

76

showed her she was wrong. They touched some chord in her, her trembling increased.

She felt a force in her blood which threatened to overwhelm her. She had tried to be blind to Joss but hate and love were two sides of one coin and now the coin spun in her, landing with the reverse side showing.

He was watching her eagerly now, his heartbeat accelerating so much that she could hear it. Involuntarily her hand moved to touch his chest, the heart thudding against her hand, the warmth of his body permeating her skin through his shirt. Joss gasped as though she offered him a fierce caress and his hand came down to press over hers, crushing it against his body. They stared at each other. She knew him to his core as though in the most intimate of embraces. He was hiding nothing from her. He never had. From the very beginning, their minds had been open to each other as though they were one being.

Joss was shaking, hunger in his eyes. "I will take you away from here," he said hoarsely. "You will want nothing, Hannah."

"And Caroline?" She already knew the answer, but she wanted to hear him say it.

"I must marry her," he said, almost impatiently. "For our sakes, Hannah. When I'm master here you shall have your own house and fine clothes, a servant to look after you."

She laughed. "I'm not my mother, Joss." She was not jealous of Caroline or any of the other women whom he had taken with such light contempt. The power of his strong, driving body was the power of the tilthammer, melting and crushing what lay beneath it, transmuting it into malleable metal. Hannah did not want his body.

It was his mind to which she cleaved, for which she starved. He was the only free man she knew, free of the shackles of convention and custom, despising them because he did not need them. He was cruel and ruthless, without mercy or scruple, but he made his own laws and forced others to live by them, and that, surely was freedom.

She saw by the working features of his face that he was trying to marshal arguments to convince her. He had come close to victory, he had been aware of her response, scenting it as an animal might, his sexual instincts telling him she was his, if he used his power.

For one moment Hannah had hungered for the sensual possession he offered her, then her mind rose up above her body and denied it all. She thought of her mother and knew that that was not her road.

"No, Joss," she said, and cold certainty was in her voice. "Oh, no."

For a moment frustration and anger flashed in his eyes, then Joss's cold, clever brain reasserted itself and he shrugged. "Maybe you're right. Now is not the time. Best for me to get into the saddle before I use the whip. They'll not get out of it now Caroline carries my child in her belly. They may kick, but they'll do what they must."

"Be kind to her, Joss, she is only a child," Hannah said flatly.

"I'll be sweet as honey to her." He put a finger on her cheek, his eyes caressing. "Be sweet to me, Hannah."

Her face was drily sardonic. "I am not the honeyed sort."

He laughed shortly. "No, damn you, you're not. A bitter sort of honey you give, Hannah. I've a powerful hunger for it, all the same."

She turned hurriedly away from the look in his eyes and Joss said behind her, "I shall be living in the house now, Hannah. Shall you like that?"

She almost ran from him, hearing him laugh behind her. That evening the servants listened as Master Shield reluctantly broke the news to his wife and brought a screaming fury down upon his bowed head.

Mistress Shield was heard slapping Caroline and then the girl's voice wept weakly before she ran from the room. For an hour the hysterical rage continued before the mistress took to her bed with a sick headache. Mrs. Poley took her up a tisane and came down looking grim. Nancy was agog, dying to know what was afoot. Apart from Hannah, all the servants knew was that something was badly wrong in the family.

In bed that night Nancy eagerly whispered, "I wish I knew what was behind it. Hannah, can you guess?" Hannah did not reply, pretending sleep, her body turned from Nancy.

In the candlelit attic Peg knelt beside her bed, reading her Bible, murmuring the words aloud in a flat voice. Did she never ask of her God that one word: why? Did she abjectly accept the way in which they all lived? Perhaps, thought Hannah wryly, it was because she herself had so large a grievance against God that she dared to stand up and ask continuously for His reasons for the way the world was ruled. Peg lived on her knees in continual reverence. No wonder she never lifted her eyes to see what went on around her! How could a creature always on its knees see anything clearly? Man had to stand to see.

Hannah was awake before dawn, her mind troubled. Dressing she slid from the bed and crept down the dark stairs, out into the cold morning air. Running through the shadows she was shaken when a rat shot across her feet. They came at night to feed on the grain in stable and stackyard, and the stablecats fed fat on them.

Sometimes Andrew came to the spinney to meet her in the dawn light. It was one time when she could be certain of seeing him safely. When she reached the spinney that morning the sky was just beginning to show a paling of light. A few birds had begun to preen, uttering sleepy calls. Andrew had tethered his bay gelding to a hazel slip and was pacing to and fro, a slender figure in a brown riding coat. He turned and smiled as she walked up to him. "I've got you something special this morning!"

She took the book and turned it over.

"What is it?" The name was unknown to her.

"Plutarch," he said in his light clear voice which was now so familiar to her. "He's an historian. Roman. You will find him very easy to read."

She flicked through the pages, reading a piece here and there. "It seems easy enough. You'll have to explain some of the words."

"Make a note of them and I will." Andrew took his duties as her tutor very seriously.

"You should have stayed at Cambridge," she said impulsively. "You could have taught there."

He grimaced. "Rough clods of boys? Not I." They both laughed.

"Caroline is going to marry Joss Colby after all," she told him suddenly.

He looked surprised. "I thought that was off."

"It is on again."

"Hades," he said, looking sullen.

She knew he enjoyed being with the girl, enjoying the pretty, delicate limbs, the eyes with their bright, moist gleam, as though Caroline were always on the point of tears. Andrew thought her silly but he liked to look at her, as he liked to look at pictures or statuary.

He shrugged. "Well, he's welcome to her. She's brainless, a talking doll. If one only wanted to touch, to be amused, she'd do very well, but surely there is more to life than talk of clothes and gossip?"

She eyed him coolly, considering him. His view of Caroline, she suspected, was much the same as Joss's attitude. Poor Caroline. Andrew flung himself down on the grass, biting at a blade of it, his teeth white and even.

"She did not mention it to me yesterday," he said, his lower lip stuck out like a spoilt boy.

"It was only decided last night." Hannah had no intention of letting him guess the reason for that decision. The fewer who knew, the better, and Andrew had a slight tendency to gossip which he had inherited from his father.

He dug a little hole with one finger, poking earth to one side. "Colby's not the man for her. He is a bully-boy, a rude rough fellow. He'll walk all over her with his boots on."

Hannah laughed. "No doubt he will, but perhaps she will enjoy it."

"That soft little creature?"

Eying him, Hannah said: "Soft little creatures sometimes like such men."

Andrew raised his head. "Do you?"

Hannah's face was wry. "Would you call me a soft little creature?"

"I do not know what to call you," Andrew said slowly. He looked at her and remembered a life so far removed from that which he now endured that it seemed to him as a period of perfect bliss. He and his friends had talked the sun up and down again in their poky rooms, by daylight or flickering candlelight, discussing life, death, the natural universe, the elements, poetry and friendship. It had been a wild awakening to the soul, a time of fierce mental excitement, and now he was flung from it, like a man once prince now beggar, into the stables and dinner table of Arandall, to starve and pine for the companionship of minds akin to his own. He had nothing in common with his brothers and father. Only in Hannah had he found a mind which could match his own, tinder to his flint.

The Arandalls had no need to search for meaning in their lives. They knew themselves to be the hub and reason for the world. Everything around them circled like stars to their sun, paying them homage. They knew their own importance. They were sure of their place. Only Andrew felt any lack, and he had never been able to talk of his feelings to any of his family, since they would have frowned or laughed, according to their mood, seeing his doubts and uncertainties with amusement or irritation, and always with contempt.

He had been feeling bored and miserable that Sunday when he first met Hannah. Her blunt, sharp speech had attracted him. He had seen her hostility to his family and been attracted to it, since by disdaining his family she was in a way agreeing with him. He found the crude materialism of his family unpleasant, their certainty infuriating.

"Are you a puritan? A dissenter?" he asked her. "Sometimes you seem to talk like one, yet at other times you mock them."

"It seems to me that religion is thrust on us like the chains that bind slaves," she said. "Our rulers use it to hold us down."

"But think, Hannah, without God what are we? Remove the sun and the world dies. Remove God and what meaning has man?"

81

"How shall we know unless we try?" she asked. "If man needs God, what does God need of man?"

As always when they argued they forgot the time and the sky filled with the opalescent mist of morning, a gauze web of gleaming white spun over the blue sky through which the slowly rising sun shot pale gold. Hannah broke off suddenly, rising. "I must get back!"

Andrew looked irritated. Time meant nothing to him. He had no duties to perform, no mistress driving him with threats of punishment. "Not yet," he complained, catching her arm. "Hannah, don't go yet."

"I must." She ran through the trees. Andrew angrily untied his horse and mounted. Hannah came out of the trees to find herself face to face with Joss on his way to the works. He stopped dead, listening to the hoofbeats of the departing horse, then looked at her, his face white with rage. "So," he said through his teeth. "He's had you, you little bitch."

Her eyes burned, their colour bright green. "No!"

The fierce tension eased in his bones. He brought himself under control. "No?" He moved closer, watching her. "Did he sigh and murmur sweet words, Hannah? Tell me. I am curious to know. How does the young gentleman court you?"

"That is my affair," she said.

"You do not deny he came a-wooing, then?"

"He's no crude petticoat-chaser."

He laughed, teeth set. "He may begin with compliments, but soon, Hannah, he'll wheedle for more than a few words in a spinney. Under that silk coat lies a man's hunger and he'll not marry you, Hannah. Your brain must tell you that. He'll not even set you up in your own house. He lies if he promises it. He'll tire of you once he's had you, and leave you with a bastard. Would you repeat your mother's story?"

"You would have me do so."

She spoke so quietly he had to bend to hear her.

"It would not be so for us," he said hoarsely. His hand came down on her shoulder, his thumb pressing into her. "Would it, Hannah?"

"What makes you think it would be so with Andrew?"

82

His breath came sharply. "You cannot prefer that white-skinned little ninny."

Her heart hurt in her breast.

"No more secret meetings with him or I'll beat you until you fall to your knees and scream to me for mercy," he promised softly. "And you'd not get it, Hannah. I'd half kill you if you saw him again."

She ran into the house, breathless, and Mrs. Poley turned from the fire to frown at her. "Where've you been? I've had all to do myself."

"I'm sorry, I was sick of a headache and went walking," Hannah said.

Mrs. Poley was too good-natured to be cross for long and, anyway, all her attention was given to Abel these days. He had changed lately. He seemed irritable and distracted, muttering to himself, grinding his teeth. He stared at Nancy all the time, a sick moon smile on his face. She, tossing her head, ignored him mostly, but that morning Hannah caught her wiggling her tongue at Abel, a deliberate invitation on her face. Abel was grunting as he watched, his eyes excited. Hannah dragged Nancy away and pinched her viciously. "Why did you do that? How can you be so cruel and thoughtless?"

Nancy giggled. "He's panting after me, Han, day and night! This morning he peered through the crack in the attic door while I were dressing. I saw him. I pretended not to." She looked stupidly knowing, amused by it. "I took my time, I can tell you. Why not? Poor mazed dolt."

Hannah felt sick. "Nancy, you would not!"

Nancy looked at her sullenly. "He's strong, Han. Look at those great muscles. What do I care if his head be full of straw?"

Hannah dug her nails into Nancy's skin. Nancy squeaked. "Han!"

"You dare," Hannah breathed. "You dare! Keep away from him. Do you hear me, Nancy?"

Nancy looked sidelong, pouting. "Very well, Han."

Mrs. Poley wearily called her. "Nancy, you must go down to the village with this crock of cream for the vicar's wife.

83

Carry it careful mind, and give her Mrs. Shield's best compliments."

Nancy went off, her shawl around her shoulders, her pattens sliding on the muddy path. Mrs. Poley gave Hannah some other task to do and turned to watch Peg delicately moulding leaves of pastry to decorate a great pork pie which Mrs. Poley had made. Abel snatched a piece, was cuffed and ran out, weeping like a small child.

In the yard he met Master Shield who cuffed him again for blubbering. "A great boy like you! No wonder your poor mother looks so tired these days."

Abel snarled at him and when, astonished, Master Shield jumped back, the simpleton turned and ran away, barking like a dog. Master Shield frowned and sighed. He hesitated over going in to speak to Mrs. Poley about the incident, so at last he went through to speak to his wife, who was grimly sitting in a chair staring at nothing with a frozen face.

Caroline was in her room. She had not left it since the previous evening. Her mother had not spoken to her in hours.

Abel shuffled along the road, his hangdog shoulders bent, muttering to himself. Just before he reached the stream, a squirrel dropped to the ground, chattering at him. Abel laughed, eyes brightening. He chattered back in mimicry and the little animal backed, red tail bristling, then ran back up the tree.

Someone laughed. Abel turned, surprised. One of Squire Arandall's daughters, Sophy, sat watching him from the back of her white mare, a wide-brimmed hat half-shading her pretty face. Abel stood gaping, his eyes filling with excitement, and the girl, seeing who he was and knowing he was a simpleton, tossed her head and asked: "What are you staring at, oaf?"

He moved to her side and she watched him advance, scorn and distaste in her eyes. Abel saw that she was very pretty, her clothes rich and bright, the red of her riding skirt spreading against the mare's white hair. He put a wondering hand to her and vaguely fondled the outline of her knee under the material.

84

"Get your hands off me!" Sophy was suddenly afraid and acted in anger. Her whip slashed downwards, cutting open his cheek.

Abel roared. The horse rose, kicking out and Sophy, caught off guard, fell to the muddy bank. Abel was on her like a wolf before she could get up. She screamed, struggling, but the boy was very strong. She could not throw him off once he was astride her. Instinct older than time was driving him and, half-child still, he had no comprehension of what he was doing. He used force since he knew of nothing else and the violent thrust of his body ripped the girl apart. Her screaming frightened Abel. It confused him into more violence. Grunting, he clumsily tried to silence her by squeezing her slender throat, his huge thumbs pressing on her windpipe. She lay still at last, the thick choking stopped. Abel smiled, content. He patted her distorted, purpled face lovingly. Then he bent his energies to satisfying the urges which had driven him so far. The girl's tongue lolled from her open mouth. Abel laughed as he looked at it, remembering Nancy's wiggling little tongue.

A keeper found them, having heard the screams and ridden hell for leather towards them. Aghast he saw Abel's huge body crouched over the girl and heard his thick grunting.

"Oh, God," the keeper muttered. "God in Heaven."

He vomited on the path twice before he had the strength to tear Abel off her. Abel was shivering by then, aware that he had done something wrong. The man was angry with him. He was looking at him in a way Abel found worrying. Afraid, Abel struggled to free himself and ran away across the fields.

They hunted him for six hours through the darkness. Mrs. Poley had collapsed and was weeping and shivering on her bed. The fields were alive with men crashing and stumbling, shouting and showing lanterns. Joss came back to the house once to check that Abel had not come back there and Hannah caught his arm between both her hands. "Joss, if they catch him he will hang!"

Joss looked at her grimly. "You did not see that girl."

85

She winced. "But he is not made like other men!"

"In some ways he is," Joss said with a grimace. "To his cost."

She felt her skin heating, shuddered and looked away, finding it impossible to believe that poor simple Abel had done such a thing. Far away across the fields, lights showed like will o' the wisps as the men moved through the night. Hannah shivered in the wind as she walked to the door with him. She thought of the poor boy cowering somewhere, too frightened to know what to do or where to go. "God help him," she said miserably.

"God?" Joss laughed harshly. "I thought you had more brains than to ask that. No gentle Jesus will stretch out a comforting hand for Abel . . ." His voice broke off as he cocked his head. "Ssh . . . what's that?"

They listened in silence. "The stackyard," Hannah whispered, a hand to her mouth. Joss nodded and pushed her back towards the house. "Get inside and bolt the door."

"Abel would not hurt me," she protested, and Joss turned a dark face on her, his eyes a flash of steel.

"Do you think I want to see you as I saw that girl? Even had he not choked her to death, he could have killed her, the way he used her."

She felt sick, her stomach heaving. "Oh, God."

"Get inside," Joss said, thrusting her inside the house. "And bolt the door, Hannah, or I'll whip the skin from you."

Joss found the boy crouching in a corner behind a stack of straw, rocking himself like a child, his thumb in his mouth. Tears smeared his face and he whimpered softly. When he saw Joss he flinched, moaning. "I'm sorry, Joss, I'm sorry. I won't do it again. Don't be angry, Joss."

Joss closed his eyes, teeth gritted, and raised the pistol he carried.

"Joss," the simpleton pleaded as Joss opened his eyes and looked at him again.

Hannah heard the retort as she waited, trembling, behind the bolted door. Her hand shook as she drew back the heavy iron bolt. She came running across the yard, her heart in her mouth, stopping as she saw Joss.

He looked at her with a hard, blank face.

"He'll not hang," he said.

Five

HANNAH COULD NOT at first take in what he had said. She stared at him, her eyes dropping from his face to the smoking pistol in his hand. Slowly she turned her head and saw Abel's body. He lay awkwardly, a hand flung up in a gesture which made her wince, his palm pink in the darkness. Dark red blood crawled across his shirt.

"Oh, God," Hannah moaned. "You killed him! You killed him in cold blood!" Her eyes went wild. Lips shaking, screaming, she threw herself at Joss like a spitting cat, her nails raking down his face. The dark side of his nature was revealed to her in all its ruthless savagery. He had showed Abel no mercy. "You shot him like a dog," she burst out, hands flailing.

Joss dropped his pistol and held her off with one hand. The other slapped her face so hard her head rocked. Her hysterical crying stopped with a gasp.

Trembling, tears running down her face, she lifted her head and they stared at each other. After a long moment he asked her: "Will you tell his mother or shall I?"

"You'd enjoy that, wouldn't you, Joss Colby?" Bitterness made her cruel. She pulled away from him and he let her go. "I will tell her," she said, walking back towards the house.

When Hannah gently broke it to her, Mrs. Poley was silent for a moment, her body shivering violently. She put her hands over her face. Hannah threw both arms around her, patting her, murmuring inaudible words of comfort. Mrs. Poley clung briefly, then she got up and walked downstairs and out of the house. In the stackyard Joss stood with a lantern in his hand. He had thrown a horse blanket over the boy's body.

When Mrs. Poley appeared he knelt and threw back the blanket, revealing Abel's still face. Mrs. Poley stood there, looking down at her son, hands clenched at her sides.

Hannah was taken aback when the mother turned and looked at Joss levelly. "Thank you, Joss," she said. He inclined his head and covered the boy's face once more.

Mrs. Poley walked away. When Hannah moved to follow her, Joss seized her wrist. "Leave her," he said shortly. "Some things are best borne alone."

Hannah was thinking. She looked up into Joss's cold face. Huskily she whispered, "I am sorry, Joss." She saw now that Joss had saved the boy from a terrible death. Abel would have suffered appallingly in gaol. Shut away from the sky he would have died a hundred times before they led him out to the scaffold. Her reaction had been blind. It shamed her now.

He looked at her without answering then walked away.

The Arandalls were shattered by the news. The terrible death of their daughter came like a thunderbolt to their comfortable world. Such things did not happen to them. At first, they found it impossible to believe. Death when it came to one of them should wear an acceptable mask. Horror, shame, rage, possessed them.

Sir Matthew rode down to the ironworks, demanding to see Mrs. Poley. Hannah stood at the kitchen door, barring his entrance. Master Shield and Joss heard their raised voices and came striding from the yard. The squire turned haggard, furious eyes upon them.

"You cheated the gallows, did you, Colby? That vile creature used my child abominably and you helped him to escape justice! Well, I will have revenge! I'll run his mother out of the country. Bring her out here. Let me see her face to face."

"You'll not see her," Joss said. "She's sick enough over what happened. God, man, do you think the poor woman wanted this? The boy was mad. We all regret what he did, none more than his mother. It is a terrible business."

"You shot him deliberately," the squire bellowed.

Joss turned his black head and looked at Hannah. She felt

the colour drain from her face at the expression in his eyes. The squire was using her own words, but in what a different fashion! They were meant as an accusation, as she had meant them, yet Joss's action now had, in her eyes, a heroic stature which shamed her.

Joss looked back at Sir Matthew. Calmly he shrugged. "The boy has paid for what happened. Let that be enough." A taut smile tugged at his lips. "We are Christians, are we not, squire?"

Sir Matthew raised his whip to slash Joss across the face, angry purple staining his cheeks. An iron hand clamped over his wrist, twisted it. The whip fell to the ground. The squire drew a harsh breath. Joss released him and he swung to mount his waiting horse.

"You'll regret this, Colby," Sir Matthew grated, looking down on them. "God damn you, I swear one day you'll pay for this."

Joss watched him ride away with a blank face. Henry Shield laid a hand on his arm, gripped it gratefully, then walked away. Joss turned and Hannah met his eyes. He looked at her coldly and she knew he would never forgive her for her outburst after he had shot Abel. There was a new distance between them. Joss walked away back to the sheds and she watched him go with a sense of emptiness.

The Arandalls buried their daughter in the family tomb. A little crowd gathered to watch. The story had already gained the status of a legend. It had all the ingredients beloved by village gossips and Sir Matthew, himself, would have revelled in it if it had not involved his own family. Whispering, the villagers stood back. The squire's family wore the haughty masks their caste learnt early to acquire in time of trial. No one watching who did not know would have guessed at the scandal surrounding the girl's death. The villagers dispersed and the Arandalls returned to their great house to try to forget.

Sir Matthew brought pressure to bear upon the vicar in an attempt to refuse Abel's body Christian burial. Mistress Shield refused to give the servants permission to attend the short ceremony and so Mrs. Poley and Joss alone walked behind Abel to his grave outside the churchyard walls. The vicar said the funeral service his face streaming with rain, his wet head bare. Master Shield arrived towards the end of the proceedings. Mrs. Poley scattered earth in muddy clumps upon the cheap coffin. Master Shield put an arm about her, face grim.

I am sorry I am late, Mrs. Poley." He had intended to be there on time, but his wife had detained him with a sudden fit of wild hysteria. The vicar closed his book and began to walk away. Master Shield touched his arm and murmured thanks. Mrs. Poley lifted her head to add her own. "I'll not forget this, vicar."

He nodded, said a few dry words of comfort, barely knowing how to speak them, it was obvious. He had never met such a situation. The customary words he would have used in such a time of grief seemed out of place for this woman. "God's mercy," he faltered and his voice died away.

Joss smiled sardonically. "Yes," he said. "God's mercy is what we must cling to, vicar, for we'll get none of man."

The vicar looked at him and moved away. Mrs. Poley walked back to the ironworks on Joss's arm, moving like an old woman. Hannah was scouring pots when they entered the kitchen. She dried her hands on her sacking apron and looked anxiously at the housekeeper. Joss sat Mrs. Poley down and went into the parlour. A moment later he came back with a glass of brandy. Mrs. Poley looked at it askance but Joss made her drink it. The spirit brought some colour back to her pale face. She smiled at Joss twistedly. "Ye're a good lad, Joss Colby."

He patted her shoulder and went out. Hannah saw the tears begin to roll down the older woman's face. She knelt and rocked her in her arms, whispering to her. "No, no, hush . . . never mind . . . there, poor soul . . ." When the tears eased she led her up the back stairs and covered her shivering body with all the warm covers they possessed and left her to sleep her grief away.

One direct result of Abel's madness was that Andrew

Arandall did not appear at the Shield house again. Hannah missed him, but she understood why he did not come. Their companionship had always been a strange one. Abel had made it impossible.

She still had the books he had lent her. Now she read them by herself, and there was no one to explain the parts she did not grasp, so she learnt to guess at them by their context. Her favourite reading was still poetry. The music of it did not need explanation. It entered her ear and eye, and filled her mind. She found herself grasping even the phrases made difficult by unknown words. Somehow the meaning penetrated, sinking into her soul like rain into dry earth.

Caroline and Joss were married on a humid day in August. The faintest veil of mist cloaked the burning blue of the sky. A distant rumble of thunder warned of approaching storm and lightning played around the trees a few miles off. The flashes could be seen as the wedding party followed bride and groom out of church.

Mistress Shield had not spoken to Joss since the day she found out that Caroline was carrying his child. When Joss walked into the house the mistress of it walked out of any room he entered. Hannah saw grim amusement in his eyes as he watched the other woman leave.

Caroline was as much under her mother's displeasure but she bore it with less equanimity. Tears pricked at her eyes when her mother ignored her. Her condition made her prone to fits of melancholy. Her moods were never predictable. She laughed hysterically or wept without warning. Abel's death shocked her into wild weeping which turned to silent brooding.

Abel's death had delayed the wedding for a few weeks. Caroline's body was beginning to round out, but tight corsetting hid it when she walked down the aisle. Her mother acted the role of hostess icily, her cold manner acting as a brake upon the gaiety of the guests for a while, but Master Shield had been generous with beer. Soon even Mistress Shield was flushed and slackening.

Caroline drank too much and had to be carried off to lie

down. The guests made crude jokes, as was the custom, their faces flushed with drink. There was dancing to a fiddler's beat later. He sat on a stack of hay, fiddling furiously, eyes bolting from his head, skin reddened and sweating. The young men danced with the girls. The old sat on long benches and passed stone jugs from hand to hand, watching enviously.

Joss carried a basket round the tables and filled it with the food which was left. "Now, don't make yourselves sick," he said roughly to the crowd of little boys following him with eager faces. They ran off with the food while Joss watched them, a faint smile in his eyes.

The only weakness Hannah had ever seen in him was towards the children who worked in the sheds. Joss was not a man for sentiment. He shouted at them, bullied them and watched them for signs of sickness, sending them home if he felt they should not be at work. Woe betide any of them who tried to take advantage of him, though. Joss had no time for sham. He saw through a wheedling tale faster than it could be told.

Nancy came up to Joss and dragged him into the dance, laughing invitingly up at him. She had drunk far too much, Hannah noticed. Nancy was over-flushed and laughed too loudly. Joss had been drinking pretty deep himself, but he had a hard head and it did not show.

"When does the new man start?" Jabey asked Hannah. She turned to look at him in surprise.

"What new man?"

"Haven't you heard? Master Colby told us a new man was coming. He had a strange look and we could see there was something behind it."

"I've heard nothing. Does Master Shield know? I wouldn't put it past Joss to be acting without his knowledge."

"He gives his orders without a thought of Master Shield these days, and they're obeyed. Joss runs the works now."

They stared at each other grimly. Hannah had seen it coming a long time ago. She was not surprised. Joss had planned it with care and determination.

Hannah accepted the jug of beer and drank deeply, flushed

93

after dancing with Jabey. Her head grew giddy, she drifted like a cloud. The jug passed on and Hannah leaned on Jabey's arm, talking to him softly.

Joss loomed up in front of them. He had undone his shirt and his black-haired chest was damp with perspiration, heaving after his dancing. Ignoring Jabey he bent and jerked Hannah to her feet. Jabey stiffened, ready to get angry, but Joss pulled Hannah into the dancers. The gleam of the lanterns made a bright circle in the yard. The fiddler scraped wildly, his rotten teeth showing between his lips as he panted.

Joss looked down at Hannah as she went through the motions of the country dance, stamping her feet, swishing her skirts. His hands locked on her waist, pulling her towards him. Her hands went to his bare shoulders, his skin smooth and damp under her palms.

He lifted her in the movement of the dance, and she looked down into his upturned face. Far away across the fields the lightning flashed. She felt as though the storm had entered her bloodstream. The air was heavy and hot. The dancers were becoming more abandoned, sneaking into dark corners to fondle and kiss. Parents had carried sleepy children off to their beds and were returning now to drink and gossip over the table. Master Shield was slumped on it, snoring thickly. His wife had gone up to her room before her drunken condition declared itself, swaying as she tried to walk with dignity.

The fiddler's arm flashed back and forth. Hannah was trembling. She felt Joss like a clamour in her blood and was overthrown by her feelings. The thunder rolled closer, reverberating in her head.

Suddenly a white streak of lightning split the dark sky, illuminating Joss's brooding face.

She stopped dead and pushed him away, turning to run. He followed, his breathing thick. Dodging from shadow to shadow she got safely to the house and fled up the back stairs. Peg was in bed. She had left before the drinking began. Now she sat up and watched Hannah splash her heated skin with cold water.

"You should not have stayed so long, Hannah," she told her sternly. "Wine steals your brains. You should not put it in your mouth."

Hannah hastily stripped off her clothes. As she climbed into the bed Peg said: "You are no Nancy to flaunt yourself before the men." Hannah laughed, her face wild. "No!" she said.

The new man arrived a week later. Hannah was sweeping the front of the house when he walked past with Jabey. They halted and she turned to smile at them.

"Hannah, this is our new workman, Aaron Hunt. He's rooming with me until a new cottage is run up."

"A fine and beautiful morning, Miss Hannah," the new man said in a voice so soft and musical that she stared in surprise.

"That's not a local accent."

He grinned, showing strong even teeth. He was a man of thirty or so, tall and straight with thick brown hair and brown eyes.

"I am from Shropshire," he told her.

"I thought you might be from Wales."

"Near enough, near enough," he nodded.

She leaned on her hazel broom, the twigs scratching the ground. "It is a long way to come to find work. Couldn't you get any in Shropshire?"

Aaron Hunt glanced from her to Jabey. "I'm from Coalbrookdale," he said.

Jabey watched Hannah wryly. Her eyes opened wide and she understood at once what it meant. Coalbrookdale. "Master Derby's works?"

Aaron Hunt laughed. "Indeed."

Joss called brusquely from the sheds and the two men bade her good day and walked over to join him. Joss lingered to eye her coldly for a moment then followed them in to the dark gloom of the forge.

The gossip was soon all round the district. Joss Colby had brought a man from Abraham Derby's works and the two of

95

them were closeted night and day, secretly talking of the smelting process.

"Joss is no fool," Jabey told her as he watched her wringing clothes. Her arms bare and dripping, she bent to the work, her forehead running with sweat. "He has book learning but books do not always tell the whole story. Joss needed someone with practical experience. Someone who knew the problems as well as the advantages. He's bought this fellow. Joss pays him apart from the rest of us – even the clerk doesn't know how much Aaron gets."

"It is cheating," Hannah said.

Jabey laughed and shrugged. "How else would Joss get to learn? You don't think Derby would be such a fool as to let Joss go there and see for himself? They've tried to keep their secrets locked up. Derby's been making iron with coal for nigh on thirty years. Few others have tried and succeeded so well. Their iron is always too dirty. Joss needs to make good, clean iron from the start."

Hannah lifted the basket of damp clothes. "And Master Shield has let Joss do this?"

Jabey looked at her. "I reckon master has no choice any more. Joss talks and master listens."

Jabey walked after her and helped her pin the clean sheets out. They flapped in an early autumn breeze. The storm on Joss's wedding day had broken the warm weather. Days of rain had followed. The gaudy brightness of the leaves was yellowing fast. Joe had lit a bonfire at the bottom of the garden. Blue smoke curled up from it. The air was filled with the tang of burning grass and leaves.

"Master's tired," Jabey said, leaning against one of the trees. "Haven't you seen it, Han?"

She had, and sighed over it. The quarrel between Henry Shield and his wife was draining him. He was allowing Joss more and more power, standing aside to let the younger man have his way. In the evenings Henry Shield sat in the parlour with a bottle of wine and drank himself into a stupor before he stumbled up to his cold bed and his cold wife.

"He is not an old man," she said, suddenly impatient. "To

96

look at him these days you would think he was finished, but he is not much above forty."

"It's that old bitch," Jabey said. "She's damn near freezing him to death."

Hannah dried her wet arms on her apron. "If he was a man he'd never stand for it. Joss Colby would not."

Jabey looked oddly at her. "I never heard you say a good word for Joss Colby before."

She flushed. "Good or bad, it is true. I can't imagine a woman who could match Joss Colby."

Jabey stood stock still, staring after her as she walked into the house. He was pale, his face stricken suddenly, a new awareness in his eyes.

Under Aaron Hunt and Joss a reconstruction was taking place at the works now. A builder from over Radshore way came into the yard and took secret orders from the two men behind closed doors. Joss wanted the rebuilding done before word of it got to the Arandalls.

The builder and his men moved in during the first week of September. They were fortunate with their weather for a while. A lazy, somnolent period went by as the men worked. Soft mists, humid afternoons, gave way to bright cold clear days when the sounds came sharply across the fields and the air was still. The leaves hung on the trees as though one breath of wind would float them off, and their colours burned red and gold and orange in the blue sky. The squire was cubbing, up at dawn and out across the stubble with his hounds baying and snuffling. The winding of the horn drifted to the iron-works and the lean-flanked dogs which hung around for scraps lifted their heads and yelped excitedly.

The alterations to the furnace which a change-over from charcoal to coke made necessary were complicated. Hannah saw the workmen from a distance, filthy from removing the old lining from the chimney and fitting the new one, their faces black, their hands cut and bleeding. Joss moved among them, naked to the waist, his muscled body gleaming with sweat, his voice barking orders. He oversaw every part of the process. Aaron Hunt hovered near him but it was Joss who was master here. None of the men even looked to see Master Shield's view when he passed slowly through the yard.

He was drinking in the daytime now. Hannah knew it by his breath and the slight sway of his walk. He ate little, picking at his food. He spoke little, too. Mistress Shield and he sat at table like total strangers, ignoring each other.

Joss lived in Shield House now. He slept in Caroline's bed and ate at table with the family. For a while after his marriage he rose when Caroline did and came down to eat breakfast in state with her, but soon after the work began on the furnace he came down while Hannah was hanging the kettle over the flames and walked into the kitchen. She turned her head in surprise and stared at him.

"Get me some bread and cheese," he ordered.

As though he had not spoken she stirred the pot of meal which had been soaking overnight and lifted it with difficulty to its accustomed hook above the fire. Joss's lips compressed. He watched her, his anger growing. He was aware that she was behaving deliberately and he wanted to hit her. He had come down this morning after lying awake half the night thinking, not for the first time, that Hannah too slept beneath this roof. His mind had been tormented with images of her in her thin little shift. Now she would not look at him or take note of him.

She turned, blank-faced, and got down the bread. He watched her saw off a thick slice. She fetched the cheese and hacked him a piece.

"We start to coke in a month," Joss said.

"So they say."

"We've seen nothing of Master Arandall for weeks," he remarked, his voice idle. Picking up the cheese he turned it round in his fingers, waiting for her answer.

"Haven't you?" She sounded amused and it infuriated him. He looked at her sharply, trying to read the averted profile but it told him nothing.

"Have you?"

She skimmed the breakfast bowls across the table without reply and Joss gritted his teeth, watching her with impatience.

"Well, Miss?" A sneer stretched his hard mouth. "I thought you were walking out with Stock of late. Are you meeting Arandall on the side?"

"Andrew has gone to London," she said at last.

His bones relaxed from their fierce tautness. "You see too much of Stock. You know he could not wed. It will be years before he's free of the millstone of his family. They need every penny he can earn."

"Jabey takes his responsibilities very seriously. He knows how things are."

Joss leaned back and eyed her closely. "Does he make love to you? I see you walking in the fields with him. Do you lie down in the long grass like the others with their girls?" As he spoke that thickness came into his voice, the words slurring together, and their eyes met in a silent duel before Hannah looked away.

"I am no Nancy."

"No," he said with an intonation close to regret, his mouth twisting. "You're made of sterner stuff, aren't you, Hannah? Cold as snow; but with that mouth there has to be a fire somewhere beneath your frozen face."

Hannah moved away to get on with her work, aware that he watched her. The silence between them was heavy with emotion. She heard feet clacking on the back stairs and Nancy came into the room. Seeing Joss she preened like an excited bird, tossing her head and smoothing her skirt down over her hips. Hannah caught the amused grin he threw the girl.

Mrs. Poley bustled through the door and looked at Joss in surprise. Since Abel's death she had been warmer with him and now she smiled. "Up early, Master Colby! Will you take tay?"

He watched her unlock the caddy and spoon the leaves into the pot. "Thank you, Mistress Poley. I will."

She laughed. "A cup for Master Colby, Hannah."

Hannah fetched one and the cup was poured. Mrs. Poley herself took it to him and he nodded to her before he drank the steaming liquid. Glancing at the remains of his breakfast, Mrs. Poley said: "That's no fodder for a man before he goes to work! You should have had oatmeal with us."

He drained his cup and got up. "I ate well enough," he said, going out.

He made it his practice after that to eat bread and cheese in the kitchen, sometimes leaving before the other servants came down. Hannah now and then found him in the kitchen when she made her way downstairs in the dawn light. He always put the kettle on its hob and slung the pot over the fire. "That's my job," she said once and he gave her a careless grin. "Well, I've done it for you. That pot is too heavy for you." He moved closer and stared at her with half-closed eyes. "You don't eat enough. You're as thin as a willow twig. I could peel you with my teeth."

She found herself laughing at the ridiculous thought, and he laughed too after a moment. It was the first time they had ever laughed together and their eyes met in startled realisation of it.

Later Hannah laughed as she made up the fire in the parlour. Caroline sat in a chair watching her work.

She was still hiding her condition by wearing tight corsets, but most of the household knew by now. Rumour and guesswork had put two and two together. Mistress Shield's anger combined with Caroline's obvious pallor and look of ailing had made the conclusion easy.

"Why are you laughing, Hannah?" Caroline asked.

Hannah looked round and smiled at her. "Oh, nothing, Mrs. Colby. How are you this morning? Feeling better than yesterday?"

"I was not sick today," Caroline admitted. "But I have a back ache and my head throbs."

She had little ailments every day. Hannah knew that women sometimes grew like that when they were breeding, as though the fact gave them licence to be as ill as they chose.

"You should not wear those corsets," she told the girl firmly. "They do the child no good. How can it grow as it should when you squash it in behind that cage of bone?"

Caroline looked stubborn. "I must keep my figure. I'll not

go about looking like a bladder of air." She sighed. "Oh, Hannah, I wish . . ."

What she wished was never divulged since Mistress Shield entered the parlour at that moment and stopped, looking from one to the other with bitter, grudging eyes. "Get on with your work, girl," she snapped, and Hannah silently obeyed. Caroline looked at her mother, her lip trembling, but Mistress Shield behaved as though she were not present, yet in so icy a manner that the girl was shrivelled where she sat and presently got up in tears and ran heavily from the room.

Hannah was angry enough at the way Mistress Shield was treating her daughter to speak to Joss when he came down next day. He listened as she sharply told him of the incident, then shrugged.

"What would you have me do? The old hag does not speak to me, either."

"You can take care of yourself," Hannah snapped. "Caroline cannot."

Joss gave her a dry smile. "You're a forgiving soul. How many times has Mistress Shield turned her spiteful tongue on you? Why should you worry over her daughter?"

Hannah made a rueful face. "Caroline is pitiful. How should I know why she makes me feel anxious for her? She's weak, that's all." She eyed him coldly. "And she's your wife! You've a duty to protect her. It's your child she carries, Joss Colby."

Joss scraped his chin with his thumb. "There's no point in talking to her mother. You should know that, Hannah. She's as stubborn as a mule."

"You must do something. Caroline is racking herself inside that corset to hide her shape. She's not eating. She's not sleeping." Hannah stared doggedly at him. "Is she, Joss?"

He surveyed her through drooping lids. "How do you know that?"

Hannah smiled tightly. "I hear her tossing and turning. Some nights she walks around the house like a ghost. It makes the blood run cold to hear her creeping from room to room like something in search of a safe hiding place."

Joss gave an irritated sigh. "I could send her to my mother, I suppose."

"Above a shop? That does not sound much better than living here," Hannah said. "There'd be no room for Caroline."

Joss gave her a hard grin. "I've bought my mother a small house." He said the words casually but his cheeks had a dark flush of triumph as he spoke and Hannah caught the intonation of satisfaction.

"What is your mother like?" she asked, curious.

Joss shrugged in his hard fashion. "Small and spare like a sparrow."

Hannah laughed. "I'd thought your mother would be made of iron," she mocked.

He did not smile, his eyes fierce. "A pity she was not – my father led her a dog's life."

"So it is him you take after," Hannah said and was surprised to get a bitter glare from him.

"God forbid," he said harshly. He looked away. "But I'll ask Caroline if she'll go to my mother."

Caroline refused. She clung to Joss like ivy to a strong oak, and, like the oak, Joss permitted it without needing that parasitic love. Hannah, watching, saw that Joss was trying to give Caroline the comfort she needed. He used a soft tone when he spoke to her, sat with her and read to her, talked to her of Birmingham and the fairs he had seen there, telling her tales of conjurers and men who could swallow swords, bears which danced and horses which could count. Caroline believed it all, mouth open, eyes wide. "I'll take you to fairs when the child is born," Joss promised. "And buy your fairings, a ribbon for your pretty hair, a ring with a real diamond."

Talking to Hannah later, Joss said curtly, "She's a child herself."

"You wed her," Hannah shrugged.

"I don't forget it," Joss snapped. "I know how to look after my own. Caroline shan't suffer from her mother's tongue when I'm there."

Hannah was learning that Joss had a divided mind where the weak and helpless were concerned. He was torn between protecting them and growing angry with them. She saw him with little Tam running at his heels day by day. Joss shouted at the boy, threw him coins or scraps of food, watched him with wry indulgence. She sometimes thought he loved Tam as he did not love Caroline. Thin and under-nourished as the boy was, he had strength which Caroline lacked. He worked for Joss without tiring. He was eager to leap to his slightest command. Joss did not find the boy's adoration unwelcome, Hannah suspected.

In October the new furnaces went into production. The whole works hovered on the first day, anxiously watching every move that was made. Joss strode around, bare-chested, his black hair ruffled by the new cold winds sweeping across the fields. Tam scurried behind him, watching in case Joss called him.

The heavy rains of August had damaged the harvest. Prices were higher than they had been for years. Bread was a luxury. Working men could not afford to eat and clothe themselves. Families starved, little children white and hollow-cheeked, some of them fainting in the sheds from lack of food.

It was not the time, the men whispered, for experiment, for dangerous new ideas.

Joss was not merely gambling with his own future but with those of every man who worked for Shields. Hating change, fearing new ideas, the workers murmured behind his back. It would not take much to bring about a full-scale revolt. Joss was not blind to their fears. He knew his men. Face to face with him they were silent, but their hangdog glowering looks spoke clearly enough for them.

The process of running in a new chimney was cautious. 'Blowing in', the men called it. It was not safe to begin to use the furnace until the masonry was thoroughly dried out to prevent it from cracking open when the immense heat began. The men filled the hearth with old timber on which they piled coke. Once the fire had reached the coke they added more coke mixed with limestone which was the flux necessary to make the unusable parts of the ore combine into a slag. Some slag was sold to builders to be used as mortar. The worst stuff was left in piles around the works. The slagheaps smouldered day and night as fresh tipping went on, a smoke rising from them.

Once the furnace was 'in blast' the loads were gradually increased. It was some weeks before the full working rhythm was reached, but the first molten iron was tapped inside twenty-four hours. The men watched anxiously as Joss took a crowbar, placed it against the clay of the tap hole and with one fierce blow of a sledgehammer began to drive an iron rod through the clay. Even the servants had crowded round the shadowy door. The iron flowed out, sparks flew fiercely. Joss snatched a lump of clay from Jabey, who stood beside him, and threw it against the opening, pressing with the iron rod to close the tap hole once more.

The iron had flowed out into a prepared bed. Now they would have to wait until it cooled to find out whether it was of good enough quality to be salable.

When Aaron and Joss inspected the pig of metal later that night, they smiled and the men threw up their caps, cheering. Relief flooded through the works.

Joss ordered beer to be brought out. The men stood round the yard, toasting the new process. Henry Shield stood almost sullenly while they cheered Joss.

When the men had gone off either to work a shift or to go to their homes, Joss brought Aaron back to the house. It was late. Caroline and Mistress Shield were in bed. The servants had gone up the back stairs leaving the house in darkness. Joss lit a candle and he and Aaron sat in the parlour drinking. Master Shield lay comatose in his chair, head slumped on his breast. Hearing loud voices and laughter, Hannah came down, ruffled where she had hurriedly thrown on her gown, her hair hanging loose around her flushed face.

"Bring another bottle," Joss ordered, showing no surprise to see her.

"You've had enough by the look of you," she snapped.

"Do as you're bid!"

"The master should be in his bed." Hannah crossed to go to Master Shield and Aaron caught her wrist, laughing. He pulled her down on his lap and brushed his mouth against her neck, nuzzling into her skin like a hot child.

Whenever she had seen him about the house or yard he had smiled at her, very friendly, but now his venturing hands were far too familiar.

Joss crashed to his feet and Aaron looked up, his head swaying on his neck. There was murder in Joss's face and even in his drunken state, Aaron read it. He stared, stupefied.

A powerful hand wrenched Hannah from Aaron's lap and thrust her towards the door. "Get out," Joss said.

She went, looking back once. Joss pushed his hands into his breeches' pockets.

"Keep your hands to yourself in my house," he said with the careful enunciation of the drunk.

"I'm sorry." Aaron spoke resentfully. The mood of happy optimism had been shattered. Henry Shield half woke and tried to stand up, something in the atmosphere permeating his clouding brain. His feet tangled and he fell with a thud into the fireplace. Aaron began to laugh with a roar. Joss joined him, dragging the older man to safety before he burnt himself. Henry Shield looked surprised, sliding along on his back.

"Hello, Joss," he said quite clearly before his eyes closed once more.

Hannah heard the two men later dragging the old iron-master up the stairs, his feet hitting the treads, bang, bang, bang. She ran after them and hissed: "No, no, take him back to the parlour. Mistress Shield will be angry."

Joss looked at her owlishly. "Let the old bat croak."

Aaron grinned, then looked at Joss as though expecting retribution. Joss ignored him, banging on the door of the master chamber. There was silence within. Hannah could imagine the old woman lying in her bed with fury and cold hatred in her heart. After a moment Joss flung the door open without ceremony and the two men dragged Henry Shield into the room.

"How dare you? How dare you?" Mistress Shield spluttered.

"Leave my room immediately! And take that drunken sot with you."

"Your husband, Ma'am," Joss said clearly. The bedsprings gave loudly. There were distinct thuds as the ironmaster's shoes were flung off. "Sweet dreams," Joss said.

"Get out, get out, get out," screamed Mistress Shield.

The men staggered out, slamming the door. Hannah watched them go down the stairs, clutching at each other, laughing ribaldly. From within the bedchamber came the heavy crash of a body landing on the floor.

"You vile sot," hissed Mistress Shield.

Hannah went up to bed.

When she saw Joss again it was well nigh noon and his face was almost waxen. His eyes were dull and heavy, he yawned, and winced at every sound. "Give me a glass of brandy," he muttered. Hannah got it for him and watched him swallow it, shuddering.

"God, my head." He put both hands to it, groaning, then he went out to the furnace to examine the progress of the new coking.

A few hours later Sir Matthew Arandall rode into the yard. Hannah heard him shouting and came out, arms wet with laundering.

Joss faced him squarely, mouth set.

"I'll hound you out of business, I swear," Sir Matthew raged. "Well, Colby, I tell you this – you'll get no more charcoal from us nor from anyone for miles. Make your iron with coke but you'll not forge the damned stuff. You cannot make wrought iron with dirty metal and coke makes dirty iron. I'll starve you out, so help me God."

Six

In early December Jabey's Uncle Will arrived to visit his sister. A seaman, he came so rarely that none of the children knew him and stared in amazement at his rough brown face as he stood at the door. He came laden with gifts from foreign parts. All the neighbours crowded into the tiny house to stare and listen to him. One of his presents was a bottle of rum brought all the way from the Indies. Will himself drank most of it and by the time his sister lit the flickering rush candle he was singing and dancing, his spare figure agile. Arms folded across his chest, he leapt to and fro, shouting a sea shanty. "Come on, lad," he encouraged Jabey, who was not backward in joining him. The sound of their merriment drifted through the village. People stopped to stare askance. Such gaiety was a rare thing these days.

Drunk or sober, Will Grey was free with his money and, seeing the plight of his sister's family he forced coins upon his sister. "What should I do with it but spend it?" he asked her, grinning. "Once I'm back at sea I'll have no need of it. Take it, girl, take it."

He had intended to spend only a day there but he enjoyed himself so much he stayed on, sleeping in a corner of the tiny room downstairs. Jabey found his uncle's tales fascinating. He could have sat and listened all day, drinking in the stories of strange lands and great oceans. "I never wed, lad," Will sighed. "Never felt the pull of a woman. If I get the urge I find a brothel but a home and a family mean nothing to me."

Jabey flushed, staring at him. Will laughed at his expression. "Have I shocked you?"

"No, no," Jabey lied. "Then you've never wanted to have

someone to go home to after your voyages?"

"Not me, lad, no. I've seen too many good shipmates broken through a woman. When a man is away from England for two, three years, he gets to wondering what his wife is doing back home. Women are easily tempted."

"Some perhaps," Jabey said soberly. He thought of Hannah. "But not all, uncle."

"Oh ho," Will said, grinning, cocking an eye at him. "Is there a pretty face somewhere for you, lad? Careful, mind. You're over young to tie yourself down."

His presence made life easier for the family. He insisted on seeing meat on the table, his pockets still full. He bought clogs for the boys when he saw that they habitually went barefoot. He filled the house with life and noise and all the children adored him. The grey struggle for survival which life had meant to them so far made Will seem magical to them now.

"He's been a blessing to us," Jabey told Hannah. "I cannot tell you what it means to have him in the house. He's sunshine on a cold day."

Hannah had liked him when they met. His free and easy ways were a little startling to her. He had grinned and hugged her waist, stealing a kiss. "So you are Jabey's girl!" Behind his kindness she discerned a surprised amusement which did not annoy her. She guessed he had expected someone more like Nancy, whom he had already met. Nancy found the jovial seaman attractive as might have been expected, and he seemed to find her very fetching.

Nancy persuaded Mrs. Poley to give her a day's holiday that week and Will took her to Birmingham. They came back by carrier next day. "Oh, we had a rare time," Nancy cried delightedly. "He's free with his money, Will Grey. Look what he bought me!" She pulled up her skirts to display her pretty legs. A red silk garter encircled the top of her thigh.

"Nancy, pull down your skirts at once!" Mrs. Poley cried in grim reproof.

Henry Shield stood in the doorway, staring as Nancy dropped her hem. She looked round and caught his glazed eye. A wickedly provocative grin flashed towards him and Master Shield went slowly out.

"Poor soul," Nancy whispered to Hannah. "The mistress keeps him at arms' length. I doubt he's seen a woman's thigh for months."

Hannah sighed irritably. "Be quiet, Nancy, do. You've only one thought in your head. Don't you ever get tired of such ideas?"

Nancy giggled and pushed her. "Get on! Of course I don't."

She visited Will Grey that evening for half an hour but he seemed weary and rather irritable. Nancy came back, pouting. "He is one of those men," she told Hannah. "Begging and kneeling for you one minute, and the next wanting nothing more to do with you." Her bright yellow head tossed. "Men make me ill."

"I wish I believed you meant it," Hannah said drily.

Nancy looked at her and laughed, changing mood at once. "Do you really not like men, Hannah? What else is there? Life would be dull if there were no men to tease and play with."

Caroline came languidly into the kitchen to ask for a drink of milk and Nancy went off, humming beneath her breath, cheerful once more. Caroline looked after her with a down-turned mouth. She sought out Hannah's company more often these days, lacking all other society. Joss was kept busy in the works and had no time for Caroline's unhappy moods.

"I wish she would not sing when I have the headache," she complained. Hannah, giving her the milk, smiled gently at her. She felt increasingly sorry for Caroline's helpless weakness before misfortune. The girl was one of those who are happy when all goes well and collapse before ill luck.

"Let me put you to bed with the curtains drawn. Your head will ache less in the dark."

Caroline was happy to be treated as a child, it restored her sense of security. She leaned heavily on Hannah as they went up the stairs, her slender little body swollen now as the child made its existence obvious.

Two days later Will Grey woke up sweating and haggard and when his sister bent over him anxiously, said wryly, "Caught a chill, my dear. Land sickness, we all get it. A seaman is best on his own deck."

"We'll nurse you," Jabey's mother assured him smilingly. "Won't we, Ruth? He'd get no such nursing on board ship."

Jabey's sister was eager to agree. She smiled at her uncle with bright eyes. "Of course we will," she told him.

Three days later spots broke out on his body and the doctor, summoned hastily from Radshore, shook his head. "Smallpox," he said, backing away.

Mrs. Stock whitened. "Never say so," she breathed hoarsely.

"I am sorry," the doctor murmured unhappily. "You will all have to be confined to the house. We can't have it spreading around the village."

"Oh, merciful Heavens," Mrs. Stock groaned.

"Where did he get it?" Jabey asked, shocked.

"Birmingham, I'll warrant," Mrs. Stock said angrily. "That trip he took with Nancy!"

"Most probably," the doctor agreed.

"The children," Mrs. Stock cried. "What about the children? My poor children!"

"I am sorry," said the doctor. "I must act for the best of all of us. The children must stay in this house until the contagion is over."

Jabey was wrung with pity for his mother and the children. He watched the doctor as he washed his face and hands in a mixture with a strong scent which was believed to keep disease at bay. "How will we live? If I cannot work or go out to get food?"

"I will speak to your neighbours," the doctor promised. "They will see you are fed."

When Joss heard he went into the kitchen and ordered Hannah to put up a basket of food for the Stock family. She went pale when she heard of the illness. "Is Jabey well? He has not caught it?"

Joss turned cold eyes on her. "I've no idea," he said. "In the same house with the sick man, he may well catch it. Smallpox is very contagious."

Jabey had organised the house as far as he could to minimise the contact between his mother and the children. They were ordered to stay in the gloomy little room upstairs. Dismal weather made their prison more arduous. They quarrelled and cried, grew fretful and difficult. Huddled together under a thin blanket they pushed each other like irritable dogs, snatching the few rough toys which Jabey had made them, grabbing little bits of food. When they grew too noisy Jabey would come up and speak calmly but firmly, cuffing a head here, slapping a hand there.

Ruth had been banished with them but within forty-eight hours it was distressfully plain that she had caught the fever. She was carried down the stairs in Jabey's arms, crying and struggling, her face hot, her eyes glazed.

Weak from months of malnutrition she had not her uncle's strength to withstand the disease. She died a day later. Her mother sobbed as she held the thin still body in her arms. "Oh, Jabey, Jabey. What's come to us? Shall we all die, then?"

Will Grey lifted his tired head and looked at his sister miserably. "T's all my fault. I brought it to you. God help me, I would not have done so for a fortune."

"We know that, Uncle," Jabey told him.

"Not for a fortune," the sick man repeated, his voice breaking. The fever had weakened him now to the point where he was shivering and grinding his teeth as though in the worst cold weather although, thanks to Joss, they had a roaring fire of coal from the ironworks. The doctor had said a good fire would help the sick man.

Will, himself, died that night, his body so hot that Jabey fancied he could feel the heat merely by putting a hand near his uncle's face. Jabey and Mrs. Stock sat all night with the two dead bodies waiting for them to be taken away.

"If you should get it, Jabey," Mrs. Stock wailed. "What would come of us all then? It'd be the parish for us, me and the children. We have no living soul to care for us but you."

"I'm as fit as a flea, Mam," Jabey swore stoutly, but his eyes were anxious. He knew that only he stood between them and the parish. Cold charity could destroy faster than starvation, he thought. His mother would rather die than go into the reluctant, grudging care of the parish.

Hannah heard at the end of that week that Mrs. Stock and one of the other little girls was sick of the smallpox. "Going through them all like a knife through butter, 'tis," Nancy said. "Shut up together like that – they'll all be dead this time next month."

"For God's sake hold your tongue," Hannah snapped, turning on her. "You like ill news, Nancy, I swear you do. If you can't say something pleasant say nothing."

Nancy looked offended, lifting her nose crossly. "I shan't tell you then that some folks in the village have got it now," she informed Hannah.

Joss reinforced Nancy's news that afternoon. "Three other cases in the village," he said flatly. "God knows where it will end. Once one of these outbreaks starts there's no halting it. It's like a fire in a wood in summer. It rages until it's burnt out."

Mrs. Stock died the next day. Nancy burst into the kitchen crying out, "Oh, Jabey's got it, Jabey's down with it now."

Mrs. Poley looked horrified. "Never! Ah, poor soul!"

Hannah straightened. "Are you sure?" she asked and Nancy gave her a cold look.

"Of course I'm sure! D'ye think I'd lie about that?"

"T's all that seaman," Mrs. Poley said. "A good soul but look what he's brought us all! It were a pity he ever came here. Nothing but death and sickness has come of it."

Nancy looked yellow pale, like creamy butter, her eyes wide. "It's mortal good luck I did not catch it from him."

"There's time yet," said Hannah angrily and Nancy gave her a furious look before running out in tears.

Hannah took down her shawl and wound it round her head and shoulders. "Where are you going, girl?" Mrs. Poley asked her.

"I can't let Jabey die alone without nursing," she said almost defiantly. "His mother gone, Ruth too. Nobody there to see his body washed if he dies. He can't be left untended, Mrs. Poley."

"He is not your concern, Hannah. Have sense, girl. You risk your own life going into that house."

Hannah shrugged. "We all risk our lives every day just by breathing. I have to go, Mrs. Poley."

Mrs. Poley shrugged too, realising she was set firm on her course. "Take some things with you, then." She began to get food from the shelves in the pantry. "Now listen, Hannah. Wrap him up well, feed him nothing but gruel and good clean water. Plenty to drink, mind, whether he wants it or not. Force it down his throat if you must. The fever is the danger. Try to get it down. It weakens the heart if you do not."

"I'll remember," Hannah promised.

She walked down the lane like a dark little ghost in her shawl. The moon was rising early over the hedges, peering at her like a curious neighbour. The skeletal trees whispered together in a cold wind. I shall not breathe this air again for a long time, she thought. Is there anything to regret in that? I should have much to regret if I let Jabey die alone without a human soul by him. How could I live with myself afterward? She stood at his gate, staring at the dark shape of the little house. The wind blew troubled clouds across the sky and she breathed deeply, wondering if it was the last time she would ever stand in the free air? Then she walked up the path and opened the door.

"No, no," Jabey cried hoarsely when he saw her bending over him. He put up a hand to ward her off as though devil-driven.

"Hush, hush," she murmured, wiping a damp cloth over his fevered brow.

The coolness brought a brief sanity. He looked at her through red eyes. "Han?" His voice steadied. "Han, is it really you?"

"Did you think I was a nightmare?" She smiled gently.

"You can't come here," he cried then, looking at her in

113

terror. "You will catch it, you will die. I couldn't bear that, Han. I would rather die myself than see you die. Go quickly. Go before anyone knows you came in here."

"Lie still," she urged, pushing him back as he tried to sit up. "Lie still, Jabey, my dear."

"Hannah," he cried out, his voice filled with desperation. "Oh, Hannah, go, do."

"Could I?" she asked him, smiling. "Could you, Jabey, if it were me lying there?"

Jabey's face worked, his glazed red skin heated until it burnt to touch it. Their eyes met and held. He closed his abruptly, sighing. Almost at once he passed back into the delirium from which she had woken him.

The room was stale and grimy, having not been cleaned for days, and when she went upstairs she sighed over the children who all burst into tears when they saw her. Unkempt, grey, their clothes stained, their hair uncombed, they looked pitiably neglected and despairing. She washed and tidied them, took their clothes away and washed them too, hanging them near the fire to dry when she had wrung them tightly. The atmosphere steamed while she made the children a hot meal. She had just left them eating it when the door burst open and Joss strode into the house.

"Are you unhinged?" he demanded as his eye fell on her. "What piece of lunacy was this, coming here, risking your life?"

"There's a sick man and three children needing care," Hannah retorted. "Would you have me leave them to die alone?"

"Why didn't you wait until I was told? You knew I'd find a woman to nurse them."

"I wouldn't wish Jabey to be nursed by someone who did it for money. It's my life I risk and I'll take nothing for it."

Joss sucked in his breath, his hands clenched at his sides. Jabey stirred on the bed and they both looked round at him. He lifted his head weakly. "Han, go while you can. He's right."

"He's wrong," she argued. "Our lives aren't worth much to

anyone but ourselves. We all put our own price on them. If I let you die without lifting a finger to stop it or ease you, I'd price myself very low."

"My own Hannah," he whispered with a weary smile. "But you must go."

"I've brought Mrs. Cregen," Joss said at her elbow. He looked down at Jabey. "I am sorry you've taken it, Stock. I'll see the children are cared for, if need be. Do not worry over them."

"I am not leaving him," Hannah said as she heard Mrs. Cregen stepping over the threshold and looking round the room with her small, bright, beady eyes.

"I've nursed smallpox before," the woman said. "I had it when I was a child and lived — you never take it twice. I'm not afraid of taking it but I am afraid of dirt and this house needs cleaning." She took off her thick shawl and rolled up her sleeves. Jabey gave a low grunt of laughter. The woman was so small, all bones, but stiff with energy.

Joss suddenly picked Hannah up into his arms, a hand beneath her knees, another round her back. "Put me down this instant," she cried angrily as he strode to the door. He did not answer and he did not halt that strong, quick stride. She looked up at the dark sky and saw the clouds driven before the wind like sheep. Joss walked without speaking, carrying her easily, as though she weighed no more than a feather. The black hair tossed in the wind and what she could see of his face had a stubborn, set determination.

"You might as well take me back," Hannah said in a low voice. "I've been there in that house, I have been close to the contagion. You cannot risk spreading the disease to Shield House and Mistress Shield would not permit it."

"I've thought of that," Joss retorted.

"You . . ." she began, infuriated because Joss left nothing to chance, he covered every possibility.

"Mrs. Cregen's house is empty. You'll stay there until you're out of danger." Joss carried her up the little cinder path, his boots grating on the shifting ground. The tiny room was spotlessly clean. "Stay here until I say you may come

115

out," Joss ordered harshly. "If you don't die I may well kill you myself. You gave me the worst fright of my life to-night."

He did not put her down, holding her tightly, scowling. "I could hit you," he said, but he kissed her instead, hard and without tenderness.

He let her drop so that she stumbled and clutched at him to steady herself. Joss turned to go then, his back to her, said in a hoarse voice, "Tam's dead."

Hannah gave a muffled cry of shock. "Oh, Joss."

"Snuffed out like a candle." Joss was very straight, his body tense. "No strength to fight it."

She leaned her cheek on his back. "I'm sorry, Joss." Although he stood so still he was trembling. She felt the slow tremors running down his body as she leaned on him. He swore in a muffled rawness, his voice so thick she could swear he was crying, then he pulled away and strode out of the door, slamming it. It blew open again and she stood, watching his tall figure vanish.

Joss hated weakness. He would not show her the grief he was feeling for Tam. He converted pain into anger which he could ease openly. The latch rattled in the wind and she closed the door, sighing. Poor little Tam. Snuffed out like a candle; Joss had said bitterly. He had saved the boy's life at the risk of his own once but nothing could save Tam when the smallpox seized him. Joss detested being helpless.

A week later she was sick to death of her own company, weary of watching the world pass by out of reach. She felt perfectly well, apart from a wish to get out of the little house and see another human face. Joss came each day to shout at her from the path. The first time she had tied the latch and he rattled it angrily until she told him she would not let him come into the house. Now he just bellowed at her for a few moments with a catechism of sharp questions about her state of health, then walked off with a movement which suggested he would like to stamp on somebody, his boots thudding on the cinders.

He had to go to Birmingham on business on the Thursday following and while he was gone Mistress Shield collapsed in the wellyard and was carried into the house by her husband, his heavy face sweating.

He came for Hannah an hour later. "The servants huddle in the kitchen like hens when the fox is in the coop and Mrs. Cregen's still nursing Stock. I know I've no right to ask you, Hannah, you owe her no kindness, but she will die if she is not nursed and I would not know what to do."

She did not want to go. She had gone to Jabey because she could not bear to think of him dying alone, but Mistress Shield had made her life a misery for years. There was nothing between them but hate. Why should she risk her life for a woman who had given her nothing but remorseless enmity?

Reading her angry, confused face, Henry Shield muttered, "I know. It is hard for you but if Caroline has to nurse her, she and the child may die. Caroline has no strength. She would be sure to take the sickness."

Hannah gave a long sigh and picked up her shawl, then she followed him back to the house. She heard weeping in the kitchen. Henry Shield said in a low voice, "Peg's at her mother's house at Radshore. Nancy would be no use and Mrs. Poley goes in dread of the smallpox. I cannot blame her – she's had troubles enough already. She is frightened of dying."

Mistress Shield lay in the great bed tossing and mumbling. Hannah closed the door and stared at her. How ironic that she of all people should be asked to come here and nurse this woman whom she had more than once wished to kill.

Mistress Shield was not an easy patient, showed an irritable hostility even in delirium, fighting against the gently restraining arms which tried to hold her down. She had the typical red-hot skin of the disease, her eyes wild and she watched Hannah even when she did not seem to know her with an excited hatred.

Joss came back from Birmingham and when he heard leapt up the staircase, his boots crashing from tread to tread. Hannah had bolted the door so he smashed his fist upon the panels, roaring at her.

"You stupid little bitch." His voice was thickened with rage and fear.

"Go away, Joss, you are disturbing her," she said close by the door.

"I could kill you."

"Joss, go away."

"Why? Why?" Joss sounded like a man at the end of his tether and there was nothing she could say to him.

"If you don't take it now, it will be a miracle," he muttered, his tone dropping. "Curse you. Die then."

She heard him walking away, then his feet on the stairs again, and she half laughed, half cried. Joss was beside himself with anger, and for a man like him his inability to do anything about the situation would be the part which angered him most. He was helpless and that would drive him mad.

I don't want to die, she thought, and looked back at the bed. Not for the sake of that woman. I must be mad. Joss is right. I should have let her die. I am weak, a fool. Pity saps one, it makes one feeble. She had not agreed to come for the sake of Mistress Shield, though – it had been for Caroline's sake that she had come, knowing she could not let the girl risk her life. Caroline carried Joss's child.

The days which followed were bitter both for Hannah and her patient. Mistress Shield recovered after a long, exhausting struggle made more painful by her hatred of Hannah's presence at her side, her dislike of having the girl touch her. It was a relief for both of them when the doctor pronounced Mistress Shield well enough to be out of all danger. Hannah still showed no sign of taking the disease but the miracle of this was explained by Mrs. Poley as she fussed over Hannah, tucking her into bed in the attic. "You had it when you were a two-year-old," she said. "I only learnt that yesterday – from Mrs. Cregen's daughter-in-law who lived two doors from you and remembers how sick you were and how your mother laughed when someone suggested that a toad be brought to sit on your forehead to take away the pits. But your grandmother brought a toad and although you came out in great spots you never died nor had a blemish after, which your grandmother laid to the door of the toad."

Hannah smiled weakly, so tired she could have cried. "My mother was a woman of sense."

Mrs. Poley shook her head. "'Twas your grannie cured you, Hannah."

"Ah," Hannah said, closing her eyes, still smiling.

"Although," Mrs. Poley added thoughtfully, "Your mother always said it was your being tied to the bed to stop you scratching that stopped you from getting great craters in your face."

Hannah slept for two days and nights, barely waking to eat or use the bucket, and when she came downstairs again she was told that the disease had raged through the village like brushfire, leaving blackened earth behind it. Many families had lost a member, some had lost several. Those remaining now had to face the rest of the winter and hunger, weakness, disease, made the prospect of deepening cold doubly chilling.

During her days nursing Mistress Shield, Hannah had lost a good deal of weight and her skin was sallow. She had barely touched a morsel of food for most of that time, sickened by the atmosphere of the room, unable to bear the sight of food.

Mrs. Shield remained upstairs, nursed now by Peg, whose company of all the servants she could most endure. Caroline came down to hug Hannah and weep. "I missed you," she whispered. "I was so afraid. I could not bear it if you died, Hannah. You are the only one who cares for me."

"Joss loves you," Hannah prompted, smiling carefully.

Caroline sighed and went quietly back to her own room without reply.

Joss called for Hannah when he came into the house. She stood before him with her hands at her waist and he stared at her in silence.

"God damn it, you look like a scarecrow!"

"What did you expect?" She lifted her head defiantly. "It was no light matter nursing that woman."

"What madness made you do it? She hates your guts and you hate her! Why risk your life for that old bitch?"

She shrugged. "How could I refuse?"

He shifted restlessly, his fists clenched. "Well, you are not to go back to work yet. You are not fit."

"I'm stronger than I look."

He smiled at that, a wry tender smile which changed his whole face. "God knows, that's true. You've a core of iron, but Hannah, even iron breaks under force."

"I'm not near breaking yet."

"Sometimes I think I am," Joss said in a low tone.

She flushed deeply, shivering. Looking away, she asked him: "Is Jabey still mending?"

"Oh, Stock's another who is tougher than he looks. He came through it after a while but he's pockmarked, they say. None of the other children took it, you'll be glad to hear."

"I am glad," she agreed, smiling, the green gleam of her eyes lifted to his face. "And glad you did not take it, Joss." The admission was husky, reluctant.

He took a step nearer, then halted and swung away, moving to the window. The watery sunshine had faded. The sky was a dead cold white. Bare twigs scratched against the fence. Sodden grass, skeletal leaves, bore witness to the winter rain.

"Since the clerk died I've been doing his job as well as my own. I could well do without it. There are worries enough with the charcoal almost gone now and the Arandalls standing firm. They are waiting for us to break first." He brought his fist up to crash against the window frame. She saw blood spring in a line along his knuckles. "They will wait a long time."

"Are the men proving difficult?"

He shrugged. "No more than I expected. What with the sickness, the hunger, they are in a mood to be violent, but I can hold them. My father-in-law is more of a problem. He wishes to make peace with the Arandalls and he'll do that by one means only, stopping production in the new furnace, changing back to charcoal." He swung to look at her. "He must not, Hannah. The future is with coke. We have to win this battle. He cannot be allowed to retreat."

"How will you stop him?"

"God knows."

"He is still the master here."

He smiled angrily. "When he's sober enough I try to talk some sense into his head but he is rarely sober these days."

"Poor Master Shield." She sighed. "He must be so anxious. His wife on the point of death, his daughter so sickly and all this trouble in the works . . ."

"I have problems as great as his but I don't drown my mind in wine!"

"You're stronger."

"Am I?" He looked almost as though she had insulted him, his eyes dark with temper. "And must I pay for that, too? It's easy for the weak, Hannah. They lie down and cry, 'I cannot', and everyone murmurs, 'Poor soul,' and lets them be. But if your shoulders are broad enough, they load them with everything they can and tell you, 'You're strong, you can bear it.'" He took three steps and halted in front of her, staring into her face. "As they did when the mistress was sick. There were all those women in the kitchen, yet they sent for you and thrust it all on you. If we are strong, Hannah, we pay for it."

She frowned up at him. "I am not strong." She lifted her arms, holding out her hands palm upward.

He took her hands by the wrists, folding them back behind her, pulling her close to him so that their faces met eye to eye. "Strength is in the mind, Hannah. The body is a willing donkey which the mind rides on a tight rein. I saw a man once lift iron more than twice his own weight because his son lay under it. We all stood and stared, not believing. His temples bulged with the effort. I'd swear I heard his body crack. But he did it, Hannah. He did it." There was perspiration on his own forehead as he spoke. It trickled down into his eyes and his lashes flickered in an effort to brush it away. "I cannot be content to be like other men and go on day after day, doing what I have always done. I have to drive myself onward, Hannah, even though it is killing me."

She was becoming more and more aware of the intimacy of the way he held her, his chest against her breasts, his waist and hips pressing on her. "Let me go, Joss," she whispered, eyes cast down.

For one moment longer he held her, watching her, then he released her and stepped back, mouth twisted.

"I must get back to my clerking, I suppose. It irks me to sit over the ledgers when I should be at more important things."

"Get someone else to do it."

He shrugged. "Who? Master Shield's no longer trustworthy, even sober. He makes mistakes, adds wrongly, leaves out figures. None of them at the works can write and do simple book-keeping."

Hannah said hesitantly, "I can."

Joss looked at her in astonishment. "You?"

She flushed. "No, it is stupid."

Joss's brows drew sharply together. "You can write clearly?"

"It would be impossible," she said, moving away.

"No, wait," he said, catching her shoulder. "Come with me."

"I couldn't."

He pushed her toward the door. "Come with me. We shall see if it be possible or not."

He made her sit on the high stool beside the desk. A ledger lay open, the long page scratched with writing and figures. "Read that."

She cast her eye down the page quickly first to make sure she understood it before she read aloud, then she quietly obeyed him. The entries were simple enough. It was a record of the amount of ore brought in to the works, where it was purchased and at what price.

Joss listened, nodding, then turned and tapped an index finger on a pile of other ledgers. "These are the records of the coke we've bought, charcoal here, limestone here. These are the sale books for wrought iron. This one is for slag. And so on . . . You've a quick mind, Hannah. You'd pick it up. A day or two and you'd know exactly what you were doing."

"I couldn't!" She was panic-stricken suddenly. She had spoken without thinking and now she had thought, and knew that if she commenced this work her whole world would change. It was tempting and at the same time terrifying. "The responsibility," she murmured. "It would be too much."

He grimaced. "As I said to you, Hannah, the strong must bear such burdens. They pay the price of their strength."

"I'm no clerk! If I made mistakes!"

"I expect you to," he said indifferently. "You are bound to. But you'll learn, as I said."

"What about the housework?"

"Someone else will do that. Anyone can scrub floors. I need a clerk badly."

"Master Shield will never hear of it."

"He'll jump at the chance," Joss said drily. "He feels guilt-stricken over you. It will give him a chance to make it up to you."

She met his eyes directly. "And when the mistress finds out?"

Joss lifted his shoulders in a shrug of indifference. "We'll face that when it comes."

"The master will never stand against her wishes and she'll not have me in here."

"My wishes matter most at present," Joss said. He touched her small face with that long finger. "For my sake, Hannah, do it. I'm weary to death of poring over these ledgers. This is one burden you can take off my shoulders."

It was an appeal to which she had no defence. She nodded, wry understanding in her eyes. "Very well."

She spent that afternoon in learning her way around the ledgers. They were very simple and once she had deciphered the different hands which had been at work in them she began to grasp a much larger picture of the ironworks, seeing that more was involved than she had ever realised. The ordering of supplies, Joss said, would be one of her jobs in future. It was essential that the intake was kept level with the output and supplies had to be ordered well in advance so that no time was ever lost in production.

In black and white she now saw the fall in production which Joss's change to coke had achieved. A large part of the income from the works was received from the various shops which bought their tools and utensils. This money had been drying up over the past weeks. The process was hastening as time went by. Soon their only income would be from the sale of cast iron itself and from the side products from the slag-heaps.

"If there were only some way to use our iron in the forges," Joss said flatly. "There has to be a process by which coke can make cleaner, more malleable iron. The stuff we're making at the moment cannot be safely rolled or hammered. It's too brittle. It breaks."

"Perhaps in time a way will be found," she said.

"Pray God it comes soon, then," Joss said.

"Do you believe in God, Joss Colby?"

He looked at her in surprise, then smiled. "I've learnt to believe in one thing only; myself. Everything else fails." He walked to the door. "I'm no man to crawl on my belly to a God I can neither see nor touch. I trust my senses and my brain, Hannah. I'll stand on my own two feet and spit in the eye of fate. If I fail, it is I who fails, not some unseen Deity. There's comfort in that even if it is a cold philosophy."

When he had gone she looked down at the neat ledger. Picking up the quill she slowly set to work, entering the figures copied from the bills of sale Joss had given her. It was a strangely satisfying process. For the first time she was using her mind as a tool instead of her body. She lit a candle when the light grew too dim and worked on into the darkness.

Master Shield stumbled through the door next day and stood, staring at her in disbelief. "What's this? What are you doing?"

She laid down her quill and stood up, curtsying. "Sir."

"What are you doing in here?"

"Master Colby asked me . . ." Her explanation was cut short as Joss came in, having heard the sound of the iron-master's raised voice. He glanced from one to the other then thrust his thumbs through his thick belt.

"I told her to come here. She's clerking for us."

"She's what?" Master Shield looked incredulous. "This girl? Why, she cannot . . ."

Joss strode over and lifted the ledger. He swung, offering it to the other man. "She's been clerking here all day. This is her work."

Henry Shield ran his eye down the entries. He picked up the neatly tied docket of bills from the desk and carefully compared them. Lifting his head, he stared at Hannah, his face blank.

"You see?" Joss grinned.

"A woman in the works? I never heard of such a thing. Women may do the lighter jobs in the works when no man may be found, but clerking? That is another matter."

"She can do the work. Does her sex matter?"

"The men won't stand for it," Henry Shield said, staring at Hannah as though he had never seen her before.

"They know she is here but they haven't said a word." Joss grinned again, his eyes amused. "I think they enjoy having her around the works. She is prettier than our late clerk."

Henry Shield scratched his chin. "How long do you mean to keep her here?"

"Give her a fair trial and if she proves useful, we shall keep her," Joss said.

"What are we to pay her? The clerk earned a good wage."

"If she does his work she must get his wage," Joss said with a casual shrug.

Hannah was amazed. The thought of money had not entered her head. Master Shield nodded, though, and went out without comment. Joss looked at her coolly. "Well, girl, get on with it!"

Two weeks later, weary and with an aching head, she straightened on her stool after seven hours. At times the words and figures blurred before her eyes. Once Joss was sure she could be trusted he piled more and more work on to her, leaving it to her to deal with the various suppliers who visited the works. She initialled the bills of sale thrust at her by delivery men, she watched the wagons unload their contents, she saw to it that the various needs of the works were kept permanently supplied, she made up the men's pay and had it ready for Joss to hand out each week. Each man's wage was carefully calculated by the number of hours he had worked, the fines he had to pay and the necessary deductions. Men argued vehemently over their fines. Hannah hated to see their strained, angry faces as they faced Joss. Even the loss of sixpence a week could mean life or death to a family when the price of bread was climbing daily.

Joss came into the little room, clicked an irritated tongue and lit her candle. "Why make yourself blind working in this gloom?"

He came and stood beside her, a hand on her shoulder, reading the ledger. "The charcoal is finished," he said flatly.

"I know. Will you be able to manage?"

"We'll stagger on, but some of the men must be paid off for a while."

"Oh, Joss," she said, aghast.

"I know, I know," he muttered, his hand clenching on her shoulder. Her fine bones hurt under his hand and she shifted uneasily, but his hand tightened.

"How will they live?"

"They can stay in their houses," he said, almost defensively. "I'll not turn them out."

"What are they to eat? Turnips?"

"God damn it, Hannah, do you think I want this? What can I do? I cannot pay men who have no work to do. Let them get aid from the parish."

"Charity? Would you want it?"

"If it is a choice between starvation or charity, they'll take the parish."

She swung towards him urgently. "Go and see Sir Matthew. Beg him . . ."

"Beg?" Joss looked so angry that she drew back in alarm. His eyes were white with rage, his nostrils flared. "I'd beg for nothing from that grasping old fool."

"Is your pride more than theirs? Why should they sink so low to save you having to ask the squire for forgiveness?"

"Ask? Hannah, he'd want me crawling on my hands and knees, and you know it."

They had been shouting without realising it and their loud voices attracted the attention of Mistress Shield. She had come out of the house for the first time that evening. For two days she had sat in the parlour for a few hours at a time, carefully moving back to normal life. She had not asked for Hannah, imagining that the girl was keeping out of her path and glad to be spared the sight of her. Henry Shield had promised to come in to supper but had not yet come so his wife walked slowly out in search of him. Nearing the office she heard the angry voices and stood, listening incredulously.

She pushed open the door. Hannah and Joss stood in the little room glaring at each other, but at the sound they turned to face her.

"What is that girl doing in here?" Mistress Shield demanded loudly.

Joss had decided weeks ago that the ironmaster's wife was no longer to be taken into account. Giving her a cold look, he said, "She works here."

Mistress Shield went white with sheer rage. Her mouth opened and closed without a sound emerging.

Joss eyed her with dislike. She had ill-treated Hannah for years. She had tried to stop his marriage to Caroline. He did not pause to think or feel compassion for the blow he was about to deliver. Clearly and icily he said: "The clerk died. Hannah has taken his place. She has an aptitude for the work. She's proved her worth a dozen times."

"Does my husband know of this?" breathed Mistress Shield in hoarse tones.

Joss gave her a cruel smile. "Of course, he knows. He is very glad to see her taken out of your hands. You'll whip her no more."

Hannah saw the pitted white skin writhe as though insects ate it. She moved towards the woman instinctively, frowning. "Don't, Joss!"

Mistress Shield turned on her furiously, her voice rising into hysteria. "You . . . keep off from me! I know what you are. I've always known. Your mother's daughter, sneaking and thieving. Oh, God, I'll have you out of here. A kitchen slut, that's what you are, what you'll stay. See if I . . ."

Her words broke off and she gave a choked cry.

Hannah stared in shock as the woman's face contorted, her breath coming in panted gasps. Mistress Shield put a hand to her breast then fell heavily, that rasping sound going on for a moment. Hannah anxiously knelt beside her.

"What is it? Are you in pain?"

The strange choking sounds stopped. Hannah looked at Joss in alarm. He knelt and turned the woman over. It was a horrible sight, thought Hannah, the face awry as though it were fixed in agony.

"What's wrong with her?" she asked Joss. "Is she ill again? Has she fainted?"

He straightened from listening at the woman's chest. "She's dead," he said coolly.

Hannah was aghast. "She can't be!" She stared at Mistress Shield with disturbed eyes. "Joss, she can't be. Dead? Like that? But why?"

"Temper," Joss said. "She killed herself with it."

"It's my fault," Hannah moaned, staring down at the dead woman. "I made her angry . . ."

"You made her angry just by breathing," Joss said. "She hated you for being what you are. You can't blame yourself. You saved her life a few weeks ago. She never thanked you for it. Why cry over her now?"

"You're hard, Joss," she said, looking at him.

"I see things for what they are," he retorted. "We're well rid of the old bitch. That's what I see." Over the dead body his long hand reached out and touched Hannah's cheek. His grey eyes were sharp. "She'll hurt you no more."

She looked at him warily. But you could, she thought. Joss Colby, you could hurt me more than anyone has ever done.

Seven

ANDREW ARANDALL HAD fled to London shortly after his sister's death, escaping the consequences as he might plague, stricken with shock and grief, yet running from his own emotions because he found them too painful to bear. His mother had reacted hysterically, screaming and raking her own face with her nails. His father had blustered, threatening reprisals against all at the ironworks. The servants had whispered and stared and listened at doors, barely hiding their excitement. Arandall House had become a house of secrets everyone knew. "Hell, I'm off to London," James Arandall said. "Coming, Andy?" And Andrew had gone with relief and shame in his pale face.

In the great city James was soon sunk in pleasure, never noticing his brother's uneasiness. Coming into the room they shared in the early hours, James drunkenly pulled off his clothes, muttering, "You should have come, boy. I had a girl of twelve. Damn it, she was good, and all for sixpence. At it since she was eight, she swore." He yawned, snuffing out the candle with an unsteady hand. "Looked twenty mind, until she took her clothes off. It ages 'em, ye know." He dropped into sleep at once while Andrew groped his way to the washbowl and threw up. A girl of twelve, he thought. Christ. He lay in the stuffy darkness, hearing James snore. I should never have left my father to carry it all alone, Andrew thought. The girls, too. What must it have done to them? A girl of twelve. How could James do it?

He dreamt of Sophy and woke up wringing with sweat and feeling guilt on his shoulders like a pall.

January brought heavy falls of snow, closing the roads out

of London, but in the spring thaw which followed Andrew came back at last, driven by ghosts which would not let him rest. In a shamed sense of new awareness he noticed the towns and villages through which his coach passed, seeing an England which disturbed him afresh: a land of contrasts stark enough to shock him, the warm, fertile fields washed by rain but so empty, the towns swollen by the influx of countrymen in search of work. The old manorial system was dead. The lessons of his own family had taught him that but now he saw it with his own eyes, the villages swallowed by enclosures, the yeomanry without support, many squires forced to sell out to town merchants. The face of England was changing. Along the road to Birmingham he noted decaying villages, hollowed hungry faces and a smouldering sense of betrayal. The farmers had known a heyday during Marlborough's wars, selling their grain at inflated prices to feed his armies, but that market had gone now and the poor harvest of 1740 had forced up prices to the level where the really poor could not buy bread.

Beggars thronged the roads between the towns, the narrow alleys and courts of the towns themselves. The new industries just growing up could give work to some but although it fed them it could not give them what their former life had given them. In the smoky, grimy little workshops and mines, a new breed was emerging: a tribe of men with dirt-grimed skins and a dark sense of resentment.

At Birmingham he hired a horse to take him home and got little courtesy from the grooms, and so he rode home and found that, even in the short space since he left, things there had altered too.

At first it was not apparent. He rode into the stableyard at the house and a groom ran, bare-headed, to hold his mount while he slid down. Knuckling his forehead, the man greeted him with a grin, and Andrew lingered to exchange a few casual words before going into the house. The dogs barked furiously, hearing his remembered steps. His father met him, brows knitted, surprise in his face, and Andrew nodded to him coolly, yet thought: he looks so old! Time had worn lines into Sir Matthew's face which had not been there last time they met. His skin had a grey tinge, his eyes were sombre.

"You did not let us know you were returning." The words sounded accusing, although they were spoken carelessly.

Andrew was surprised to find himself touching his father's arm and asking: "How are you, sir?"

Sir Matthew stared, frowning, searching his son's eyes. "Well enough, well enough. You? You have not been ill, Andy?"

"No," Andrew said, looking surprised.

"You look as though you have been."

Andrew stared at him. "So do you," he said, and they were both silent.

They were both aware of what the other was thinking. Their eyes disengaged and sought the ground. Sir Matthew shifted his booted feet noisily, a flush stealing into his pale face. He tried never to think of his dead child. He had lost others but none of those deaths had had the catastrophic effect of that one. Sophy had not been his favourite child but she had been pretty, a lively, rather wilful girl with bright eyes, and her murder had destroyed something in him.

Joss's intervention in the events which followed, his rebellion over the use of charcoal, had in some strange way become confused with Sophy's killing, and Sir Matthew found in Joss a target for all the pain and hatred burning inside him, so that now he almost believed that Joss had been responsible for everything. A recurring dream had begun to trouble him in recent months. He dreamt he saw Sophy in her wide hat and bright riding habit, smiling and calling him, and then she was unseen but heard, calling, calling in a child's voice filled with fear and panic, and he could not find her. He would run, panting, but always the voice was out of reach, the terror mounting, until he burst out from crowding trees to see her lying on the ground and a man lying above her. The squire's heart would seem to crowd into his throat. He gasped and cried out and the man would lift his head. He was always smiling, sardonically, mockingly, and it was always Joss.

Now he looked up, his broad body shuddering, and

Andrew saw the grief in his eyes and was shamed all over again, for he had known that his father was suffering this and he had run away.

In an impeded voice he whispered, "Father!" He put an arm shakily around the other man and Sir Matthew cleared his throat, looking away.

"You'll need a drink after that ride, m'boy. Come along."

For a second Andrew looked as if his father had hit him, then he smiled briefly, understanding, as only Sir Matthew's son could, knowing his father's dislike of anything personal, anything hinting at emotion.

"Thank you, sir. I'm as dry as a kiln," he said, following him along the passage.

"How's my mother?" he asked later, his boots on the table in the library which still served as his father's favourite refuge.

Sir Matthew looked away. "Took it hard but she's more herself, now," he said, and Andrew caught the flicker of something in his father's eyes which worried him.

In the bedroom above Lady Arandall was lying under one of the grooms, a wiry brawny boy of seventeen, his skin redolent of stableyard smells, straw and horses, his healthy body sweating as he drove into his mistress again and again while she moaned with satisfaction. Lady Arandall had tired of the household servants. They had a tendency to become insolent. Jacob, the boy pleasuring her now, spoke rarely and seemed to forget what she let him do in these moments. When she rode his blank eyes showed no flicker of awareness. He never hinted at their private meetings. He neither blackmailed nor showed emotion. His mounting of her had an animal starkness which she found peculiarly satisfying. When he had finished, and lay panting on her afterwards, she stroked his bare arms, pleased by the firm swell of his muscles beneath the spare flesh, a faint smile on her painted face. She was beginning almost to be fond of the boy.

She lay and watched him dress in his rough shirt and breeches. He turned to the door, knuckling his forehead. "Good day, my lady." She heard the door close as he stole away and laughed, almost wildly. The laughter died and tears came instead, suddenly, without warning. She brushed them out of her eyes angrily and rose from the bed, biting her lip. Stupid, she thought. Stupid, stupid.

In the library Andrew was listening in stupefaction to his father's account of the split between themselves and the iron-master. "Do you mean they've bought no charcoal since October?"

Sir Matthew's teeth ground together. "Not an ounce. I've seen to that."

"But have you sold it elsewhere, then?"

"Some of it." His father's face was set rigidly, little flames in his eyes.

"And the rest?"

Sir Matthew came to his feet. "Questions, questions! You'll find out soon enough, boy. Ride to the forest. Take a look for yourself." His mouth writhed as though in torment. "Take a look for yourself, Andy, and tell me then if Joss Colby doesn't need shooting. I'd take a pistol to him myself if I thought I'd get away with it. He's behind everything that's happened to us this past year. The man deserves the worst I can do to him."

"What is the worst you can do?" Andrew asked shrewdly.

"Starve him out, him and his men."

"And is it working?"

"Of course it's working. Their forge has been silent this month or more."

"You've been down there?"

"No need, I hear the tales soon enough. There are plenty of idle tongues around here, you know that." Again that writhing of the mouth, the bitter flash of the eyes. "Gossip thrives here."

Andrew winced. "Yes," he said heavily, then added in a cool tone, "Sir, one of us should take a look down there all the same."

"The ironworks?" Sir Matthew peered at him, brow heavy. Malice glinted in his eyes. "Still chasing Colby's little bitch of a wife? She's breeding, they say, never leaves the house, reared too delicate for her station in life. All the fault of that mother of hers, no doubt, a pasty-faced little wench, no stamina." He gave a spiteful grin. "If you fancy the wench, why not, boy? That would stick in Colby's guts. I owe him a reckoning."

Hannah was working late in the office when she heard the tramp of feet out in the lane, then the low mutter of voices. Curiously she opened the door and glanced out. The day shift had gone off an hour since. What was afoot? Across the yard she saw the gathering shapes in the trees. A few carried rush lanterns, the eerie gleam throwing strange dancing illumination over the pale faces. Hannah began to recognise them and then to feel her heart beat thick and heavily. She looked over at the furnaces and saw Joss look out, the red glare of the fire behind him, his strong body bare, arms rippling with muscle as he moved to get a better view. Some of the night shift crowded behind him and Joss put his hands on his hips, squaring to face the newcomers as they surged forward suddenly.

They halted a few feet from the furnaces. Joss surveyed them coolly, head thrown back, thick black hair ruffled by the night wind. "Well?" he demanded in a tone as calm as though he suspected nothing of their purpose.

The crowd shifted their feet, pressed close together like sheep huddling against the winter wind, then there was a convulsive movement among them and one man was pushed forward, facing Joss aggressively. She knew him at once – Jem Tiler was a small, skinny Birmingham man with a rough temper and a quick tongue. He had been laid off when the forges went out of work.

"We've had a meeting, Joss Colby," he shouted.

"Have you now?" Joss commented softly, and she saw the silvery flash of his grey eyes as his head moved to take in all the faces in the crowd. "I thought some of you had more sense. D'ye think the magistrates will let you roam around in a mob like this and take no note?"

"Are you threatening us?" Jem asked. "We've rights, Joss Colby, like it or not. We don't have to stand by and see our children go empty and our wives clem for nothing but your pride. T'old master likes it no more than we do, we know that. The works belongs to the Shields, not you, Joss Colby. While t'old master had charge of things we could count on a fair wage and we'll not stand for being laid off."

"Aye," the crowd murmured in a deep sigh. "Aye, tell 'im, Jem."

Jem shifted his stance and eyed Joss in a menacing fashion. "We want our jobs back, Joss Colby, and we want them now. Tonight. Give us your word the forges open again or . . ."

"Or what?" Joss broke in with a deep, angry question. He had stood there, feet apart, face impassive, listening, but now his powerful arms shot out and before the crowd had notice of it, Jem Tiler was caught in his strong hands, struggling like a rat in a bulldog's teeth, shaken and helpless.

Was Joss mad to lose his temper in the face of such a dangerous crowd, Hannah asked herself, instinctively moving forward, her mouth dry and her heart hammering?

Joss was throttling Jem Tiler, who was making choking sounds, his hands vainly trying to free his throat from the grip on it. "I'll teach you dogs to come snarling at me," Joss shouted, and Hannah suddenly saw that she was wrong. Joss had not lost his temper. The silvery eyes were cool enough. It had been one of his calculated risks. He suddenly flung Tiler from him and faced him, crouched in a wrestler's stance, as men did at the local fairs when they wrestled naked for a pig. The men moved back, formed a ring, shouts coming from them. In the light of the lanterns Hannah saw Jem pick himself up, fingering his bruised throat, watched the fear come into his thin face as he saw Joss face him.

Jem looked round at the faces of the other men, swallowing. "Mates, this isn't the way," he shouted. "We didn't come for this, did we? I'm not afraid of Colby but I won't pretend I'm a match for him. Look at the size of him, mates, it would be like wrestling with a bear. What will it prove? That I'm a runt beside that great rutting boar? We came to get out jobs back, see our children fed. Don't play into his hands, curse him."

"Shall I tie one hand behind my back, Tiler?" Joss jeered. "Will that suit you better?"

Jem looked at him, flushing darkly, then whirled and snatched a lighted brand from the hand of one of the men and flung it towards the stackyards, the light flashing and flaming through the dark as it flew. "Let's see you fight fire, Joss Colby, for if we don't get our jobs, so help me God you'll have to or the whole place will burn down around your ears."

The brand fell among straw and began a sudden fierce blaze. The younger men were bellowing with excitement. One or two ran to light other brands to whirl into the stackyards. Hannah thrust her fist into her mouth, shivering. At the kitchen windows the servants crowded to stare and quiver. The night shift had moved out to watch, too, silent in sympathy with their workmates.

Joss pushed his way out of the ring and within a moment had sent both boys crashing across the yard, his body weight put behind the blows, the jar of bone on bone making the men gasp.

They watched as Joss flung a bucket of water over the blazing straw and stamped out other sparks with his booted feet. Then he turned and faced them, jaw belligerent.

"What now? I'm not giving way to threats. You don't know me if you think I would. Come on, there are twenty of you and only one of me. Let's see what you can do, or are the odds too high for you?"

His contempt slashed the men and began a stirring among them, an angry reaction which Hannah felt to be more dangerous than anything that had gone before. She could listen to it no longer. She ran out and faced them, trembling, white-faced, scornful. "Is this the way to see your children fed? Threats, violence, setting fire to the place? Can't you see what will come of it? Some of you will get hurt, some of you may go to prison, but there are some who will be shipped off to exile or even hanged. That's what happens to men who roam around in mobs and offer violence and murder. Will that feed your families? Will it comfort your wives when they have to go on the parish? Have some sense, all of you. Go home to

136

your wives now before you go further." She looked round the circle of lantern-lit faces and saw their eyes gleam in the pale light. "Go home," she said desperately. "For your own sakes."

Jem Tiler pushed her abruptly backward. "Out of the way, girl. Hold your tongue."

She fell as he pushed and in a second Joss was at his throat, face wolfish, teeth bared. "Strike a woman, would you? I'll teach you to treat a woman in that way."

She scrambled up, head aching where it had hit a wall, blood on her white face. "No," she screamed, dragging at their arms as they fought. She was lifted out of the way and looked up into Jabey's serious face. "Stay there, Han," he said gently, then he went back to where Joss and the little man were fighting. Jabey's arms plucked Tiler away and Joss found himself facing Jabey suddenly. Breathing heavily, chest rising and falling, Joss crouched, his eyes on Jabey's calm face.

"That's enough," Jabey said, looking at him. He turned and looked at the men. "Go home. You'll do yourselves no good here."

They hesitated for a few seconds but Jabey's voice impressed them. After a while they went, their feet shuffling. Tiler went last of all, his face bruised and bloody. Joss slowly straightened, eying Jabey in a strange fashion.

Jabey turned his back on him and looked at Hannah. "Are you hurt, Han, love?"

"No," she whispered shakily. "Thank you, Jabey."

He brushed down her dusty skirt and ran his hands over her untidy hair, smiling at her. "I could wish you weren't so brave, lass," he murmured. "Best go indoors now. The air's cold."

She reached up to kiss his cheek, her arms round his neck. "Jabey, dear, thank you."

Then she ran into the house, forgetting the candle she left burning in the office, and the other servants burst out with questions and comments, excited by the night's events.

In the yard Joss turned on the night shift and bellowed, "Get back to work, this isn't a fair day." They vanished and he looked at Jabey. In silence the two men stared at each other, their faces set in hard lines. Joss's hands were clenched at his side and Jabey glanced down at them shrewdly, his eyes narrowed, then he turned and walked away while Joss stared rigidly after him.

Caroline had not left her bed since her mother died. She lay in it like a doll, her swelling body hidden under the covers, her hands lying on the quilt immobile, without occupation. She had abandoned her sewing. She never read or played her flute. Hannah often wondered what she thought about all day in her idleness.

Hannah, herself, had no time for rest. Since Mistress Shield's death the management of the household had fallen on to her shoulders. Mrs. Poley managed the kitchen as she had before, but Master Shield clung to Hannah as a drowning man clings to a drifting spar, insisting that she take over the tasks Mistress Shield had performed, making the daily decisions about the running of the house.

"You're my brother's child," he said drunkenly, maudlin in his cups. "I'll make it up to you, Hannah, for it all. You've Shield blood in your veins. It is your home too."

She still worked in the office each afternoon but her mornings were now fully occupied with the arrangements of the house, and when Joss realised how much of her time was necessarily spent out of the office he rode to Birmingham and came back with his youngest brother, Matt, to serve in the office as her assistant.

A tall, very thin boy with thick brown hair and brown eyes, Matt was fifteen. He had learnt to cipher and count stores at his uncle's shop but he had hated his uncle, as Joss had, and leapt at the chance to get away from the tyranny of the cane and the angry blow.

Hannah had taught him all she knew patiently, realising at once that Matt's shy silences concealed an able mind. Soon she could leave him in charge during her absences, although his youth made him an easy target for the men's teasing. They mocked and bullied him, chaffed him about his smooth boyish skin, asking, "Does your mammy know you're out?"

and argued with him over the fines book, claiming he had made a mistake over this or that. Matt retained a hold on his temper, smiling good-humouredly at them.

When the doctor visited Caroline he always nodded smilingly to Hannah, greeting her as nurse. "How's my patient today, Nurse? Any change? You look hale enough, God knows. Lend her some of your roses."

Matt's arrival had made life easier for Hannah. She was free then to spend time with Caroline, trying to tease her gently into some sort of activity, although her visits did little good, since Caroline was obstinate in her refusal to get up.

"She wants to hide," Hannah said to Joss. "She's too frightened to come down here. Up there, she feels she's safe. Nothing can get at her."

He moved restlessly, eyes angry. "What can get at her, for God's sake? You talk as though the house were full of wild animals."

She eyed him slightly mockingly. "Perhaps she feels it is."

He caught the tone and his face changed. He looked down at her, brows rising. "Me, you mean?"

Her eyes gleamed as green as rushes. "If the cap fits."

He smiled, amused. "You're an insolent little wretch, Hannah. I would say you were getting above yourself, drunk with a little power, if you had not always been as sharp as a knife."

She lifted her thin dark brows. "Drunk with power? What power?"

He gestured. "Who is it runs this house now? Who is beginning to rule the yards with a rod of iron? Why, yesterday when you came into the yard the men stopped swearing and some of them even smiled."

She laughed, eyes glinting. "That must have been a rare sight. They don't smile for you, do they, Joss Colby?"

He frowned. "You know damned well they don't. And you know why." He pushed his hands into his breeches. "I'm trying to get some iron from Naylors over at Pymming but so far no luck. If I could only get my hands on some charcoal but nobody around here will sell it to me and if I bring it in from farther afield, our profit margin will be too low."

She put her hand on his arm urgently. "You must do something, Joss. There's real hardship among the men. Some of the children look like wraiths. It makes me sick to see them."

"I know, damn you," he muttered, the muscles under her fingers tightening with anger. "I'm trying."

She glanced at him in wary appraisal. "Joss," she began, and he interrupted her, his face black with temper.

"No! I know what you are going to say, and the answer's no. I'll not go to Arandall on my belly to beg."

"Pride won't feed the children!"

He caught her shoulders and shook them. "I'm the sort of man I am, Hannah. Don't try to change me. I risked everything when I changed to coke and I'm not backing down now."

She looked up, helpless in his strong hands, the thick red-brown hair hanging down her back in soft little curls which brushed his skin as her head moved. Although she had been working hard lately she had been eating well, sleeping well and with the grim shadow of Mistress Shield removed she had been gradually putting on weight, her skin and hair gaining a lustre which altered her whole appearance. She would never be pretty but when she smiled and her eyes gleamed bright green she had a beauty which startled the unwary eye. She was wearing one of the new gowns which Master Shield had ordered Peg to make for her. The white kerchief crossed across her bosom was fresh and crisp. Her blue gown had a smooth texture which outlined her slender body closely. Joss stared down at her and something flickered in his grey eyes.

He bent his dark head and she gasped in shock at the feel of his mouth on her shoulder, pushing aside the kerchief to glide over her skin. He moved nearer so that their bodies touched. She heard him breathing thickly below her ear, his lips hot on her neck. "Hannah," he muttered.

"Don't," she whispered unsteadily.

His arm slid round her waist. His breathing quickened.

"You get more lovely every day," he said, his face hidden from her.

She thrust at his broad shoulder but the feel of his body under her hand sent a shudder through her which horrified her. He heard her rough-drawn breath and pulled her closer, his hand pressing her back, moving slowly up her spine.

She was tempted and Joss knew it, he sensed it with that animal instinct of his, his blood informing him before his brain. He had been under stress for months now, bearing the full weight of the conflict with the squire, with no help but his own will and intelligence to carry him through that time. His desire for Hannah had been forced out of sight during those months. Now it burst out from the shrouding bands and she felt it in every nerve.

"Oh, God," he groaned, seeking her mouth with a twist of his black head.

A liquid heat flowed through her. Silently she yielded and he took her mouth with a hunger which fed and fed and would not be assuaged. They pressed together, seeking the satisfaction which had become a nagging necessity, then suddenly heard running steps outside and sprang apart, breathing heavily, their faces flushed. Hannah was sickened by her own folly, her moment of weakness.

The door opened. Nancy ran in gasping, excitement and panic in her face. "Miss Caroline . . . the baby . . . Hannah, come, Mrs. Poley says we must send for t'midwife, but you must come now."

Hannah did not look at Joss. She picked up her shawl and ran, winding it round herself, and as she crossed the yard rain began to fall in light, thin spears around her, dampening her hair and running softly down her face.

Caroline's screams could be heard from outside the house. A few of the men were gathered there in the darkness, staring. She passed them and went into the house, hearing the screams grow louder as she came up the stairs. Mrs. Poley was in the chamber with Caroline but she was doing no good and her face was flustered and anxious as Hannah ran to the bed.

"She won't lie still," she whispered, trying to hold the girl's writhing body down. "She's like a mad thing. Hannah, she looks so ill."

Hannah looked at Caroline quickly and saw the red, sweating little face contorted with the ugly sounds emerging from the open mouth. She took a deep breath and her hand slapped sharply over the girl's face. The screaming stopped dead. Caroline looked at her incredulously, hurt. Then the tears ran faster than the rain dripping down the windows. "Oh, it hurts, Hannah, it hurts," she moaned, and Hannah held both her twisting, perspiring hands and said gently, "I know. Shush now, lie still."

She did not, however, like the look of Caroline at all. The girl's body had an unhealthy, swollen look, even her small face seemed to be twice its normal size, and her legs and ankles were puffed like balloons, reminding Hannah of the bladders which were carried by clowns at fairs, the skin a dead, flabby white. The midwife was out when one of the servants knocked at her cottage, but the doctor happened to be in the cottages visiting a dying old man. He came an hour later when his patient permitted it and shook his head over Caroline, his eyes grave.

"Birth fever," he said. "There's water in her body, see." He poked the swollen ankles with one finger and the dent sank into the flesh lividly.

"Can you do anything for her?"

He shrugged. "Give her release from some of her pain, but it may kill the child if I do." He looked over his shoulder at Joss, who stood in the doorway, listening. "Well? It is your child."

Hannah met Joss's eyes and saw the stark indecision in his face. He gnawed his lip and she thought she saw him look at her as though to beg her to make the decision for him. Caroline gave a short, sharp scream of such agony that they all winced, turning their heads to look at her. She was squirming on the bed, fighting the pain weakly, and it was clear to Hannah that the girl's small store of strength was failing.

"She'll not survive the birth if this goes on," she said to Joss flatly.

He jerked his head at the doctor. "Do what you can for her," he said, turning away.

It was little enough. The doctor made Caroline drink a cup of some dark liquid which almost made her vomit. After a while, however, it calmed her and she dozed on the dark edge of sleep, twitching, wincing. The doctor went downstairs with Joss and Hannah stayed in the chamber with the sleeping girl. Caroline's eyes had a doped dullness which erased her personality entirely. Her body continued to perform the act of birth despite her drugged state, however, and Hannah held her hands while the girl jerked and grunted like an animal.

Once before the end Caroline opened her eyes and there was clear intelligence in their depths for a few moments. Wearily, she said to Hannah, "Never lie with a man, Hannah, or you'll come to this and it is a worse pain than I have ever known. I wish I were dead."

"No, no," Hannah protested, patting her. "When the baby is born you'll be happy, Caroline."

"I'll be dead," Caroline said bitterly. "And that will be the happiness I want." She closed her eyes, grunting again with that thick animal agony which seemed to be growing stronger now.

Hannah called for the doctor but when he came there was little he seemed able to do but sigh and shake his head. Caroline was screaming again now and he said he dared not give her any more physic. "It would kill her," he said flatly. "We must trust to God."

Hannah almost laughed but there was no laughter left in her as she clung to Caroline's sweating hand and watched the girl suffer. Her delicately made little body had never been intended for an easy birth, the doctor said. She was too frail, too slightly built, her hips too narrow.

Hannah was lashed with a self-hatred and guilt which bit into her conscience. While Caroline lay screaming with pain as Joss's child fought to leave her body, Joss had been holding Hannah in his arms, kissing her with a hunger she had returned without reservation. That ate at Hannah now. She closed her eyes and shuddered, remembering the feverish pressure of their bodies as they kissed, knowing that if Joss had not been stopped he would have taken her. She had not put up any fight. It was a bitter admission for her as she held Caroline's small trembling fingers and silently wept.

Caroline died in the early hours. There was chill silence in the house although the servants sat huddled in the kitchen listening to the cries above. The air was heavy with that marrow-freezing cold which comes before the dawn. Hannah shivered as she watched the sweating doctor wrestle, bare-armed, to drag the child from Caroline's dead body. His white shirt was daubed with blood, his wig had long since been thrown to the floor and his short hair bristled on his flushed scalp.

Hannah felt sick but she would not look away. She forced herself to see the indignity, the violence done to the dead girl. She had betrayed Caroline in Joss's arms earlier. Now she suffered all that happened in a need to make retribution.

"God damn it," the doctor gasped in one last effort, then shot back, holding the blood-masked child in his hands.

It was a boy. Hannah saw that at a glance. Then the doctor's heavy silence sank into her brain and she saw the cord around the baby's neck, the lolling head and terrible stillness. The doctor acted feverishly but it had been too late long before the child had been dragged forth. Joss's son had never lived to take a breath.

Eight

JOSS DID NOT say a word. He sat alone in the parlour in his shirtsleeves, his head in his hands, the black hair ruffled as though he had run his fingers through it again and again during the long night. He would have heard Caroline's screams even with his hands over his ears, and being Joss, he would not have shut them out. He would have sat there listening and even though she could not see his face she could guess at the stony blankness of it.

Hannah repeated the stark sentence. "Both dead." She did not try to soften it. How could she? To another man she might have offered comfort, soothing lies, tried to wrap up the truth in some fashion, but to Joss she gave the fact bare, shorn of all pretence.

After a moment he asked harshly, "Was it a boy?"

"Yes."

And then he laughed. Hannah winced and her hand came down on his shoulder, her nails biting into his body.

"Don't, Joss."

The doctor had offered to break the news and she had refused. She had left it to him, instead, to tell Master Shield, who had drunk himself into shielding stupor and lay on the floor of his bedchamber snoring thickly.

She looked down on the bent black head and saw blood on his knuckles. At some time in the night he had bitten his hands, she recognised the teethmarks for what they were.

"I did her a terrible wrong," Joss said in that hoarse, dull voice. "She was a pretty child. It need not have come to this but for me."

If he could cry it would ease him, but he would not. Under that hard face he was fighting still, struggling with his own pain and remorse. He was too strong to surrender and the battle would drain him.

She could have moved her hand to his hair but she dared not. He might then have turned and let the terrible seed between them flower. Even in her compassion for. him she could not permit that.

"Caroline loved you," she said, but it was the wrong thing to say. She knew it even as she said it. Joss lifted his head from his hands then and glared at her, eyes wide and tearless yet glittering as though tears were dammed up behind the bright iris.

"Do you think I don't know that? That makes it worse, it makes it damnable. It is my crime, my punishment."

She understood. He had charmed Caroline deliberately and taught her to love him, yet he had never loved the girl. He had taken her slight, childlike body and used it for his own ends, and he had killed her, as much as if he had cut her throat.

Joss put out a hand suddenly and she drew back, flinching. Their eyes held silently, and there was no need for words in what he was asking of her, what she was refusing. His nostrils flared white above the tormented mouth. He got up and pushed her from his path.

"I'll find my own road out of it then," he said, as if she had spoken.

She watched him pour brandy into a glass and swallow it, then pour another. Quietly she went out, returning upstairs to help Mrs. Poley with the necessary tasks. She was growing used to washing the dead, she thought, as she worked beside the weeping old woman. It would have been joy to have a living child to welcome but she found it harrowing to bind the child and lay it in its mother's arms, waxen pale upon that still breast.

Weeping, Mrs. Poley went out and Hannah watched beside the dead. Sunlight glittered on Caroline's bright hair. A bird flew past the window, darkening the light briefly.

Joss staggered into the room and hung on the doorframe,

his fingers spread to support his weight. His haggard face was darkly flushed now. The odour of the brandy came with him.

He stared at the child. Taking two steps he lurched to take it from its resting place.

"No, Joss," Hannah said, and he thrust her away as she tried to take the child.

He tore off the white garment, breathing heavily. She saw his eyes wince, close, then open. In death the child had a perfection which cleft the heart. Joss touched the tiny fingers, brushed a hand over the sparse black hair. Under his breath he was muttering oaths. "My son," he breathed, but it was not sorrow, it was rage. His face was torn by it.

He had not even looked at Caroline. Hannah firmly took the child and Joss let her. While she gently clothed the cold little body Joss went out and she heard him crashing down the stairs, swearing.

Caroline and her child were buried two days later. Master Shield was sober on the day of the funeral but that night he went to Birmingham, leaving the house in a state of flux. The servants did nothing but whisper. Even Mrs. Poley sat in a chair, her skirts drawn back around her knees, warming her legs at the kitchen fire, uncaring if any work was done or not. Peg had leave to visit her family at Radshore. Nancy was off on some amusement of her own. Hannah worked in the office for a few hours but an unseasonable heat had fallen upon the works. Spring blazed briefly into summer. Golden light poured down upon the fields and the air smelled of flowers. It was impossible to work in such weather. Giving Matt leave to go fishing, Hannah shut the office and went out herself to look for Jabey. He was on night shift, she was told. The men grinned, winked at each other. Hannah retreated before their knowing grins. She would not wake him, she decided. He always slept well, his body worn out with work.

Feeling the heat of the afternoon press down upon her she went into the stables to fondle the horses, feeling the silken inner skin of their ears crumple beneath her fingers. Their rough tongues licked her salty skin and made her laugh. Caroline's little mare shuffled its feet and whinnied. Buried one day, she thought. So short a time and yet already life was marching inexorably on without the girl.

Climbing the ladder she lay down in the hay loft, inhaling the warm, summer scent of the dried grass with pleasure. There were swallows swooping round the yard outside, their restless darting flight punctuated by grumbling calls to each other. How light and free it would be, soaring far above the earth, able to range at will in the blue sky. If one had no body at all it would be sweeter. Freedom, she thought sleepily. Caroline had it now. Was it sweet to her?

She drifted into a relaxed sleep. She would do nothing at all for the whole day, she thought. Nothing at all. It was so long since she had had time on her hands that it was too precious to spend in doing anything.

From below came the sound of the horses shifting their feet, blowing through their nostrils as though they laughed. The swallows made little chirruping sounds like the groom when he brushed the carthorses before setting off to deliver a load.

She brushed aside a brittle stem which was tickling her cheek, and yawned widely, catlike, her mouth triangular, her teeth small and sharp. What o'clock could it be? She was aware of having slept but had lost all sense of time.

She froze suddenly, hearing Joss's voice below. A little giggle followed whatever he had said. Hannah listened, then crawled silently to the trap and peered down.

Nancy stood in the stable, her pretty, silly face flushed with heat and excitement. She had unlaced her bodice partially. Her white breasts showed to the nipple.

"What sort of girl d'ye think I am, Joss Colby?" she asked, tossing her yellow head, her eyes provocative.

"I know what sort you are," Joss drawled, mocking her, his thumbs in his wide leather belt, his strong body at ease. "You've been begging for it for weeks and I'm disposed to give it to you now. There's no soul in earshot. We'll not be interrupted."

"You speak so rough, Joss," Nancy pouted. "I'm no slattern to be taken in the straw without so much as a kiss."

"Oh, is it kisses you want?" Joss's eyes sparkled derisively. He pulled her into his arms and kissed her brutally, biting into her soft pink lips, bruising her mouth, ramming it back upon her teeth.

Hannah heard Nancy squeaking and her eyes burned with anger. Poor silly fool, she thought. He will eat her up and spit out the pips. Nancy had stopped giggling now, struggling, a weak, helpless thing in the talons of a bird of prey.

She gasped as Joss lifted his head. "You hurt me!"

The hard mouth grinned. He kissed her again, silencing her cries of protest, and Hannah did not need any close scrutiny to know that Joss was taking what he wanted from the girl's limp body with merciless efficiency and total lack of feeling. It was amusing him to hear her moan and squeak in his grip, he was a tiger playing with a kid, ripping it to pieces merely to hear it shriek. Caroline's death had shocked him into self-contempt and anger and now he was taking those feelings out on Nancy, imposing his bodily strength in order to release the powerful emotions Hannah had refused to satisfy. When he again lifted his dark head from Nancy's half-fainting body she expected to see blood on his mouth. He stared down at the girl and there was amused satisfaction in his face.

Nancy tried to pull from his arms, shaking. "You are a devil, Joss Colby, I want no more of such kisses. Let me go."

"Not without what you came for," he mocked, the white teeth predatory between his lips. One hand slid down her body, fondling her.

"I will not let you," Nancy mumbled, wriggling at the caress of his hand.

"Half the lads in the works have tumbled you, you little liar, and you've been giving me the eye for months." Joss thrust her backwards as he spoke and Hannah watched, stiff and sick, as Nancy fell on the straw and Joss lunged down on her. She tried to close her eyes but they remained open, staring, as Nancy struggled like a moth on a pin, softly moaning, while Joss pushed back her skirts and took her. Nancy cried out in pain and shock, beginning to cry.

Joss Colby had a dark side which cherished pain. She had

149

always guessed it, Hannah thought, now she knew. He enjoyed inflicting pain, he was amusing himself now with Nancy, tightening the screw of it to the pitch he needed.

Hannah had never seen humans couple before. She had seen animals and known how it was done, but now she could not move, held in disgust and fascinated revulsion. Joss drove into the girl with the regular thud of the tilthammer as it came down upon hot metal, his body stark and powerful, uncaring that Nancy was wincing and sobbing below him. Her voice rose to a high shriek. "Oh, God, no, Joss, no."

He put a muffling hand over her mouth and over his fingers Nancy's eyes begged for mercy, tears running down her face. Hannah hated Nancy for a second, sick with jealousy because the girl lay merged with Joss in such intimacy, of mind and body, without knowing anything of him. Hannah understood him and hated him for what she knew.

A strange, pulsating heat began to grow in Hannah. She ran her tongue over her dry lips, shivering. She could not take her eyes from him. She realised she had always known how he would make love, as if she had already experienced it, but now she was an unwilling observer and her blood was beating in rhythm with the downward plunge of his body.

Suddenly he dropped his hand from Nancy's face and her voice emerged from her parted lips, rustily groaning. Her body writhed under him as if she were impaled and dying. "God, Joss, you've hurt me so," she cried and then she began to whine, her voice high with a drained pleasure Hannah could feel in every nerve. Hannah's stomach was cramped with a hot sickness. The bodies moving in the straw seemed to dissolve before her eyes. The sounds they were making ran inside her head like the mad delusions of a nightmare. Joss was grunting now in deep, physical satisfaction, and she hated him with a feeling which burned her insides like swallowed acid.

Never, she thought. It must never happen to me. She looked again and Nancy lay still, white and limp and exhausted. This was what he did to women. Her instinct had warned her. He used them with the full extremity of passion and they died of it.

Caroline had said, "Never lie with a man or you will come to this."

Joss pulled himself away. Nancy was weeping. She dressed herself where he had pulled her clothes apart, then scrambled to her feet. "You're a brute, Joss Colby, a cruel brute."

"You got what you came for," he shrugged. "Why complain?"

"I didn't come for that!" Nancy's face was smeared with tears. "I wanted a little loving not to be mounted as though I were a mare."

"A fine mare you'd make," Joss grinned. "You'd breed nothing but geldings."

"All you gave Miss Caroline was a dead child," Nancy said, and Joss's face burnt suddenly with rage. Hannah saw it flare blackly into his face. Nancy fell back from him, trembling, then ran from the stable.

Joss was swearing viciously. He smashed his fists down on the iron manger on the wall. Blood flowed over his skin but he struck again and again, breathing heavily.

At last he stood still, head hanging. She could not see his face. He looked at his hands, then walked towards the door. Hannah waited until she could hear no sound. Softly she stole down the ladder backwards, turning to creep out.

Her breath caught. Joss stood in the door wiping his hands on a kerchief. For a moment they stared at each other. He wore a strange, startled expression. Then his eyes flared.

"You were up there," he said, lifting his eyes to the trap into the loft.

Without answering she turned her head away.

"It serves you right, then," he said, his eyes on her profile. "You should have come down at once."

Still she said nothing and he moved nearer. "It meant nothing," he said, his voice suddenly thick.

She did look round then, her eyes contemptuous. "Do you think you need to tell me that? Nancy may be a silly slut but that gives you no right to use her as you did. Men are all the same. Trampling like pigs in a sty, grunting, snatching what they can . . ."

He went white, his eyes dark flames beneath his brows. She was surprised to see pain in his face. He breathed hoarsely, "You frozen little fool, what runs in your veins? Vinegar? By God, I'd like to change that look on your face!"

He took a step nearer before she could move and caught her. The hard mouth swooped but before he touched her lips he was pulled off her. Dazed, they both stared as Jabey's presence came home to them. His face was angry, the brown eyes lit with rage.

"Go to the house, Hannah," he said quietly.

She would have argued but he flicked her a look. "Now, Hannah," he said, and she went. Jabey kept his eyes on Joss as he took off his shirt.

"I'm going to kill you, Colby," he said.

Joss laughed contemptuously. He stripped and the bare brown body rippled like water in sunlight as he moved. His eyes were amused, yet there was calculation there, too.

"She wants me," he said, watching Jabey's face.

The pockmarks showed more lividly but Jabey did not answer. Instead he crouched, fists held rigid. Yet it was Joss who moved first, as fast as a snake, and his blow sent Jabey reeling through the open door into the yard. He climbed to his knees, gasping, and Joss hit him again. Jabey's eye socket split under the blow. Blood ran down his cheek.

Men came out of the works, drawn by the sounds of blows and grunted breath. They stood, bare-chested, around the furnaces, staring. Joss's arm smashed down again towards Jabey but Jabey had his measure now and ducked, crouching, to take him round the waist, catching him off guard midswing, throwing him bodily backwards against the stable wall. The impact left Joss gasping for a moment, then he straightened. His upper lip curled back in a wolfish snarl of rage. Jabey saw his eyes before Joss got to him. The great hands fastened round his throat like grappling hooks and Jabey didn't have a chance. Joss forced him slowly, choking, to his knees in the dust. The muscles in his arms clotted as his grip tightened.

Hannah had watched it from the kitchen. Her anger with

Joss deepened as she saw Jabey on his knees in front of him, wrestling to be free of those powerful hands. Without stopping to think, she snatched up a bucket of ice-cold well water and ran out there. She flung it and in surprise Joss let go of Jabey, looking up at her, face dripping.

"Leave him alone," Hannah shouted. She went on her knees, tears in her eyes. "Oh, Jabey, you fool, you fool," she whispered, looking at his bruised and battered face. "You know you aren't up to his weight."

Joss watched them bleakly for a moment then he turned his head and roared at the men to get back to work. They went and the yard lay sunnily empty. Hannah helped Jabey to his feet, her arm around him. Joss walked away without a word.

"Whatever made you do it?" she asked, bathing his eye later. "Joss is stronger than any of the other men."

"He did not fight fair," Jabey said, and she laughed wildly. "Did you expect he would?"

Jabey smiled wryly. "As you said, Han, I'm a fool. I thought he was going to kill me. I read it in his face."

"He's a vicious cur. Stay out of his path, Jabey." She sighed, inspecting his face. "You're a picture now. Oh, Jabey. Why tackle him?"

"I ran into Nancy crying her eyes out," Jabey said, a frown in his eyes. "I asked her what the matter was but all she could say was that Joss had hurt her. Then I saw him with you." He looked away from her, then back. "I saw his face, Han. I don't want you in the house with him at nights."

"I can take care of myself," she said without real confidence.

"Let me have the banns cried," Jabey said very quietly.

She hesitated then bent her head. "If you like, Jabey," and he kissed her very gently before he went.

Master Shield came back fighting drunk from Birmingham a few days later and slept it off all afternoon. When he came downstairs he was a sickly yellow, his eyes red-rimmed.

Hannah was in the kitchen alone, calculating the dry stores. He called her into the parlour and when she obediently went to him, he waved a hand impatiently at one of the chairs.

"Sit down, Hannah."

She had never been invited to sit in his presence before and her astonished face betrayed it.

"Sit down," he repeated irritably, and she obeyed him, placing her hands in her lap, waiting.

He sighed. "I've not long to live," he said. "I've no child alive but I do not want my mill falling into Colby's hands. I want to see it go to my own blood, Hannah." The sore eyes blinked at her. "You're all that's left. While I was in Birmingham I made a will leaving it all to you."

She was too astounded to do more than gape like a landed fish. He saw her look of disbelief and nodded heavily.

"I know, I know. You've not expected this. But who else is there? If I die Colby will get it all."

Hannah found her voice. Faintly she said, "But Joss is your son-in-law."

"He killed my child. When he came here I had a wife and daughter. My mill was my own. Now I've nothing. He has destroyed Caroline and taken my mill. I drink because I can't stand up to him and prefer not to face what I've become."

Slowly she said, "He won't accept it."

Master Shield took her hand. "He will. If you wed him."

Her hand went ice-cold in his grasp. "No," she said. "No."

"You could not run this place alone," Master Shield told her. "And if you married young Stock, Joss would kill him inside a week."

Her eyes flew to his face in appalled understanding. Of course Joss would, she thought.

"Joss would not stand for watching another man take over the mill," Master Shield said flatly. "He's done too much to get it."

"I could not marry him," she said in a voice that shook. "I'd rather die."

"You're my brother's child. Bess's daughter. I've done you grievous wrong in the past. I want to right it now. I want to know that when I'm gone there will be children with Shield blood living here. Colby's a ruthless devil but you'll need him to run things. Stock would never do. He is a good lad but Colby will knock him to kingdom come if Stock tries to take

154

what Colby sees as his. You'll need Colby to run the works. He's clever and he knows what he's doing. He must stay."

"Then let him have the works," she cried. "Does it matter?"

"It matters to me," he groaned. "I know you owe me nothing, Hannah, but I beg you. Do it for me. How can I die in peace knowing he gets it all? I must have my own kin here. If I'd had sons . . ."

"You still could," she said desperately. "You're not too old."

His face contorted bleakly. "I don't want them now. All I want is to finish with it all."

His tone pierced her with compassion. He looked so ill and weary, his skin like aging parchment over his bones. "I know that I'm to blame for it all. I brought him here. He never cared a straw for Caroline. I knew it all along but she wanted him and I needed him, so I let it happen. I've that on my conscience. I want to go in peace."

"What peace would I have?" she asked, expecting no reply. There would be none with Joss. She had looked through the outward mask of his face and seen that the dark core was adamant, implacable.

He would take her, crush out her essence and leave her empty, a husk. She had to save herself, escape his possession, as she would the demonic possession of her soul by evil forces, starving the clamour in her blood which demanded the satisfaction of surrender to his body. His freedom was bought at a high cost by others, by all those with whom he came in contact, since he must impose his will upon them, like an incubus, sucking them dry to feed himself. She had known that for a long time, never putting it clearly into thought until she saw him using Nancy's helpless body to renew his own strength. She had been aware of his need for that renewal after Caroline's death when she silently refused to give him what his look and seeking hand had warned her he wanted. So he had gone to Nancy for it. Fate had shown her what she had feared all along.

"I cannot marry him. I am afraid," she said.

"You're strong," Master Shield said obstinately, setting his lower lip. "And I think you are the only human being I ever met who could stand against Joss Colby."

If he will let me, she thought grimly. He would not leave her a spare inch of her soul if he had his way.

"Oh, God, Hannah, don't say no," the old man groaned.

"There's Jabey," she whispered and already she was weakening. He could see the conflict in her white face.

"Stock will survive. And, anyway, I think he's not the man for you. He's too weak."

"Jabey's not weak," she said, indignantly. "He's strong."

Master Shield eyed her gravely. "If you marry him, Joss will kill him, sooner or later," he said.

She flinched. "Oh, God help me," she moaned, and the conflict was over. He could see surrender in her face. He got up and poured her wine, made her drink it. She was shaking, her teeth chattering against the rim of the glass.

While she held the glass they both heard Joss's boots as he came down the passage. Hannah stiffened, staring at the door. Master Shield patted her shoulder. "Stay here," he said, and met Joss at the door, putting a cheerful arm around his shoulder. "I want a word, Joss," he said, and Joss looked past him at Hannah, his eyes piercing, then he followed the old man out.

Hannah sat down, her knees giving. She must be mad. Even to think of it was total madness. She heard the servants coming into the kitchen, heard voices and laughter, the clink of pans, the sound of water splashing.

The door opened and Joss came into the room. She did not look up. He walked quietly over to her and stood there. She could see the black gleam of his boots.

"You know what Master Shield just told me," he said, and she heard the thick flare of triumph in his voice.

"Yes," she said, somehow making her voice emerge coolly.

He drew a long breath, "Hannah," he said, and his hands came down to lift her to her feet. "Oh, Hannah," he muttered, his fingers flexing on her shoulders. She lifted her head. A blind hunger filled his face. His eyes were closed and he was breathing roughly, lips parted.

"I would have asked you, anyway," he said, putting his lips to her hair. "But this way I get it all." He moved away, opening his eyes, and smiled, his face glittering like the moon on dark water. "I never suspected he would leave you the works. You've worked your way into his heart, Hannah."

"You have not asked me yet," she said in a still, quiet voice.

"Shall I go on my knees?" He was laughing, teasing her, then he looked down into her eyes and the smile went as he saw her expression.

"You want the works, don't you, Joss?"

His eyes narrowed and a shrewd fixity came into his face. "You know I do. But I want you, too."

"You can't have me."

He stood very still. After a moment he said, "The old man said you had agreed."

"To wed you," she said, nodding.

"But?" he asked with a rasp in his voice.

"I'll make a private contract with you first. You'll get the mill, but I want your oath that you will never touch me."

"Don't be absurd," he muttered. "You think I'd agree to that?" His eyes half closed, calculating. "This is because of what you saw from the hay loft. I told you, Nancy means nothing to me. When I'm hungry I eat and if there's nothing but dry bread, I eat that."

She flinched at the cruelty of that, remembering Nancy's hurt. "You'll not ease yourself with me," she said.

She could read the flicker of thought in his eyes. "Old Shield will make you marry me," he said.

Hannah looked up into his eyes, cool and certain of herself. "No man can make me do anything."

"I can," he said. She had been waiting for just such a move but he was too quick for her, all the same. Although she knew him so well she could not always anticipate his move in time. His hands held her, his mouth searched for hers, found it. She struggled to hate and knew her senses were reeling under the impact of being touched by him. His hand forced her head to stay where he wanted it and the kiss grew deeper and deeper, a strange mixture of demand and pleading, hunger and tenderness. Yet it was not the kiss which undermined her. It was the fact that Joss was trembling. His body was pressing against hers and he was shaking. Hannah dragged herself back from the brink of surrender under the lash of her cold little conscience, forcing herself to remember all she knew of him. She had to stay free of him or be destroyed.

Her hands against his chest broke him out of it. Breathing thickly he looked down at her, eyes dazed.

"The mill or nothing," she said. "This is your last chance. Jabey puts up the banns next week."

He let her go then, staring at her, disbelief in his face. "If you marry Stock I'll have to kill him," he said almost as though it were so obvious she should have known it. "I'll not let him have the mill . . . or you."

"You made use of Caroline," she said. "You admitted it to me the night she died. You will not make use of me except by my agreement. I'm prepared to marry you and let you run the works but I'm not prepared to have your hands on me."

He went a deadly white then, watching her and seeing she meant every word. Hannah walked over and got out the great family Bible, laying it on the table. "Swear on this," she said.

There was a long pause then he walked over and put his hand down on it. "What am I to swear?"

"Just that you will never lay hands on me," she said.

He said it expressionlessly and then she felt tired as though she had been through some terrible ordeal. White-faced, she sat down and gripped her shaking, icy hands in her lap. Joss turned and looked at her without a sign of feeling in his face.

"Why are you doing this, Hannah? Caroline? Or Nancy?"

"Neither," she said. "It is you."

"Me?" She saw he had not expected that. He sounded outraged. She could almost have laughed.

"When Caroline was dying I struggled to keep death at bay but I failed. I wasn't strong enough. I watched her eyes glaze and I hated death. Have you ever watched the life go out of someone's eyes, Joss? It is hard to explain. At that moment I

158

felt very aware of being alive. Never so aware before. That's how I feel about you, Joss. You are a destroyer and I won't go down before you."

"Thank you," he said bitterly.

They were silent and she could not guess what he was thinking. The sound of the servants drifted to her again, laughter and chatter, the sound of someone scrubbing the table, feet tapping on the floor. The sun had slid down into the distance and the room grew cold. She shivered and Joss lifted his dark head and glanced at her. He walked to the door. "I'll tell Stock," he said.

"I'll tell him myself."

"You won't see him again," Joss said, his eyes bleak. "After our marriage you'll never see him alone again. If I can't have you, no one shall."

"I owe it to Jabey to explain."

"No."

She eyed him coolly. "Yes."

She felt the hot tension of his rage across the room but her head stayed up, her eyes defiant.

"Damn you," Joss said and strode from the room. She closed her eyes. She had won. But at a cost to herself she could not yet calculate. She had held him at bay as an invaded country might the invader by scorching the earth in front of the enemy, leaving him no comfort or aid, and like the blackened countryside destroyed to save it from rape she felt totally empty, lifeless.

And she still had to tell Jabey.

Nine

SHE CALLED AT his house next afternoon. He was just up, his rough hair splashed with water where he'd washed his face. A heel of bread lay on the table beside a mug of beer which smelled stale, the odour of it filling the little room. Jabey listened, turning white. His shirt needed washing, she noticed, and wondered who would do such things for him. The little house was stuffy and cluttered, needing a woman's presence. She ached for him and tried to smile. "I've no choice, Jabey."

There was so much he could have said but he said none of it. His brown eyes were lightless as he bent his head. She waited for him to speak, praying he would say something, anything, feeling as though she had stabbed him through the heart.

When he did speak it took her breath away. "Be careful, Hannah," he said gently.

"Careful?" She could not help the bafflement in her voice.

"I'm not blind. He's been after you for a long, long time. I even think he truly cares for you, as far as Joss Colby can care for anyone. But remember Caroline. When she came back from school she was as bright as a new penny. He broke her in a year. I've known him now for long enough to see how he enforces his will. He has to be master, Hannah. It is in his blood. Mostly, men bear it, since they must, and they recognise it in him. But you'll not put up with that, so I say be careful. I've no wish to see you look like Caroline inside a year."

She was dumbfounded. "Jabey, Jabey, is that all you are going to say? I gave you my word and I'm breaking it."

He looked up then and smiled. "I somehow never thought I'd ever wed you, Hannah. Even when you said I could have the banns called I couldn't believe my luck. There was always this feeling down inside me . . ."

She put her arms round him and kissed his cheek. "Oh, Jabey, love, the truth is you're too good for me."

"The boot's on the other foot."

She shook her head. "No, I'm not fit to wash your shirts, Jabey. There is more of Joss Colby in me than I care to admit."

Looking at her, Jabey nodded. "I've known that for longer than I remember. You're clever, Hannah, and you're strong. Colby's your natural mate."

She winced, heat in her veins. When she was going she told him softly, "I'll always love you, Jabey, in many ways. I respect you. I would have been happy as your wife."

"Would you?" He shook his head, eyes sombre. "Your wings are too strong for that cage, Hannah. It would have been a crime to pen you up with me."

Working in the office later, Joss came in and glanced at her. "Seen Stock?"

"Yes." She added nothing and he asked nothing.

His mouth harshly tightened. He picked up the invoices and scanned them. "We're running low on lime. Get some more, will you?"

"I've ordered it."

He gave her a dark look, anger tightly reined but unhidden. She made herself meet those cold eyes but she was trembling. Sometimes the way he looked at her made her feel like a field-mouse when the harvesters tread too close, their iron sickles slicing down the sheltering corn. Instinct prompted her two ways: to hide or to run. When Jabey asked her to wed him she had seen a refuge and taken it. Jabey would have been both shelter and escape from Joss, but now she was exposed to all the bitter temptation of a passion which could only destroy her, and she looked into the future with a bleak face.

Her hands shook as she picked up her quill. The figures in the ledger swam before her eyes. Why didn't he move? Why did he stand there, his hands clenching and unclenching, as though he fought down a need to hurt. Her body shuddered in expectation as she heard him breathing beside her. Frustrated, Joss would become cruel. She recognised the cold glint of his eyes in those moods, a need to hurt, to impose himself, to dominate. He had offered her tenderness and she had refused it. Now Joss would give her coin of another kind.

Joss turned away and began running an index finger down the coke ledge. Gradually, Hannah breathed again, but she was more alarmed than ever.

Next day Andrew Arandall came to the house as Hannah was giving Mrs. Poley her day's instructions. They laughed at each other as they stared, both saying: "How you have changed!" Although it was only months since they met it had been a very long time to each of them and much had happened. "What has happened to you?" Andrew demanded, surveying the changes in her and Hannah rapidly told him all that had taken place.

He said suddenly: "I've missed you, Hannah."

She stared at him, searching the bright blue eyes as though suspecting they must hold mockery, but they were perfectly serious, their gaze intense.

She felt herself blushing, looking away. He had surprised her by what he said and she did not know how to reply.

"I'll not ask if you've missed me," he said ruefully. "You've been too busy. I fled the path of duty and sought pleasure and it leaves a taste of ashes in the mouth, I find. I wish I had stayed, Hannah."

"You did not like London?"

"London is a sink where all the vices drain. Did you know that you may buy a girl of twelve for sixpence there?"

She gave him a horrified look.

He caught her expression and his pink mouth hardened into sick distaste. "Oh, I've no fancy for such purchased vices, Hannah. It would give me no pleasure to abuse a child." He laughed bitterly. "Although, I think my brother James would tell you that I was a eunuch, sexless. He mocks me for my lack of sexual curiosity and would have me grovel in the gutter with him like a pig in a sty, rutting without a care."

Her eyes widened and stared and Andrew gave her a flushed grin. "I beg your pardon. That was no language for you to hear."

"Do not put a guard on your tongue for me," Hannah said soberly. "I prefer honest speaking, even if it startles me. It takes courage to resist temptation, Andrew. I admire you for it. Especially when your brother laughs at you for your pains."

"There's no temptation in it," Andrew retorted. "I felt no flicker of interest in James's little pleasures."

Peg rustled in with a tray and Hannah asked Andrew if he would take wine, politely gesturing towards a chair. Peg eyed him with unhidden suspicion before she went out and Hannah hid a smile behind her hand. Peg felt that gentlemen had no business spending time alone with her.

"I've been to the charcoal heaps today," Andrew said suddenly.

She glanced at him in sharp interest.

"They terrify me," he said. "They're as high as mountains. The charcoal-burners are being hurt by this business, Hannah. It is not only your men and their families who need to see it settled. My father and Colby are both pigheaded. They must be brought to see reason."

"Do you expect me to give you ammunition to use against Joss?" she asked him, her eyes searching.

"You're angry, I can tell." Andrew stared into her eyes. "Your eyes go that green when you are laughing or in a rage. Hannah, there has to be a way of settling this – we must find it."

"I never knew of anyone who settled Joss," she said drily. "He is like some great rock. One cannot move him."

"My father is another," Andrew sighed.

She made a grim face. "They need to have their heads banged together."

Andrew roared with laughter. "I'd like to see it!" His face sharpened and he stared at her. "Damn it, why not?"

She was startled, then wry. "Joss would never go to see him."

Andrew shook his head. "But you could go, Hannah."

"I?" She gaped like a stranded fish. "Don't be foolish, Andrew."

"Why not?"

"He would never listen to me! Sir Matthew Arandall listen to a bastard kitchen maid?"

He looked her up and down, brows wryly flickering. "You are not that any more, Hannah. Take a look in your mirror someday. My father may turn difficult but I've a fancy you could handle him. You'd take him by surprise, anyway, and maybe make him listen."

"I couldn't."

"Will you try?" he asked nevertheless.

Hannah hesitated. Then she shrugged her shoulders and made a face. "Why not?"

Andrew stood up and stared at her again, from head to toe. "Is that your best gown? Haven't you a green one?"

Startled, she said, "Green?"

"Aye, green is your colour," he said as soberly as though he were a dressmaker. "You need tutoring in fashion, Hannah. That style is five years out of date. I must take you in hand."

She laughed, amused at the notion of a young gentleman teaching her the rudiments of fashion, but after a while she obediently went off and changed into her only green dress.

When she returned Andrew sighed over her gown. "The wrong shade of green," he told her. "'Tis too pale for you. But it will serve in lieu of a better."

On the way to Arandall House she peered over his shoulder and asked him shrewdly, "Did you come here today to end this quarrel?"

Her hands were round his waist, holding him lightly. He looked down at them and knew he found it pleasant to have her ride so close to him, her body leaning on him.

"Yes," he admitted. "It has gone on long enough. I've no wish to see my family bankrupt. Nor Colby, neither. We need each other. My father will not see that, nor will he see that in a few short years the charcoal market will be running lower and lower until it ends altogether."

She absorbed this remark thoughtfully. "Then Joss is right? About coke?"

"Colby knows what he's doing," Andrew nodded. "He's not the only one to change to coke and he won't be the last. My father has to see it before it is too late. If he goes much further along this path he'll ruin the family."

Hannah felt a sudden affection for him and leaned her cheek against his slim back. "You're very honest, Andrew."

He put a hand over hers and laughed. "Why, so are you, Hannah. I think it is what we saw in each other from the start. It is not often that minds meet as ours did on sight."

She laughed teasingly. "What nonsense. I hated you on sight, Andrew Arandall. A pretty, dressed-up puppy I thought you, lording it arrogantly over everyone in sight. What you thought of me I don't know, but from your insolent smirk, I'd hazard it was nothing flattering."

He looked startled, remembering suddenly the Sunday morning when he first set eyes on her, the flushed defiance in her face, the brilliant hazel eyes flashing green as they always did in anger, James had mocked her. He had a vision of her sprawling in a weedy ditch, glaring up at them. It seemed so long ago, a lifetime, and he had stepped across a great divide that morning, a chasm he had only dimly recognised at the time but which now he knew to be of vital importance in his life.

"You taught me to look below the surface, Hannah," he said very seriously. "Before I met you my thoughts were dragonflies skimming over deep water, but now I have learned to think and see more clearly."

She wriggled slightly, embarrassed. "Don't flatter me, Andrew! I'm no Nancy to be lured with a spoon of honey."

"Nancy?" He did not know whom she meant.

"The other maid at the house."

"I don't recall . . ."

"With yellow hair and a pretty face," she prompted.

Andrew shook his head. "I can't remember her."

Hannah looked at his silvery wig just in front of her eyes. Nancy, she thought, would never have believed it possible that a young man could forget her but remember Hannah.

The grooms in the stableyard stared in curious surprise at Hannah as Andrew lifted her from the horse's back. He put a hand under her arm to lead her into the house. "We'll find my father in the library," he said.

"And your mother?"

His skin flushed dark red. He did not answer. The stable had once been safe from his mother's engrossing attentions but now Andrew found himself sick whenever he glanced at one of the strong young grooms, only easy now with the older men whom he need not suspect of helping to cuckold his father. As his horse was led away he had already noted the absence of Jacob. It had grieved him. He liked the boy. He was calm, kindly, quiet-tempered and loved the horses. Now Andrew knew he would never feel at ease with the boy again.

Hannah had heard vague rumours and she glanced at Andrew shrewdly, sorry for the angry flush on his face. She should have held her tongue.

Before they reached the door of the library they heard the deep, droning snores. It sounded to Hannah as though a bee had been shut into the room. She giggled, glancing at Andrew.

He opened the door and stood back to let her enter. She glanced across the room, then back at Andrew. "Leave me alone with him," she said softly.

He looked surprised, then worried. "Hannah, I don't . . ."

"Go, Andrew," she said, smiling, pushing him out of the door.

When it was closed behind him she advanced across the library and sat down in a chair drawn up opposite Sir Matthew and waited.

Her eye began to wander round and round the rows of shelves, intrigued by the names she knew and the names she had never heard before, saddened by the moth-eaten spines, the peeling gilding of the titles, staggered to see so many books in one room. After a moment or two she got up and softly walked to a shelf, selected a book of poems by an author of whom she had never heard. Chapman, she thought, amused at the idea of a poet with such a common name, then sat down and opened it.

Almost at once she was sucked into the verse by the towering magic of the story. Names she knew stalked in the lines: Achilles, Hector, Paris and Agamemnon. She had met them in one of the works of Greek history which Andrew had lent her, but here they were transformed by the fact of being in verse.

When Sir Matthew snorted out of sleep and sat up she was too engrossed to notice. He stared at her as though she were a ghost, looking from her bright brown head in the wintry afternoon sunlight to the pale green gown which fell to her small feet.

"What the devil are you doing?" he bellowed and she jumped.

Eyes startled, she looked at him and dropped the book. He bent to pick it up, eying the spine.

"What's this? What's this?"

"It is Chapman's Homer," she said frankly. "I borrowed it to read until you woke up."

"Chapman's what?" He was dumbfounded by her soft burring voice, her self-confidence. She was not a servant, he thought. She dressed too well. She was not one of the gentry. She was too direct and easy. Who the devil was she and what was she doing in his library?

"Homer," she told him, smiling into his baffled eyes, and he scowled, largely because she was unlike anyone he had ever seen and he did not know how to treat her. Had she been of his own class, he would have politely but bluntly seen her out. Had she been a servant, he would have roared at her to leave. As it was, he merely gaped and Hannah, seeing his expression thought he wanted her to explain Homer to him, sensing he did not know the name.

"It's about the Trojan war," she expounded. "The battles and killings."

"Is it, by God?" He stared down at the old-fashioned print with its hooked 's' and heavy black lettering, then he gazed at Hannah. "D'you like books about wars, Miss?"

"War is stupid," she said. "Men get killed, and for what? They would always do better to sit down and talk before they get to killing each other, for when they're dead their quarrel is ended, anyway. There is always a peace, isn't there, in the end?"

Sir Matthew considered this and grunted. "You don't understand, Miss. Men fight to settle an argument when sense fails."

"Better to be sensible first, then."

"Maybe," he said, suddenly amused, grinning at her. "Now, Miss, who the devil are you?"

"I'm Hannah Noble," she said.

He frowned. "Don't know the name. Noble . . . there was a fellow called Noble teaching at the village school once."

"My grandfather," she said clearly, meeting his eyes. He stared, open-mouthed. "Then you're . . ."

"Yes," she cut in crisply, daring him to smile. "I am."

He cleared his throat. "Just so." His eyes slid away. "Well, what can I do for you?"

"I've heard it said you are a gentleman," Hannah said coolly.

The lowering eyes swung round to her. "What?" His bellow was like that of a bull. "You impudent hussy!"

"Act like one," Hannah said, lifting her chin.

"What the devil are you talking about and who gave you leave to come into my house and insult me, you saucy little witch?" he asked. But now there was amusement in his eyes because in the pale sunlight Hannah had an engaging charm, her brown hair gleaming, her eyes very green, her rounded chin high. Sir Matthew was not immune to charm or spirit in a woman and he had taken one of his rare fancies to Hannah.

"I'm talking about the ironworks," she said.

He was on his feet at once, purpling with rage. "Get out! Get out before I have my footman throw you out."

"There, I knew you were not a gentleman," she said with apparent satisfaction.

"God curse you," he muttered, taken aback. "What d'ye mean by it, coming here, talking to me in this fashion?"

"Will you listen or not?" she demanded.

He stared at her, his jowls trembling. Then he laughed. "Damn me if you aren't the living spit of your mother." He gave her a sly little glance. "I tried to get her into my bed once, girl, but she sent me off with a flea in my ear. Lively creature, your mother. I can see a likeness."

"If you try to get me into your bed you'll see it, I promise you," she said, laughing.

He grinned, slapping his knee, a bawdy amusement in his eyes. "What's your name, did ye say?"

"Hannah," she told him. "Are you going to listen to me, squire?"

"Why should I?" His face darkened again. "Colby's going to pay for what he's done to me."

"He won't be the only one to pay, though, will he? You'll pay, too, Sir Matthew."

He leaned forward. "Is that a threat, young woman?"

"It is a prophecy," she said. "You know I'm right. Your charcoal must find a buyer soon or you will grow desperate short of money."

His eyes narrowed. "Who says so?"

"I do," she said, meeting his eyes. "It is true, isn't it?"

"I can wait. Colby can't."

"Ah, but he can," she said quietly. "He can buy iron for the forges, squire."

"Who would sell him iron? A rival ironworks? Do you think me a fool, girl?"

"They need not know who is buying it," she shrugged. "He has a relative in Birmingham, an uncle, who can act as go-between."

Sir Matthew's face sharpened and his eyes grew steel bright. "Is that so? And where does he plan to buy this iron?"

She laughed. "Perhaps he has bought it already."

"Has he?" Sir Matthew did not move, all his attention on her now.

"I suspect he may have – his brother has been to Birmingham on private business."

"Why should you tell me this?" Sir Matthew asked, scowling.

"I hate to see children go hungry!"

"D'ye think I like it? Colby mut be taught a lesson, though."

"He is as thick-skinned as you, Sir Matthew," Hannah retorted with a flash of her eyes.

"Get out of my house, you insolent cat!" Sir Matthew strode to the door and flung it open, bellowing for his footman. "I'll have no bastard servant telling me my business. How'd ye get in here, anyway?" The footman hovered outside but Sir Matthew had turned back into the room again, his brows knit. "Who the devil put you up to this? Who brought you into the house?"

"You have a son with brains in his head," Hannah told him.

He gave her a stare from his side of the room. "Aha. Andrew. Damn the boy. Is he mad?"

"He is the sane one, Sir Matthew."

"Get out!"

The footman slid forward, smirking. Hannah gave him a cold glare. "Come one step near me and I'll scratch your eyes out," she promised him.

The man looked into her bright green eyes and something in her face stopped him in his tracks. Sir Matthew growled, "Take no heed of her, you dolt. Throw her out. Jumped-up little hussy."

"My uncle has changed his will," Hannah said.

Sir Matthew's whole face changed, eagerness coming into his eyes. "Cut Colby out, did he? Of course. The girl's dead, isn't she? Who gets it now?"

"I do," Hannah said quietly.

There was a silence. The footman, sensitive to the change of mood, backed slowly out, and Sir Matthew stood with his mouth dropped open and a glaze of thought in his eyes.

"Well, I'm damned," he muttered. She saw him turn a benevolent beam upon her. "And so you've sensibly come to make terms with me, eh? Colby is finished then." He came forward, rubbing his big hands. "He's cut his own throat, the insolent swine." Bowing, he took her hand and kissed it with an air which made her smile. When he chose he could turn courtly, she saw, and he chose now. "I congratulate you, Miss. Your uncle's done the right thing. So, you will be needing our charcoal at once, eh?"

"At once," she agreed. "Just as soon as you can come to terms with Joss Colby."

Eyes bulging, Sir Matthew spluttered: "What? But . . ."

"I am wedding him," Hannah said softly. The sudden blow took all the colour from Sir Matthew's face. He had risen to a height of triumph only to tumble in shock and dismay. He stared at her, swallowing.

"Why, you little . . ."

"Sir Matthew, you've no need to climb down, you know. Send Andrew to come to terms with Joss. You will not lose face."

"You think I'm frightened of that swine Colby?" he blustered.

Hannah saw it was time to charm him if she could and gave him a bright, eyelash-fluttering smile, mimicking the flirtation she had watched Nancy offering Joss from time to time. "Oh, I am very sure you are not," she assured him softly, and her hand crept up to touch his sleeve, fingering the thick, muscled arm beneath the cloth. "But you're too proud, Sir Matthew, too strong. You must not refuse to let poor Joss climb out of the pit he's dug for himself – that is being cruel."

He shook his head as though to clear his brains, but he was not untouched by her flattery, her vivid smile.

"All you have to do is let people think you're ill – you have the gout again – and that Andrew is managing the estate for you. Let Andrew make terms with Joss.

Sir Matthew had a sudden, cunning glint in his eye. "What's all this of Andrew, girl?" His lip curled back from his teeth in a wide grin. "I'll be sworn you were the piece that fetched him to Shield House so often in the past!"

She blushed and he laughed uproariously. "The sly dog. So he has beaten Colby to you, has he?" Slapping his thigh he turned and bellowed, "Andy! Andy, you there, you dog?"

Andrew came in sheepishly, giving his father a nervous

look. Sir Matthew leered at him.

"She's a fetching little piece, boy, and I'd love to see Colby's face when he finds out you've been before him." His thick laughter made Andrew's face burn and Hannah met his astonished eyes briefly before she looked away.

"You've given us some of our own back, at least – let Colby ride as high as he pleases – every time I see him now I can think that you enjoyed his wife before he did."

Hannah quietly slipped out of the room and left Andrew to talk to his father of the terms they would ask from Joss. When they rode back to the ironworks later, Andrew asked her: "Why did you let my father believe you to be my mistress?"

"It seemed to be what he wished to think and it helped him swallow his pride."

After a pause he said, "And it did not shame you?"

"If it had been true it might have – but knowing it for a lie, I was able to smile."

"What if Colby learns of it?"

She was silent. "That is a bridge I shall cross when I come to it," she said at last.

"Colby would kill you if he heard it from my father." Andrew had a disturbed note in his voice. "Hannah, do not marry him. I did not like it when I heard of it first, but the more I think of it the less I like the idea. I hate it, to speak truth."

She felt the tension in his body as she leaned against it and she was disturbed herself, aware of feelings in Andrew which had not been present in the beginning but which made her anxious as she felt them now.

"I have to," she said in the end, roughly.

"Your uncle bids you?"

"Yes."

"Must you obey him? He has no right in law to order you."

"He is afraid to let Joss take the mill. He wants to have it pass to blood of his own, lawful or not."

"I see," Andrew said, sighing. "You have changed me, Hannah, did you know? Before we met I was drifting like a feather in the wind."

"Much has happened since we met," she agreed.

"Some of it too bitter to be borne," Andrew said and she knew he was thinking of Sophy. His sister's murder had altered the whole structure of his life. He might imagine it had something to do with herself, but Hannah guessed that he had been shown in one terrible shock how fragile life could be, how open to the blows of fate, and it had changed the colour of his mind. He had been shown not the reason but the unreason of the universe and it had raised questions in his mind which Hannah had been asking since she was a child.

"What do you want life to give you, Hannah?" he asked.

"More than I have had so far. I want a reason for living but I've never found one yet. Peg would say God was the reason, but he perplexes me. He cannot be a cause for living and a cause for dying – there's too much he does not answer. Ask and every time you come up against the wall of his silence."

Andrew sighed deeply. "You run dangerous close to atheism, Hannah."

Her eyes on the blue-hazed horizon she saw the sun sink in a glitter of gold and remembered Homer, the clash of a conflict long silenced on the shores of time, wondering if conflict was the reason and the essence of the world.

Ten

JOSS SHOWED NO pleasure or even relief when he realised that the Arandalls had climbed down. He sat in the parlour with Andrew and when Hannah brought them wine, Joss watched her, his eyes narrowed, before he turned his black head to scrutinise Andrew's purposely blank face. She quietly left the room and for an hour heard their voices rising and falling, sometimes angry, sometimes quiet.

Andrew left without seeing her. Joss went out to the yards to tell the men that the feud with the squire was over. Their sick relief erupted into a night of wild gaiety. They danced and sang in the yards, their wives and children joining them. Joss broke some barrels of ale and the men kept it up for hours before they drunkenly stumbled home.

Hannah found herself crying as she watched the dancing. There would be no more hungry little faces in the lanes, no more sullen looks and weary bodies. She had not been able to bear to see the children these last months.

Later she found Joss in the office talking curtly to Matt whose ears were red. "Your scrawl is like a cat's scratching. You'll learn to write legibly or I'll knock your idle head off your shoulders."

"He is improving," Hannah said, smiling at the boy, whose eyes glowed gratefully.

Joss snarled to his brother, "Get out." Matt shot from the room without a word, his feet stumbling as he ran.

When he had gone, Joss turned on her, lips drawn back from his teeth. "You get above yourself! I'll not have you step between me and my men. I've told you that before."

"Matt does his best!"

"If that's his best he can try again." His face was taut, the bones beneath the brown skin sharp and angular, as though he gritted his teeth and held his features in a vice. He was angrier than she had ever seen him, and Hannah was surprised. Although he often scolded Matt with the same peremptory tone he used to the men, he had a hidden affection for the boy which she had noticed more than once.

He stared down at her. "You've been conspiring with Arandall behind my back, haven't you?"

She saw the true reason for his rage, then. He had guessed she had a hand in the sudden change of policy in the squire's family. Hannah tilted her head, her chin defiant.

"What if I have?"

"Don't be pert, Miss," he said through his teeth, his eyes flaring. "Or I'll shake you. And more." His voice thickened. "Much more."

He moved closer and her body was enveloped in a rolling tide of heat which ran up to her temples, leaving her flushed, glowing like a poppy, her heart beating hard under her bodice. Joss's grey eyes narrowed. He concentrated his stare on the blue vein in her throat which pulsed and throbbed as he stared at it.

"I won't have other men near you," Joss said huskily. "Do you understand me, Hannah?"

She struggled to fight down the sensations he had awoken in her.

His face altered as he watched the effect of his words. He laughed under his breath, very softly, and Hannah knew it had pleased him to overthrow her and make her tremble and blush.

He walked to the door, still smiling. "I'll see less of young Arandall, thank you. Give the young gentleman his dispatch, Hannah, or I will do it for you and he'll join his ancestors sooner than he thinks."

The forges swung into full production and the figures climbed week by week. Joss was stepping up production way beyond the amounts Henry Shield had produced. Joss was a born ironmaster – he had an instinctive love of making

175

iron and a fascination with the process which kept him working after hours at improvements in their methods. The wagons began to roll out of the yards weighed down again and the men whistled as they walked to work. Joss might drive them hard but their families were full-fed once more.

As production mounted so Hannah found herself doing more of the clerical work than ever. Matt did what he could but with Joss so deeply engaged in the production Hannah had to do many of the tasks he had once done. Henry Shield was always too drunk. He sat in the parlour at night or walked down to the village alehouse. His life was seen always through the bottom of a glass since Caroline died.

Joss relied on her to pay the wages, deal with the men's complaints and requests, check in the wagons and check them out again. When he did come into the office he was in a curt, brisk mood and Matt would cringe over his desk while his brother snapped questions at him.

Hannah intervened one day, sending Matt on an errand. "You terrify the boy!" She looked at Joss impatiently. "Why snarl at him?"

He eyed her, irritable and tense. "I am sick of his feeble ways."

"Matt is not feeble! I rely on him!"

"No wonder he grows silly, with you patting his head all day," Joss said jealously, his eyes angry. He had been watching Hannah and his brother working together and felt a pang of resentment because she never gave such warm smiles to him.

Hannah looked at him in surprise and speculation. "He is your brother, Joss. You should be kinder to him."

"Why should I bother? He gets enough kindness from you!"

Hannah watched him swing away from her, his face averted, and told herself she was imagining the jealousy his eyes revealed.

Joss looked at the candle flickering on the desk, his face sombre. He wanted Hannah's whole attention, needing it as a child needs that of its mother, craving it angrily because it

176

seemed his right, a right she denied. He hated to see her softened face when she talked to Matt or Jabey Stock. Joss's childhood had been so short. Other babies had come so fast, pushing him from the centre of his mother's world. The frustrated, angry desire of a child for a mother's love and whole attention had become in him a hunger for success, but running alongside that was an instinctive blind need which had for a long time been centred upon Hannah.

"Do you want me to smile at you, Joss?" Hannah asked huskily. "Be kinder to Matt."

"I'm not crawling on my knees to get a smile from you," he roared, turning violent, his face darkly flushed, then moved to the desk and snatched up some ledgers in a pretence of ignoring her, his mind on other, more important, things.

"Tiler's fines keep mounting." He laid the ledger on fines before her, pointing with one long finger. "If there's a rule to break, he breaks it, and I heard him arguing with Matt last week, trying to wriggle out of half his fines."

"Tiler's wife has consumption. Did you know?"

"Should I? What has that to do with it?"

"It's what makes him angry."

"Is it what makes him late every day? Does it cause all his clumsiness? He has too many fights and he answers back too fast. He's a damned sight too quick-tempered."

"His wife will die," Hannah said, looking at the strong, fleshless hand holding the fines book.

Joss slammed the book shut. "If he goes on making trouble, he's out. Tell him that from me."

"Tell him yourself." She stood up, gritting her teeth.

"What do you want? Am I to turn a blind eye to his behaviour? The men will think I've gone soft."

She laughed coldly. "Who would think that?"

Joss turned his grey eyes on her face. "You had better not," he said, then he went out, slamming the door.

She spoke to Tiler a day or so later. The skinny little man looked at her belligerently, his jaw stiff. "I work hard enough, believe me. Some mornings my wife can't get up and feed the children. What do you want me to do then? Leave them to scrounge food where they can? The youngest is only two."

There was a dark flush on his face but she saw misery in his eyes. "Is your wife worse?"

"She won't see another winter," he said. "And I can't say I'm sorry for that. She suffered badly in the last one. Being laid off didn't help. We all went without food but she wasn't strong enough to bear it."

Hannah sighed. "Couldn't you get one of the other women in to help?"

"They'd want paying and I've no money to spare. What I have got goes in food."

Hannah thought of Mrs. Cregen. She was still looking after the children but she had to take in washing and needlework to make ends meet, and meeting her in the yards the other week Hannah had noticed how much weight she had lost.

"I know of someone who could help," she said. "If you could hold your temper down and not pick fights you would not lose so much in fines. You're losing money every week."

"He fines us for everything he can," Tiler retorted.

"It's the custom. You know that."

"He drives us harder than flesh can stand."

She shivered. Yes. "I'll see what I can do about your wife, Mr. Tiler, if you'll see what you can do about your temper."

He stared at her hard then gave an abrupt nod. Turning, he halted. "They're saying in the works that you're going to wed him."

"Yes, I am."

"What about Stock?" He surprised her by the sharpness of his tone.

"That's none of your business," she said, flushing.

"I like Stock. He's a man I trust. You'll make a poor exchange if you take Joss Colby instead."

"Good day, Mr. Tiler," she said coldly.

He would have gone but he turned back again. "Lookee, Miss. Stock loves you. Think on that."

Tears pricked at her eyes. "Do you think I don't know that? I'm not a fool, Mr. Tiler. Good day."

She walked down and saw Mrs. Cregen next day. The woman was easy to persuade. Hannah offered her sixpence a week to go in and help Tiler's family and the bargain was soon concluded. For another sixpence Hannah offered her out-work from the Shield house, sewing and washing which would take the load off Mrs. Poley's back. When she left both she and the other woman were well content.

Tiler kept his word. From that day his fines dropped. Hannah saw Joss glance down the fines book and lift his brow two weeks later. He shot her a look. "Speak to Tiler, did you?"

"Yes."

He did not ask how she had done it. He merely looked at her, those bleak grey eyes piercing.

"For decency we must wait six months before we wed," he told her. "Do you agree?"

"Yes."

"No hurry on your part," he murmured coldly.

"No," she agreed without looking at him.

"No," he said and walked out. She looked at the door and thought: he is always walking away from me now as though he cannot bear to be in the same room. Their relationship had changed since she forced him to their bargain. He looked at her with dislike, a scarcely hidden animosity in those cold eyes. Yet they worked well together. The reins of the ironworks were running smoothly in their hands. Joss left much of the office work to her and when he discussed it with her he did it as one equal to another, listening to what she said. Once she had woken in the mornings with a sense of dread in the face of the day, but now she woke eager for what the day would bring. She still slept in the attic with the other women although Nancy jeered at her for it and made spiteful remarks about it no longer being her place.

Mrs. Poley had been told she was to marry Joss, of course, and that meant the others knew. Nancy's reaction had been to stare first, incredulously, and then to burst out with bitter, malicious words.

She kept up these outbursts for days. When Hannah walked

179

into the kitchen that evening Nancy was alone, scouring a pan, and looked round, her face darkening. "Oh, it's you. I'd have thought you were too grand for the kitchen now."

Hannah ignored that. She took off her shawl and sat down, her mind and body tired. Although it was almost summer the evenings were cool and it was pleasant to feel the warmth of the kitchen fire on her chilled body.

"I can't imagine it," Nancy said. "You and Joss. What could he see in you? But you're sly, Hannah, aren't you? For all your high minded ways you've never been without a man. Two-faced, that's what you are."

"I reckon 'tis Jabey you love and always have, yet you're wedding Joss for what he'll give you. I told Joss so." Nancy turned up her nose, sniffing. "I told him straight. I don't mind admitting it. She's marrying you for the works, I said, but it is Jabey Stock she loves."

Hannah shrugged. "He knows. I told him myself."

Nancy looked furious. "So he said. It beats me. You hate each other but you're wedding. I don't see virtue in that. I see greed and a cold heart. Joss will get nothing from you. I told him that, too. At least I give men a little fun."

"Don't let me stop you," Hannah smiled.

Nancy did not like that, either. She looked at Hannah like someone searching for a tender spot to place a knife. Then she said softly, "Maybe Jabey'll need some fun now."

Hannah looked at her angrily. "Leave Jabey alone." It would lower Jabey in his own eyes for him to take what Nancy had offered so many others. Hannah knew Jabey too well not to guess that.

Nancy's eyes quickened. She grinned. "Oh ho, now you're jealous. I was right. It is Jabey you care for." Then she went off laughing and Hannah wished she had hidden her reaction.

Walking through the yards a week later she saw Nancy talking to Jabey by the base of the charging platform. He was laughing, his teeth showing white in his blackened face. Hannah looked up and was anxious. Jabey wouldn't. He couldn't. Nancy suddenly began to tickle him and Jabey burst out laughing. Hannah turned away, shivering, and bumped into Joss. He looked up at the other two then down at Hannah's white face.

His face was expressionless. "You shouldn't have let her see you were jealous of Stock," he told her flatly. "She's gone all out to snare him."

"If she can, she's welcome," Hannah said bitterly. "A man who can let Nancy catch him isn't worth worrying over."

"You ask too damned much of a man," Joss said in a sharp tone. "Did you expect Stock to be a bachelor all his life for you? Men are built otherwise."

"You should know." She walked away and Joss followed her. As she entered the office he said, "It is time you slept downstairs. You're no servant any more. Take Caroline's room."

"When we're married."

"Now," he said. "Nancy will have her claws out for you all the time from now on. Your place is at the front of the house now. I'll move my things out of Caroline's room and you can move in."

She abandoned the argument. Next day she began sleeping in the pretty bedroom where Caroline had died. The first night she lay wakeful, shivering in the bed, but she was surprised to see how quickly all that faded and she began to feel as though she had always had a fine room of her own instead of sleeping with three others in a low-ceilinged attic.

She had come a long way since the days when she had stood at the attic window watching Joss walk past at dawn. Why was it that life never turned out as one had expected it? Eating an orange once she had thrown the pips into the fire and watched them fly out again in different directions with a little pop. She had tried to guess which way each would go and how far, and had failed completely. Life was too unpredictable, too strange, to be sure of where one would end up or with whom.

Had she married Jabey she would have been an iron-worker's wife all her life. Jabey was a good man and she was fond of him, but Joss was like a dark river whose source and destination were unknown. She could not guess how far he would rise and what they would make of their lives together.

Sir Matthew had been as good as his word. Andrew had taken over the management of the charcoal business and he took to riding to Shield House from time to time, ostensibly on some excuse of business, but always managing to spend time with Hannah while he was there. Joss did not like it but when he angrily warned her to keep Andrew away she asked him how she could when they had to see each other to talk of charcoal deliveries and occasional faults in the quality they received.

"Matt can deal with him then!" Joss snapped.

"You know Matt would be too awestruck to say a word."

Joss looked as though he wanted to break things. "Very well," he said thickly. "You will always see him in the office and always have Matt present."

"Very well."

Her very lack of argument irritated him. "And you'll stop calling him Andrew," he ordered. "Master Arandall is no friend of mine."

Hannah flicked him a dry glance. "I cannot suddenly change to such formality! I've always called him Andrew."

He lost his temper. It flared up like a rocket and he grabbed her arm, his face fiercely angry. "You obstinate little bitch," he hissed, bending towards her.

She put a hand against his chest, pushing him away, sensing the danger in his loss of control. "Andrew wondered if you might consider taking him as a partner," she said to distract him.

It distracted him at once. He stood still, eyes narrowed. "Did he indeed? Is that his interest, I wonder? What did he have in mind? Did he say?"

"He wondered if you needed capital to build a new mill to supply all our orders."

Joss grinned. "Of course I need capital but I should not go to him for it. I'd go to the bank. Dace drives a hard bargain but he has a shrewd eye for making money. His bank would suit me better as a partner than Arandall."

"You think Mr. Dace would lend you money to build a new mill?"

Joss shook his head. "Not yet. I'm still paying for that long gap in production. We must wait. No point in trying to run before you are walking."

"But we are doing so well."

He looked smilingly at her. "We're picking up."

"I've been looking back over the books," she said.

"Have you, Hannah?" He sounded dry. "You alarm me. You know too much already. And what did your curiosity discover?"

"That our profits have shot up compared with last year's and the year before."

"You've been looking at the monthly figures. Look at the annual total. We have a long way to go. When the time is ripe I'll think of expanding. Not before."

There was a tap on the door and Jabey came into the room, halting in obvious surprise when he saw Joss. Joss shot a look at Hannah then glared at Jabey. "What do you want, Stock?"

"I wanted a word with Hannah."

Joss's face flushed darkly, surprising Hannah. "Miss Hannah," he said through his teeth. "And when we're married, Stock, you'll call her Mrs. Colby."

Jabey's gaze was level. "Yes, Master Colby." He spoke calmly and without insolence but the effect was to make Joss look more dangerous than ever.

"What do you want then?" he asked Jabey who did not budge an inch.

"A private word, sir," he said in the same level voice.

"Anything you have to say to Hannah, you can say to me," Joss grated.

Hannah looked steadily at him. "Excuse us, will you, Joss?"

He opened his mouth to refuse but something in her face made him turn and storm out, banging the door.

Jabey looked at Hannah and shrugged. "I annoyed him."

"It does not matter. What do you want, Jabey?" She was stiff with him because she was angry. He had been seeing Nancy a good deal lately. Nancy had made sure she heard of it and it had lowered Jabey in Hannah's opinion.

"I wanted to tell you I'd decided to wed Nancy," he said.

Hannah thought for a moment she had not heard right. She gaped at him foolishly. Then she burst out angrily, "You can't mean it."

Jabey did not answer, merely looked at her.

"Jabey, it would be madness. You know what she is, what she has been, what she will be in future." She felt both impatience and pity for him. "Nobody else has thought it necessary to marry her to get her body, why should you?"

"I don't like to hear you talk like that, Han," he said. "I do know Nancy. And I'm not wedding her to get her into bed. She's carrying Colby's child."

Hannah sat down. "Does he know?"

Jabey nodded.

"What did he say?"

Jabey's face was stern. "Asked how she could even guess whose child it was."

"Oh," Hannah said, shuddering. Then with a wry face, "Well, it is a question anyone might ask. Nancy gives her favours lightly."

Jabey nodded. "I'm not concerned with Nancy but the child. I don't pretend to love Nancy and I've had her body as freely as everyone else."

Hannah flinched at that and Jabey saw it. He stopped dead and stared at her. She looked away and Jabey came close and touched her cold face. "Han?"

"How could you?" she asked him in a low voice. "Jabey, how could you do it?"

His voice trembled. "Are you jealous, Han? I never thought you'd care."

"Of course I care. Oh, I'm not petty enough to mind if you marry, Jabey. I'd expected it. You're a man who needs a home and a wife. But Nancy . . . she's not your sort. It hurts me to see you fishing in such muddy waters."

His hand dropped away. "I see."

"Don't marry her, Jabey, please." She did not mind if he thought she begged. She could not bear what would become of him if he married a girl like Nancy. "She'll drag you down, embitter you. You'll never have a moment's peace and you'll always be wondering who is having her when she's not with you. Girls like her don't alter. Nancy needs to be desired. She has neither shame nor conscience."

"But she has feelings," Jabey said. "And Colby has hurt her. He treats her like a whore."

"She behaves like one."

"That's no reason for unkindness. Anyway, I've said I'll wed her, and I will." He walked to the door and Hannah stopped him, her hand on his arm.

"Don't go in anger, Jabey. I wish you very happy, even if I don't think you'll be happy with Nancy."

He turned slowly and sighed, then smiled. "Han."

She let him take her in his arms and turned up her face. Jabey looked at it for a long moment then he kissed her as he had never kissed her before.

She put her arms round his neck and touched his rough hair and Jabey groaned deeply, kissing her harder, his arm fierce around her slender waist. Suddenly he let her go and muttered something she did not hear before he pushed his way out of the office.

She stood, breathing fast, astonished by the force of his kiss. Jabey had always been so gentle. It did not please her to wonder if Nancy had changed him.

Next Sunday Jabey and Nancy walked to church. It was a nine days' wonder. Hannah heard the men laugh behind Jabey's back and was very angry. Nancy's reputation made the story spread like wildfire. Even men who liked and respected him, grinned behind his back. He was marrying a girl whom many of them had enjoyed, and it made him a figure of fun.

Joss commented on it to Hannah as they worked in the office next day. "Does it make it easier for you that if you had wanted Stock you could have had him?"

"I'm not talking of it to you."

Joss looked at her under his lashes secretly. "She's with child, did you know?"

"Yes," she said, looking back at him directly.

"Stock told you?"

"Yes."

"Did he tell you whose child she claims it to be?"

"Yes."

He laughed savagely. "What a fool Stock must be, taking that little slut and her bastard! But then I suspect he feels that by taking her from me he's getting some of his own back."

"Jabey wouldn't . . ."

"Wouldn't he?" Joss stared at her. "I watched him kiss you in this office the other day. He was well nigh desperate for you."

Her face flooded with colour. "You watched!" Then, her temper getting the better of her, "When did you take to peering through keyholes?"

"I saw it through the window," he said, then, savagely, "As any of the men could have done. I don't want that happening again. You didn't discourage him, did you? Put your arms round him, stroking his hair, kissing him back. Perhaps that was what he wanted, to make you jealous enough to get you back."

"Jabey and I were saying goodbye," she said, staring coldly into his eyes.

"I hope you meant it," he said. "Or you'll regret it." There was a pause and then he asked, "Do you love him?"

"Yes," she said.

It was not a lie. She did love Jabey. But it was spoken in self protection in the hope of keeping Joss at bay and she saw his face close up coldly as she spoke.

"So Nancy was right," he said. "That's why she went after Stock, you know. She wanted to make you jealous." The grey eyes surveyed her chillingly. "And she did, didn't she? How does it feel, Hannah, to burn with jealous love?"

She could not speak because his tone had lowered to a hoarse urgency and she knew what he was feeling because the same emotion was pouring through her veins. If she spoke, if she looked at him, he would catch a glimpse of it, and she would be lost. She thought of turning to him, lifting her face, touching him, and she felt sick with desire. He moved closer as though scenting her feelings. He was breathing beside her and she was dry-mouthed, aching. Oh, Joss, she thought silently. Joss.

Still she did not move and at last he swore and went out and the room swam round her as though she were fainting but her mind was clear and cold. She wanted him, but instinct warned her too strongly for her to give way.

After a few moments she was sufficiently under control to get on with her work.

Nancy was all spiteful triumph, eyes glittering with it. Hannah got her alone after she had pranced around the kitchen showing off to the others and said to her coldly, "Make Jabey a good wife, Nancy, or I'll see you rue it."

Nancy grinned. "Poor Hannah. Jealous as a green-eyed cat. You can't have your cake and eat it. You can't have Joss and Jabey."

"Just remember what I say," Hannah repeated.

Nancy put a hand over her waist. "I'm going to have a baby," she said, watching Hannah. "Can you guess whose?"

Hannah looked into her silly, sly eyes. "It is Jabey's child," she said.

Nancy opened her mouth and Hannah put a hand over it smartly. "It is Jabey's," she said, staring at her. "If you've any pride, any honesty, make it Jabey's child. You owe him that at least."

Nancy's eyes stared at her over the muffling hand, and Hannah was reminded of the anguished way she had stared at Joss as he used her roughly in the stable. Under the girl's sly spitefulness there was a trace of something childlike, she thought, almost an innocence. It was ridiculous, of course, to use that word. Vulnerable, she thought. That was the better word. Nancy could be hurt. She had been hurt. Was that what Jabey saw in her? She slowly took away her hand and Nancy cried miserably, "Has he talked to you about me? What has he said? I'll not be patronised. Did he ask your permission to wed me? He knows what he can do with his wedding ring. I won't be made respectable, wed out of pity."

Hannah gently brushed her hand across the girl's grubby wet face, wiping away the slow tears running down her cheek.

"Jabey could come to love you if you let him. He's a man with a good deal to give. You're very pretty, Nancy, and if you try you could be happy with him."

Nancy sniffed, wiping the back of her hand across her face with a rough gesture. "For all he's so noble he wants the same as other men." The blue eyes darted maliciously at her. "Have you had him, Hannah? Or shall I tell you how he is in bed?"

It was useless, Hannah thought. There was no way she could reach that closed little mind. She feared for Jabey as she walked away with Nancy's high, mocking laughter ringing in her ears. How would he bear what Nancy would bring him, the shame and mockery of the other men?

When the banns had been read they were married in the little church and if the bride was by now obviously with child, the parson turned a blind eye to it. Such things were the custom rather than the exception among their class, and although he looked sternly at them he said nothing. Jabey took Nancy home to his little house and she darted around it excitedly, glowing with the pride of having her own home. "I'm no servant now," she crowed to Jabey. "I'm my own woman." Flinging her thin little arms around his neck she kissed him and Jabey smiled at her, brown eyes warm. "I will make you happy, Jabey," she whispered. "I will."

He stroked her pretty hair, watching her eyes sparkle. "Nancy, love, I want to make you happy. Nothing bad shall touch you again."

She lowered her lashes demurely and her hands began to touch him, coaxing, teasing. Jabey took her wrists and pulled her hands away. She looked up, startled.

"Not like that," Jabey said. "Never like that again, Nancy." He lifted her into his arms and kissed her cheek. "You are my wife, not an easy slut."

Nancy closed her eyes as he carried her to their bed but the blue eyes were burning angrily behind those shielding lids.

Eleven

THE HARVEST WAS safely in, the weather showed fine, yet Sir Matthew Arandall felt gloomy. Last week, that damned Colby had married the little Noble girl. He had not, of course, attended the wedding, but he'd heard every last detail of it from his son. Sir Matthew had been enraged when he heard that Colby had invited Andrew. "Damned insolence! Who does he think he is? Invite an Arandall to a country bumpkin's wedding?" Then he had roared, his face darkly red. "He wouldn't have you there if he knew you'd enjoyed his wife, boy. Damn me, the joke's on him. I'd like to tell him so, watch his face. That would knock some of the arrogance out of him."

Colby had had his whole family there, fine as can be, the gossip said, with his mother in a silk gown and his brothers in brave broadcloth.

These jumped-up bastards were all the same, Sir Matthew thought. Put every penny they could scrape together on their backs. People said Colby had armed his mother like a lady, daring anyone to smile. They'd grinned behind his back, no doubt. A common blacksmith's wife wearing silks and mincing about on little red heels? They would all laugh. But secretly. None of them cared to risk laughing while Joss Colby was around.

"The girl's a fool," Sir Matthew had told Andrew. "Colby will knock hell out of her. He once tried to take a whip to me." He had rationalised the incident when Joss snatched his whip and stared him down, and now saw it as an unprovoked attack upon himself.

Andrew had said very little. Sir Matthew got the impression that his son had not enjoyed the wedding, and who could blame him? He was losing a pretty mistress to a hard-headed boor.

"The ironworks are working all out," Andrew had said, and Sir Matthew's gloom had intensified.

It was absurd to feel like that, he told himself. His own fortunes were bound up with Colby's, God knew. Yet he would have got pleasure out of hearing that Colby had failed in something. The man was too damned lucky.

The door opened. Someone tapped as they entered. Sir Matthew glared round. "Knock first, dammit."

"I'm sorry, Papa," Andrew said, eying his father's heavy jowled face with hidden amusement. "I wanted to talk to you about Charlotte's wedding."

"Wedding? Wedding? I'm sick of weddings," Sir Matthew burst out. "Why can't gels get married quietly? Why all this fuss? Lawyers and settlements and wedding breakfasts. Anyone would think she was a member of the royal family."

"I will not detain you long," Andrew promised, smiling.

"The second of 'em in three months. Marriage mad, that's what they are. It spreads like the plague once you get it in the house."

Andrew laughed. "They catch it from each other. But they only marry once, Papa. By the way, I've had a letter from James. He can't get down for the wedding. He's sick."

"Eh? What's the matter with the boy?"

"Just a rheum of some kind," Andrew lied, not wishing to admit that James had written that he had a dose. It was not the first time that James had contracted the pox. He would recover, no doubt, in a few months, dosed with mercury or some such vile concoction. The cure was almost as foul as the disease, Andrew thought. James was a fool. Why did he go on running such risks? Diving into the gutters of Mayfair after diseased little whores could surely give him little pleasure?

Part of the blame could be laid at their mother's door. She had never disguised from them her penchant for sexual pleasure. James had learnt early to fondle the maids or tumble the local village girls. He rode hard, played hard but he did little else.

"Well, what about the wedding?" Sir Matthew demanded and Andrew pulled himself back from his bitter thoughts to speak calmly to his father.

In her bedroom Lady Arandall was on her knees. Jacob was gasping at what she was doing to him. "My lady, no," he muttered, his normally phlegmatic face shocked. Her long nails dug into him to hold him and she threatened with her teeth on his throbbing flesh until the boy stood still. Triumphantly she lifted her head later and Jacob hit her, his skin flushed hot.

"Even animals don't do that," he whispered. "'Tis unclean."

"You loved it," she retorted. He had lasted longer than any lover she had ever had. It made her half mad sometimes to admit how much of a hold he had on her. She longed to find him boring, to make him cruel.

His strong gentleness infuriated her. She had mocked him, hurt him, been harsh with him and he had taken it all so quietly that she was driven insane. Now for the first time she had got under his skin and the knowledge delighted her.

"Now do it to me," she murmured, watching his face.

"No," Jacob said, revolted.

"You will."

"No, no," he denied, pushing her away. He dragged on his clothes while she laughed at him.

"You little prude! Send James to me, then."

Jacob turned his slow, direct gaze upon her. "No," he said.

She quivered, smiling. "Jealous, little man?"

Jacob drew breath then said nothing, walking out. Lady Arandall cursed violently and threw a glass bowl at the mirror in which she saw her naked body too clearly.

Meeting James in the passage Jacob turned his head away. The footman leered at him. "Keeping you busy, is she? Rather you than me. I'd had enough after a week. She's never satisfied."

Jacob went down into the stables and the head groom gave

him a sharp look. "Those brasses look dull," he said. "Give them a good rub, boy."

Jacob silently got on with the work. He had a good place here. He ate well, got well paid. He did not want to leave it. But he might have to, he thought. He was sorry for her. It had been no hardship at first. He had been too awed by her to argue when she first seduced him. He had been inexperienced, innocent of women, but she had given him insights into her sex which had disgusted him gradually. He spat on the horse brass in his hand, his face stolid. He would not do that to her, whatever she said. It was one thing to lie with her as a man should. That was something else.

Andrew Arandall strode into the yard and called for a horse. The head groom yelled to Jacob to saddle one and the boy ran to obey. Andrew turned his head away as Jacob led the animal up to him. Jacob felt himself redden and hate flowed through his veins. He liked Andrew Arandall. He felt it when the young man deliberately avoided his eyes.

When Andrew had ridden out, Jacob went back to his polishing. I'll keep out of her way in future, he thought. She'll not get me into that room of hers again.

In the mud-floored little cottage which was now her home, Nancy dragged herself irritably to the open door and leaned against the frame, watching the lane. She was bored. She had not spoken to a soul all day. Bessie was with the clerk's wife. Jabey was at work. The autumn sunshine glittered on the distant fields and a scent of smoke hung in the air. Nancy was weary of her heavy body, weary of the suffocating smallness of her home, weary of Jabey's stern kindness.

They had had a quarrel that morning in the dawn darkness. She had woken him late and he had had to hurry or be fined, going through the early chill of the day empty. As he dragged on his work clothes he had quietly pointed out how important it was to them that he should not be fined. "We need every penny I can earn if the child is to be fed and dressed when it comes."

Irritably she had shrugged and said the unforgivable. "'Tis Joss Colby's brat. Let him pay for it."

Jabey had gone white, looking at her coldly. "I don't want to hear you say such things again. I'm the child's father, Nancy. Is your baby to grow up hearing you say such things? If we are ever to be a family you must forget the past."

"Do you?" she had asked spitefully. "D'you think I don't know that every time you lie with me you remember how many others did it before?"

Then Jabey had walked out and she had pursued him in the quiet morning, her voice high and angry, because she could not bear his ability to control his temper. Another man, she had thought, would have struck her. Joss Colby in his place would possibly have killed her. Except that Joss would only laugh if she said such things, those grey eyes mockingly indifferent. Joss did not care. He would not care if she gave herself to every man in the works. Jabey cared. Yet he bore it calmly, with dignity, ignoring the lewd jokes, the looks, the secret amusement of his mates without once losing his temper with her. Nancy could have wished he would, just once, fly into a rage.

She had shut up at last, watching him stride through the dark, and had gone back into the little house weeping. Jabey was too kind, too gentle. He never brought up the past. It was always she who did so, flinging it into his face. When he kissed her she would eye him triumphantly. "Want me, do you, Jabey? Well, you've paid the price, so why not? I gave it to Joss and the others for free, but you've had to pay, so I can't say no, can I?"

Why do I say such things to him? Why do I mar what we could have? Jabey tries. It is I who don't. She sighed, a hand to her aching back. This great belly was dragging her down. She would be glad to be rid of it, except that she was afraid of what must happen first. Miss Caroline had died in labour. Nancy had heard her screams and shivered. Was it always so?

Joss and Hannah had been wed a week. Nancy had not gone to the wedding. Hannah had invited her but she had refused. She had stayed indoors and heard the wedding party pass without so much as peeping out. Gossip said it had been a fine affair. Joss had been generous with victuals and drink. Hannah had been pale, though, folk said. But then it was no easy thing to wed a man like Joss Colby. No doubt she had had fears.

Nancy thought of that night. Jabey had lain beside her stiffly, not touching her, but she knew he lay awake. She had listened to his even breathing angrily. Her temper had flared out at last. "They'll be awake too," she had said nastily. "Joss is a hard lover. Hannah will ache tomorrow."

Jabey had not answered. He had turned on his side and pretended to be asleep, and she had silently cried, hating herself, hating him.

In the morning she had stared at his white, blank face with a mixture of anger and jealousy. Jabey had never said so but she knew he loved Hannah. Nancy had never thought she loved Jabey but he was her man, and he had no business lying beside her thinking of another woman. For all his goodness, she had told herself, he was just a man and she knew all about men.

A neighbour came out of her house, a basket on her arm, and Nancy prepared a bright smile, but the woman turned her head away and did not look at her. "Miserable old cat," Nancy said aloud, angrily, then went in and banged the door. They would see if she cared. Ever since she moved into the cottages they had ignored her icily, turning up their noses at her. They gossiped and visited each other freely enough. She saw them at their doors in sunny weather, lazily leaning their backs against the doors, laughing or nodding as they talked. They shut up when she came out. Their eyes bored through her back as she walked past. They never spoke but when she had gone by they whispered, faces coldly virtuous. Sometimes she felt like whipping round and flinging it into those self-satisfied faces, crying out which of their men she had lain with and what they had said or done. But she had held her tongue so far, not because she feared them but because she feared Jabey. He would be so angry and the quietness of his anger was worse than any rage.

The dust of the lane was disturbed a moment later as Andrew Arandall rode past. Nancy heard his hooves and peered out, spite in her face. Going to see Hannah, she thought. How did Hannah get away with that? The squire's son called on her almost daily and stayed for hours, yet nobody breathed a word against Hannah. Oh, she was careful, clever as a trained bear doing tricks. She entertained him in the parlour with Peg waiting on them in her neat dress, in and out of the room all the time, so that no one should question what took place.

I'll swear Joss does, thought Nancy. He won't like that. He always hated seeing the young gentleman sniffing around Hannah. Nancy had been quick to notice just how much of an interest Joss took in the men who came near Hannah. She had learnt to play on that. She found Joss exciting when he was in a temper, and he flew into one whenever she told him gossip about Hannah.

How did Hannah manage it? Holding Joss and young Arandall on a string so openly without folk talking? She looked so pure and demure, Nancy thought bitterly. There had never been talk of Hannah and men. Nancy had seen her once a few weeks back walking with young Arandall near the house. Hannah had worn a very fine gown, finer than any Nancy had seen on her before, and she had walked in a different way, her body swaying. Nancy had recognised it as a seductive movement and been infuriated. Hannah had changed a good deal. She wore her hair dressed prettily and it was always clean and shining. She had filled out to a rounded shape, although she was still slender and small breasted. When Nancy visited the kitchen once Peg had told her in shocked tones that Hannah was learning French. Peg disapproved of that. Peg disapproved of everything, though, Nancy thought. She was another virtuous woman. They were all the same.

In the parlour Hannah curtsied carefully to Andrew who observed her with close interest. "Better," he nodded.

"I've been practising in front of my mirror," she admitted.

"It shows."

"Joss came in and asked if I'd gone mad," she laughed, remembering Joss's astounded face.

She caught the look on Andrew's face and dismay flickered inside her. She had tried to ignore the feelings which had been growing inside Andrew but she had been unable to pretend they did not exist. Andrew said nothing but her own sensitivity to Joss had made her far more aware of the emotions of other people. Whenever she mentioned Joss to him, Andrew frowned and his eyes held an unmistakable jealousy.

Hurriedly she asked: "Will your brothers be coming home for your sister's wedding?"

"James is sick," Andrew said shortly. "And my elder brother is in Italy. He should have been home months ago. Enjoying himself too much, I dare say." His mouth writhed between laughter and bitterness. "Oh, we're quite a family for enjoying ourselves."

She felt sorry for him and wanted to show her sympathy but she was growing more careful now, afraid of what she might release if she let him come too close. Joss was right. She should put an end to Andrew's visits, but how at this stage could she without precipitating what she most feared?

When he left she walked over to the office. Matt was working on his high stool, his shoulders hunched. He looked round and smiled at her affectionately.

"You can leave now," she told him. "I'll finish that."

"Joss is in a temper," Matt muttered uncertainly.

"When isn't he?" She pushed him, smiling. "Off you go."

An hour later Joss strode into the office and halted, staring at her head bent in the candlelight. "Where the hell is Matt?"

"I sent him off. He looked tired. He works too hard."

"At his age I worked like a dog and nobody gave a damn."

"Is that a reason for making Matt's life a misery?"

He looked at her harshly. "Why do you never spare any of your sweet sympathy for me? I work harder than Matt."

"Do you need my sympathy, Joss?" She caught the bitterness in the tone and put a hand on his arm.

He looked down fixedly at the hand. "The next time you

196

touch me I'll make you wish you had kept your hands to yourself."

She snatched her hand away as if it had begun to burn. She could not be unaware that Joss was driven more and more, frustration tautening his features, his body like a coiled spring whenever he was near her.

"Arandall was here," he said.

"Yes."

"Was he pleased with your curtsy?" His tone lashed deliberately.

"Delighted."

His mouth twisted tormentedly. "He should have been a dancing master. He's taught you how to walk and curtsy like a lady born. Who the hell does he think he'll fool? However you look and behave, you'll always be a bastard kitchen maid to women of his class."

"Thank you," she said, curtsying low.

Joss looked down, his eyes fixing on the upward thrust of her white breasts against the stiff neckline of her gown. She heard the thick inhalation of his breath.

Deliberately he put a long finger on the visible cleft between her breasts. "So that's why Arandall likes to watch you curtsying to him!"

The touch of his finger on her body made her burn as though that light caress went through her from head to foot. She rose, scarlet, and turned away. Joss laughed harshly. He went out and crossed the yard as it began to rain. Jabey was drinking from a jug outside one of the workshops, his chest bare, sweat on his forehead. Joss met his blank eyes aggressively.

"Get back to your work, Stock, or I'll fine you for loitering."

The men hammering in the forge looked up, their naked chests flushed in the flickering light of the fire. Jem was holding a red-hot iron rod in the tongs while another man hammered at it. "Hell on two legs," Jem muttered to his workmate. "By God, I'd like a chance to hammer at that face of his!"

Jabey walked past, his face bleak. Jem watched him starting work again. "If I were Jabey I'd cut his throat for taking my girl."

"Would you, Jem?" The other man grinned. "Man, he'd eat you for breakfast and never notice!"

Joss stood on the filthy earth floor, throwing a hard glance around at the men, his hands on his lean hips. His eyes fixed on a thin boy at the fire who was helping one of the older men. "Hey, you!" Joss roared suddenly. "That boy's dead on his feet. Get him outside."

"Aye, Master," the heavy-set worker muttered, still hammering at the glowing metal which the boy held.

Joss took three strides. The men watched as the boy was swept off the floor and carried out into the sunlight.

The boy's workmate leapt backwards as the red-hot metal which the boy had held plunged to the floor. "God damn it," he gasped. "God damn it."

Joss dumped the boy on the ground, forcing his head down between his knees. "Tiler," he bellowed over his shoulder.

Jem went out. The boy's face was the yellow of tallow and he was trembling violently. Joss looked up, his face harsh. "How many times must I tell you men not to drive the boys so hard? I'll not have slavery in my shops. That's a man's job he was doing. Next time I catch one of you men making a boy do a man's work, I'll flay you alive."

"Yes, Mr. Colby," Jem said with the nearest to liking he had ever come towards Joss.

Joss released the boy's thin neck. "Leave him here for an hour. Don't stop it from his wages."

"Aye, sir," Jem said, a half smile on his face.

Joss turned glittering eyes on him, daring him to smile. "I've not gone soft. Don't think that. I make my rules and I expect them to be kept. The next man I see driving a boy too hard is paid off for good."

"What's wrong with him?" Hanley grumbled to the others. "He wants t'work done, doesn't he?"

None of them cared much for Hanley who was brutal and ill-tempered. They did not answer. Joss strode away and Jem walked back into the forge. "You heard him," he said to Hanley. "Go easy on the boy or he'll have you."

Autumn passed into a melancholy opening to winter, rain lashing down day after day, turning the lanes to muddy swamps, their surface deeply rutted by wagon wheels, the streams filling in a rushing floodtide.

The Arandall wedding took place on a day of torrential rain. The bride wept as she saw the leaden sky. Her finery was ruined between the coach and the church porch and the guests darted through the mud with irritable faces. After the wedding there was dancing at the great house and many drunken scenes of revelry. Lady Arandall sank several glasses of wine and danced sedately with her guests. Andrew, bored, lounged in a corner and thought how much he disliked being among his family. The men talked of the Spanish war and he listened irritably. German George, he thought. What a king to have. Secretly he lifted his glass in a toast to the king over the water. The true sovereign was left to dwindle in foreign parts while this uncouth little fellow wore his crown and had his dull mistresses. Folly. It was all folly. Hannah would say they were both as bad as each other. That made him smile. One day he was certain Hannah would see it from his point of view. She was too clever to stay blind.

Lady Arandall was bored. She glanced around the crowded, noisy room and could stand no more of it. Slipping out by a side door she went out to the stables. The place was quiet, all the men enjoying the kitchen hospitality. Jacob was in a stall rubbing down one of the horses. He looked round and froze.

"You have been playing games with me, little man," she said, her elaborately curled white wig shimmering in the lantern light. "I am very cross with you."

"I'm very busy, m'lady," Jacob said anxiously, looking past her in case anyone else was around.

She watched his angular young features with a strange sensation in the back of her throat. All the men she had ever known had gone whistling down the wind since she met this boy and Lady Arandall knew herself trapped in an emotion her mind rejected and her shallow heart could not endure. She had used men without conscience for years. It irked her to admit that for once her feelings were engaged by a graceless, stumbling stable lad.

She walked forward, her long silk skirts brushing through the straw. Jacob saw the expression in her eyes and whispered miserably, "No, m'lady. Don't."

Sir Matthew put down his empty glass and looked sluggishly around the crowded room. His head ached. He heard the wind rattle the sashes and drew a shaky breath. Damn it, he thought. A hard ride across the park would cool his head. With an unsteady gait he walked from the room and Andrew watched him go with a frown. He had noticed his mother's secret exit earlier and felt a flare of alarm, wondering if Sir Matthew had gone in search of her. The guests were talking loudly at each other, few bothering to pause for answer. Andrew made his way to the door and followed his father, hoping their absence would not be noticed.

He heard his father's slow steps on the cobbled yard ahead but as he came up behind him Sir Matthew stopped dead.

The stall door swung open. In the lantern light father and son saw the little tableau clearly like a scene from a play. The elegant woman in her silk dress on her knees in the straw and the unhappy looking boy groaning out, "No, m'lady, no."

Andrew's stomach heaved. He looked hurriedly away. Christ, he thought. What has she sunk to?

Sir Matthew stared, his face a livid white and could not look away. He had a brief memory of his wedding night, the trembling young girl who blushed if he looked at her, who cried the first time and hid her face from him in their pillows.

Suddenly dark blood rushed into his face. He gave a wild, sick bellow like an enraged bull and staggered forward.

Lady Arandall heard him and half rose, terror striking into her. Sir Matthew caught at a leather strap hanging on the stall door among the other tackle Jacob had removed from the horse.

Jacob fumbled with his clothing hurriedly, not daring to look at his master.

Sir Matthew did not even look at him. His eyes were on his wife's pale face as he brought the strap flailing down. She screamed, her hands flying to her torn cheek, and the strap came down again.

The terrified horse reared, legs pounding the air, nostrils flared in reaction to the unknown violence suddenly surrounding it. At that instant Lady Arandall rolled away from her husband's descending arm. The hooves smashed down and Andrew shouted, "Mama!"

Jacob instinctively flung himself at the horse's long neck, dragging it back, soothing it, talking softly, while his eyes stayed on the limp body in the straw.

Andrew slowly knelt by his mother's side. His father stood stricken, breathing irregularly, the strap still hanging from his hand.

"Oh, my God," Andrew moaned. "My God. Mama."

Jacob led the sweating, trembling horse into the next stall and came back to ask quietly: "Shall I fetch the doctor, sir?"

Andrew looked up blankly. There was blood smeared along one side of his hand where he had felt his mother's neck for a pulse.

The boy, supposing him not to have heard, repeated the question, and Andrew said roughly, "She's dead."

Sir Matthew dropped the strap. The words were echoing inside his mind but he made no sense of them. His eyes had a dullness which groped for meaning as he stared at the shattered mask among the straw. She had always been so pretty, too quick for him, he knew that. As a girl she had flashed into rooms like summer sunlight, taking his breath away. She had made him feel slow and stupid. Sometimes she had laughed at him but he had imagined tenderness in her laughter and been content. Now he looked back and wondered. He had had suspicions many times before but pushed them away as worthless lack of trust. Only since Sophy's death had he really asked questions, not wishing for answers. There had been a terrible gulf between them since Sophy was killed. They should have come together over it, comforted each other, but somehow they had become enemies, strangers.

What did he know of her? What had he ever known? Looking back his life had been one round of eating, drinking, hunting, sleeping. What had hers been? He had never asked.

Seeing her on her knees in the stable before a half-clad boy doing those foul things to him he had felt his mind explode. It had been worse than when Sophy was killed.

In his mind Sophy had still been a child and the gross brutality done to her had seared his mind, haunted him, but seeing his wife do such things, forced to witness his own shame, hers, had burnt in the back of his throat like acid. It burnt there now. Oh, God, he thought, how could she? He was not incapable of fondling a servant girl himself. He had now and then strayed from the marriage bed in the past. Once or twice there had been brief liaisons. But it had always been the simple act, done quickly and forgotten. Not that. Whores might do it. He knew of such things. He was no innocent. But his wife . . . she had not merely betrayed him, she had broken his pride by what she did. He could not look at the silent boy beside him. It would have been easier if he could have blamed the boy but he had heard too clearly the note of shame in the boy's voice as he begged her to stop.

He straightened his body without looking at his son or the boy, then turned and walked out of the stable with a heavy tread.

Jacob knelt down on the other side of the body and stared down at the tangled hair, the bloody features. He could not recognise anything in the ruin which had once been a woman.

In the house the guests laughed and danced. Music drifted out on the chill night air. Andrew shivered. Where had his father gone? Ought he to follow him? Papa might do something stupid. Who could blame him if he did? Andrew swallowed on bile. Christ. To see one's mother . . . no, he could not, would not think of it. And James in London buying little girls. Son of his mother. Was there a curse on the whole damned family? Too much inbreeding in the past, perhaps. They said it led to insanity.

"Shall I carry her into the house, sir?" Jacob asked him and Andrew started. He looked across the body and a dark flush ran up his face. His eyes skidded away from the boy. "I will do it," he said. He wanted to scream out: do not touch my mother! But the boy's face was so gentle. There was quiet strength in it, a pity he hated but could feel. All the same, Andrew could not stand the sight of him. He would never want to look on his face again. Hoarsely he said: "You had better go."

"Go where, sir?" Jacob asked without surprise.

"Damn you, I don't know. I don't care. Just get out of here. Don't let my father see you again."

Did he have to explain it to this numbskull? Couldn't he see, feel what his presence did to them?

He put both hands under her and sweated as she bonelessly yielded in his arms. Her head fell limply back across his arm. He averted his eyes from the bloody features. Walking across the yard the wind lifted her hair in a winnowing caress, blowing strands of it over his sleeve. Her wig had been left on the straw. He had not cared to pick it up. She had not had her head shaved for some time and the little curls were childlike, fine and soft, the same colour as Sophy's had been.

What had made her as she was? As she had been, he thought. Death ended chance, the possibility of change. She was fixed for ever in his mind at a moment of horror.

Sir Matthew went out into the stableyard ten minutes later and vanished into the lantern-lit stalls. A shot rang out. There was a slow rustling in the straw and then a thud.

Walking back, his pistol in his hand, he met Andrew running full tilt. "Papa," Andrew gasped, catching his arm. His blue eyes fixed on the pistol.

"Don't be a fool, boy," Sir Matthew said heavily, seeing the look on his face. "I shot the horse." Then he walked past his son into the house again and Andrew stood in the night air with tears running down his white face.

Twelve

JABEY SAT HUNCHED in the sun eating a mess of cold pease-pudding. It was all he had had to eat since an unsavoury supper the night before. Nancy had slapped it before him, her expression daring him to say a word, and grimly Jabey had eaten the stale barley bread and sweating cheese, knowing the larder held nothing else and that there was no point in chiding her since that would only lead to tears and violent counter accusation. The baby had been crying in its cradle. Even the fire, with rain spitting down the chimney into it, had had a sulky air.

Summer's somnolence lay thickly on the works. The men stretched out for their brief midday meal enjoying the moments in the heat which was so unlike the fiery blast of the furnaces, a warmth that relaxed and calmed, making one think of cool streams and the shade of moving branches. Jabey grimaced. Except that the little stream near the works which had once run crystal clear was now the colour of blood, polluted by the iron ore which lay in vast heaps beside it. The banks were trodden mud, even in this weather, the stench carried by the water flowing on with it for half a mile.

Glancing up Jabey saw the new maid at the house industriously washing the dust-laden windows, her trim body moving with quick, neat gestures. Some of the men whistled, watching her, and she turned her black head to give them a pert smile.

"There's a dainty piece," Joe Herrot grinned, stretching his bare arms above his head. Sweat glistened on his skin turning the grime encrusting it to running ooze. He brushed a hand against his face and the smears made him a comical sight. "Hey, Marian! How about a walk with me on Sunday?" he bellowed.

"I'm not that hard up for a man," the girl retorted, but she half smiled. Joe Herrot had a brawny body, thought Jabey. He was a man girls looked at and he knew it. He knew little else. He spent his hours after work drinking at the inn, bowling, wrestling, gambling on the cocks which were set to fight to the death behind the inn. His money went in his pleasures. Of course, he had no family to feed. He had drifted here from the north and settled like driftwood caught on an ebbing tide and stranded high on a beach. It was, Jabey told himself, typical of the man that he exerted no will to stay or go. Marian would get an ill bargain if she let him push his way into her life.

Hannah had engaged her in the village. She had replaced Nancy. Jabey finished his distasteful meal and swallowed some beer to wash it down his throat. Jem Tiler appeared in the workshop door and shouted to the men. "Get back, you lazy crew. Time's up."

The men, grumbling, got up and began to troop back to work. Jem glanced at Jabey and nodded. "How's the babe?"

"Better this morning," Jabey said, his face sombre. Little Ruth was not a strong child. She ailed from time to time with a weakness of the bowels which Nancy found difficult to cope with, sickened by the necessary tasks the illness forced upon her.

"That's good news," Jem said, watching him, a frown between his brows. He and Jabey had become good friends over the past months. Jem's wife had died in the harsh days of spring, leaving her little ones motherless and Jem bitter with fate. Jabey had felt a kinship with him in those weeks. Hannah had arranged to have the children cared for by Molly Cregen, but although Molly did her best for Jem, the man had turned to drink to sink his sorrow and Joss had threatened to dismiss him after a succession of violent incidents. Hannah had spoken to Jabey, and Jabey had made it his business to stick close to Jem out of work, drinking with him if he insisted, challenging him to bowls, walking with him across the fields as spring became summer. They had talked as they walked and come closer as each recognised in the other the seeds of chill disillusionment. Their talk was never of the true subjects occupying their minds. They ranged from politics to work, arguing, laughing, grimacing, yet by skating over the surface of their problems they grew to understand each other.

Jem knew very well that Nancy, after a brief period of amused delight in her baby, had grown sulky and bored. He knew that Jabey resented her refusal to accept the life he offered her. He might wonder if Jabey knew how often, during his night shifts, Nancy left the house, but he never asked, nor did Jabey ever tell him. If Jabey knew of his wife's secret meetings with Joss Colby, he never gave a hint of it. Why had he married her? Jem often asked himself, but he never asked Jabey.

Jabey's stolid calmness under his misfortunes had its effect on Jem, all the same. He gave up drinking. He worked harder. He toned down his sharp retorts to Joss. When Hannah, however, suggested him to Joss as the new forehand, Joss looked at her incredulously. "Are you mad?"

"Poacher turned gamekeeper," she said lightly, smiling. "It's an old story, Joss, and I think it is right for him and us."

Joss surveyed her with drawn brows. "He's very thick with Stock, I notice. Your doing?"

"He and Jabey comfort each other." She neither denied nor confirmed it, her expression calm.

"So long as you give Stock no comfort," Joss said with a slow, searching stare.

"I'm too busy," she returned. "But will you give Jem the job?"

"Has he asked for it?"

"Of course not," she sighed. "Now would he? I doubt it has entered his head. He's the right man, though. I am sure of it. The men have always listened to him."

"He's a firebrand." Joss did not like him, his spine stiffening at sight of the man. Jem was a hothead, he thought, dangerous. Was Hannah losing her wits to suggest him?

"Give him a trial," she suggested. "Tell him he's being

considered for the job and let him see if he can keep the men in order. For a month, say?"

"No." Joss turned away but her quiet voice halted him.

"I think we should." She made it no stronger but he knew that note in her voice and his hair bristled angrily on the back of his head. It was rare for them to argue. It was always over something of this sort, one of her strange, quixotic ideas about the men. There was her idea of buying a boar and two sows to breed from so that each man could be given a piglet to rear in his garden on scraps from his table. Joss was scathing at her first mention of that, but the men had been delighted as they carried home their squirming pink prize. Several had died but most had fattened and now there was an air of excitement abroad in the works as the men competed to see whose pig would grow fattest. The children doted on the animals. Hannah had laughed saying that when pig-killing time came their tears would flow even if it meant sausages hanging in their larders and salted pork laid down for the long cold winter.

Her innovations had not stopped there. On a visit to Birmingham she had bought a bulk order of cheap material which she stored at the works and which the men could pay for over the year week by week so that when their wives needed clothes for themselves or the children, it was there for them. Although she did not stop the fines system she began a counter-measure by offering a bonus to any man who could show a clean slate at the end of each month. Joss had laughed at that, too, but it had amazed him by proving extremely productive. "The carrot not the stick, Joss," she had said and she had proved right. "This is not a charity," he had bit out, and Hannah had said, "No, indeed, it is common sense. Men do not always work hardest for the man with the whip."

So in the end he had given way over Jem Tiler. It infuriated him when she proved right again. Jem was astonished by his promotion, but although he would not drive the men he could, it seemed, coax and push them into working. He had stayed after his month's trial.

Although he had never been told so, Jem suspected his rise

to be due to Hannah's influence, and his respect for her had deepened. Now as he and Jabey turned to go back to work she emerged from the house and Jem halted, saluting her. "Good morning, Mrs. Colby."

Jabey looked round reluctantly. She crossed to join them, walking lightly in heeled shoes whose silver buckles shone in the sunlight, her body slender in the fashionable olive-green walking dress she wore, her throat and breasts half revealed by the square-cut neckline of the tight bodice, her features softly fleshed, coloured with health. The hazel eyes flashed green towards Jabey. "How are you, Jabey?" she asked gently. "How is Ruth?"

"Still ailing," he said, looking away because it hurt to see her. She had changed so much since her marriage, he thought. She had a presence she had never had before. The men looked smilingly when she passed them, eyes eager for her notice. Although Colby's iron hand still governed the works it was to Hannah that the men turned for comfort, advice or help, and she always gave it freely. Between shifts she let it be known that she was in her office if she was needed, and sometimes a little queue formed to seek her counsel. Joss, if he strode by, would eye it grimly but he said nothing.

Old Shield still lingered in the house, stumbling from room to room in drunken boredom, but he rarely ventured to the works, and his skin had a yellow tinge which deepened as time passed. It was a marvel he had lived so long, the men said, shrugging. He had saturated himself with drink. Pickled in it, they grinned. Perhaps it now kept him alive like eggs preserved in brine.

His hostility to Joss had become a grim resignation, partly because he relied on Joss to keep him company in the evening now and then, the old affection between them surfacing when they drank together. Joss was hard-headed. He never drank too much. He was too strong to be prepared to let his mind drown, but he would match the old man drink for drink at first, giving him the illusion of comradeship.

Some nights Hannah would hear them coming up to bed. Joss had to half-carry Master Shield, his strong arm round the old man's shrunken body, helping him as he stumbled on a stair. Once, hearing a crash, she ran out in her nightgown and saw them both lying tangled at the foot of the stairs. Master Shield was laughing drunkenly. There was blood on Joss's face where he had cut it on a nail projecting from the stair.

Joss hoisted the old man, swearing under his breath. When he saw Hannah he gave her a brief level look. "Open his door. My God, he weighs like lead."

She stood in the doorway and watched as with rough impatient tenderness Joss pulled off the old man's boots and breeches and covered him with the quilt. Almost at once Master Shield snored thickly. Joss came out, closing the door.

"Why do you let him go on drinking?" Hannah asked angrily.

"It's as good a way of killing yourself as any other," Joss said drily.

"If he wishes he were dead, that's your fault!" she accused.

"Everything is my fault," Joss said in grim humour. "I know that."

"You know why he drinks!"

"What do we ever know about each other?" Joss asked with a twisted little smile. "Why did he let his wife whip you for every little thing? Why did he stand aside and let me take the works? When he's drunk, d'you know what he talks of all the time? Your mother. I think since she died he has never cared if he lived or died at all. When I walked in, he was ready to welcome me with open arms because it left him free to kill himself his own way."

Hannah stared at him in amazement. "Is that what you tell yourself? Does it ease your conscience, Joss?"

"Conscience be damned," he ground out, his eyes angry. "The old fool has been dying of love for years. I just helped him on his way." He looked fiercely at her. "Women are sweet poison which a wise man shuns."

She turned away from the expression in his face and went quickly into her own room, bolting the door. Joss laughed harshly as he heard the bolt go home.

Looking at Jabey as she stood in the yard, Hannah

remembered her own trembling emotions as she stood listening to Joss laughing outside her room. They were all trapped in a situation which was growing more dangerous every day, but did Jabey guess that?

Once she had known Jabey's thoughts as easily as she knew her own but he had put up a shutter against her months ago. It disturbed her to see the difference in his eyes whenever she met him.

The sound of hoofs made them all look round. Jem glanced at Jabey and then looked away, pity in his face.

Andrew rode up and Hannah left the men to smile a greeting at him. Jabey stared in rigid attention. How did Colby like that? he asked himself. He hoped the bastard was eaten alive with jealousy.

Joss had taught himself to hide his reaction from Hannah but his anger festered beneath the surface of his controlled face. He stood at the office window now, watching Andrew smiling down at Hannah in an intimacy that was gall and wormwood to the man watching them.

He could be patient, he reminded himself. Time always brought a chance for revenge. Andrew Arandall should pay for what he was doing. Hannah should be the bait with which he lured the young gentleman and when she realised that, Joss smiled, she would rage helplessly. And she should pay too. She most of all. He clenched his fists, aching to have his hands on her.

He was meeting Nancy again on the nights when Jabey was on the night shift. Joss had not planned to start their involvement again. Nancy had come to him, sidling like a little cat, her sly blue eyes filled with invitation.

"Baggage," Joss had grinned, slapping her shapely little rear. "Be off with you. Do you want Stock to turn you out of doors?"

"I don't give a damn," she had spat. "Thinks himself better than me, does he? I'll show him."

Joss had raised a dark brow, understanding. "So that's the maggot in the apple?" He was tempted as he looked at her rounded body, much improved by her pregnancy, fuller and more inviting in those soft curves. Joss was sick of frustration, burning with impotent rage against Hannah. He had not had a woman for months and he suddenly succumbed to the physical need.

The girl never hid her hatred of Hannah. Her eyes spat it jealously whenever she mentioned Hannah's name, yet her emotions were more complex than straightforward jealousy. Nancy resented her husband's feelings for Hannah. The human heart was capable of oddly twisted reasoning, Joss thought. It stung in Nancy's breast that Jabey patronised and criticised her while placing Hannah on a pedestal. "She's no plaster saint. No better than me. Worse, if the truth were told. She's got them both dancing on a string, Jabey and the squire's son, but breathe a word against her round here and they are all up in arms for her." Then she would glance shrewdly, slyly at Joss, her blue eyes sharp. "You, too, I'll lay, for all you come to lie with me on moonlit nights. Is her bed closed to you, Joss? Is that it? I've seen you watch her. Is she cold? The men do not see it. She's bought their love with those damned pigs. Even Jabey has one but it doesn't do. It ails like the child."

My child, Joss had thought without deep interest. He had seen it. It bore too much resemblance to Nancy for him to recognise it for his own. Blue eyes, pale hair, a waxen complexion. No, Joss felt nothing for the pining little thing.

He had a bit and bridle on his temper where Hannah was concerned, but with Nancy he gave the wild steed free range, loosing the pent violence within him, using her sensuous little body forcefully. It was what she came for and what she got, sometimes more than she was prepared for, he realised. Some nights she cried after he had done. But she came back for more. Almost, he thought, as though she needed to be a victim to his freed violence, as though it redeemed her.

He needed it himself. If he had not had Nancy for an outlet he might have lost all control one night.

He turned away, gritting his teeth. One night, he thought. That thought was all that kept him sane. He carried it with him as a talisman. Murmured it to himself silently. One night he would tame her, crush her, inhale the fragrance of her surrendered body in all the exultation of triumph, but first he would have destroyed Andrew Arandall. He had already had his revenge on Jabey. It had been made easy for him by the fool's own actions. No doubt Jabey Stock had imagined that in wedding Nancy and fathering her bastard he was hitting back at Joss. Why else should he have done it? Well, he had been wrong. He was paying for his folly now, and would pay more in the future.

Nobody made a fool of Joss Colby.

Andrew was laughing at Hannah's French accent. "My God, they'd laugh you out of Versailles."

Unabashed, she grimaced. "I try to mimic you but it is not easy."

"My accent is appalling," he agreed cheerfully. "Must you learn French? Why in God's name? Do you mean to go there?"

"I mean to read French literature," she said. "They are our enemies, after all. It is wisest to know your enemy, Andrew."

And I know mine, he thought. That husband of yours. He grows like a beanstalk and we all stand in his shadow. Except perhaps you . . . He smiled at her and she smiled back, unaware of his thoughts.

People had ceased to raise their eyebrows at his constant presence at Shield House. When Hannah began to have dinner parties for ironmasters and their clients, Andrew was a regular guest. He gave their table cachet. His business dealings with Joss made it respectable and his polite manner to her in public underlined it. When Joss and Hannah were invited back, Andrew was frequently asked too. People began to couple them all together, as though Andrew was a member of the family.

"How's trade?" he enquired now, closing the French book which lay on the table.

Peg came in demurely with the tea tray and Hannah gestured to her to pour it. "We're doing very well. Better every day. We've more orders than we can fill."

He glanced at the pretty filagree necklace round her throat. "That's new."

"Joss gave it to me for the Naylor dinner," she said, fingering it, and looking down as it prompted a memory of Joss clasping it round her neck while he watched her in the mirror in their bedroom, the room he did not share and never had. Master Shield had insisted on giving it up to them, blithely unaware that the great bed only held Hannah afterwards. Joss used the small spare room. As Joss's fingers lingered on her nape she had been aware of his driving needs, tense until he moved away. He rarely touched her but when he did, however tight a rein he maintained on his features, she felt his emotions as strongly as he did, terrified of them.

"Very pretty," Andrew said. "His taste is good."

"Don't sound so surprised."

"Do I?" He caught Peg's disapproving eye as she passed his tea and smiled cheerfully at her to Hannah's hidden amusement. Dear Peg. How she grieved over Andrew's visits here, seeing them as what she called 'serpent visits', the temptation offered to Eve in the Garden of Eden. "You call this the Garden of Eden?" Hannah had teased her, laughing. "I hope God provided better than this for our ancestors." Peg had given her a horrified stare, lacking all humour. "I am sure Master Colby does not approve," she had said. Hannah had not answered. She was sure of it, too, but she had no intention of allowing him to interfere.

"How's Master Shield?" Andrew never let a visit pass without enquiring after the old man, partly from courtesy, partly from genuine interest.

"Well enough," she sighed.

"Still at the bottle?"

"He tries to stay away from it but . . ." She shrugged. She had abandoned all her attempts to save him from himself, seeing now his slow descent into the grave as a chosen path from which he would not be deterred. Joss had stolen his child and his manhood, in his eyes. He had the querulous temper now of the impotent, resentful of Joss, jealous of his energy yet abdicating all chance of defeating him. "He has given up hope, I am afraid."

Andrew looked down into his cup. "It shows in their faces, doesn't it?" Since Lady Arandall's death he had read it in his father's face.

Peg had stolen out, reproval in her face. Hannah glanced at Andrew soberly, wondering how much truth there was in the wild gossip which had circulated for months past about Lady Arandall's end. She had never mentioned it to him, nor he to her, and she never would.

"How is your father?" she asked instead and he expressively shrugged.

"Does all he used to do. Rides, hunts, drinks. But there's no heart left. He goes by habit as a dog follows old trails, old scents. He does not care any more."

She had watched Lady Arandall's silver-handled coffin carried through the churchyard on a windy winter morning. The villagers had crowded to watch her go with a sense of loss. She had been an indifferent patroness, selfish, shallow and proud, but she had provided them with endless gossip and they missed her. In their daily lives such creatures were like the eerie gleam of will o' the wisps at twilight. Even if they led the traveller astray they gave some touch of comfort to his gloom. Lady Arandall was a myth they liked to retell over winter fires. All the family provided them with the stuff of legends. They lived fully and although that pace consumed them young it gave out a great light by which the common people could see more clearly and which warmed them from a safe distance.

The whispers had been strengthened by Jacob's dismissal that night. He had vanished but was soon heard of working on a farm some miles off. Someone saw him at a fair and probed him with questions but the boy was not disposed to be talkative. They got no answers from him.

Even if Jacob had talked, his answers might have explained nothing. What could he tell them of Lady Arandall's mind? What could anyone else know of someone's motives? People did the strangest things and for the oddest reasons. She had

214

spent long hours herself in puzzling over Jabey's reason for marrying Nancy and come to no conclusion. He had told her himself that he did not love the girl and Hannah knew perfectly well why – Jabey still cared for herself and that touched her, hurt her. She felt the same fondness for him that she had always felt, but nothing more. Why was love given so uselessly, like water poured into sand?

Shaking herself out of her sad mood she asked Andrew: "How is your brother James now?"

He shrugged. "He has the pox, did I tell you?"

Hannah bit back a smile. "You did not need to – I had heard."

"Yes," he said drily. "One cannot keep a secret around here. His letters grow strange. It affects their minds, you know, sends some mad. He's taking the cure but even that can kill, I've heard. One takes one's life in one's hands every time one lets a doctor into the house."

"Peg would call it retribution," Hannah murmured.

"I wouldn't call her wrong." Andrew's eyes had a sombre intensity. "I often ask myself how much of it is fate and how much the result of the past. The Arandalls have led a wild life for years. Maybe we're paying for it now."

She winced, remembering his mother. "And your other brother?" she asked. "Is he still in Italy?"

He nodded. "God alone knows what he's up to – we don't. He never writes except to ask for more money. Which my father sends. Well, it is his, I suppose – it all comes to him in the end. The estate's entailed, of course. I shall get a pittance."

"It seems unjust when you have done so much to keep the estate solvent."

"I've enjoyed it. I find I've a taste for business, shameful though the admission seems to my father. My brothers would say I had the heart of a tradesman. Maybe I have. At least I am keeping Arandall afloat."

"While all they do is eat its profits."

"We must keep the land together. I'd die rather than sell a yard of Arandall land. Every acre is precious. If my brothers get their hands on it, it will all go down their gullets or into their bellies."

"Or on some woman's back," Hannah commented drily.

"Precisely." He grinned. "Thank God they can't sell. The only land I own is further down the river at Timperley. I've a fancy to build myself a house there some day. It's a pretty spot; good building land, level and dry, yet with a view of the river. When I've some capital I'll build my house."

"Is it part of Arandall?"

"No, I inherited from my aunt."

"The one who left you a small income which would not keep you in coals?" Her eyes danced green and teasing and Andrew laughed back at her.

"Aunt Hatty, yes. Good old soul. She fancied I'd a look of herself. She was a tartar. I'm not sure I'm flattered."

"Oh, I think you would pass in a crowd," Hannah teased, laughing.

"Would I, Hannah?" Andrew's eyes fixed on her face, that look in them again and she instinctively backed.

The door opened. Joss lounged in the doorway, his face coolly shuttered, but his eyes piercing as they shot from Andrew to Hannah. He nodded to Andrew. "Arandall! Been here long?"

Andrew looked at the mantel clock and made a face. "Too long, I'm afraid. I've outstayed my welcome."

"Oh, I'm sure you haven't," Joss drawled and his hard mouth held a smile which sent the blood to Andrew's soft-skinned face. He leapt to his feet, mumbling apologies. Joss watched mercilessly as he stumbled from the room after kissing Hannah's hand.

She sat facing Joss, her face expressionless. They heard Andrew ride off and in the silence which followed Joss sat down, his long legs flung out, his eyes on his boots.

"What was that about some land he owns?"

"Eavesdropping, were you?" Hannah looked at him angrily.

Joss's lip curled. "If I'd a taste for watching your lover court you, I'd sit in here and enjoy the spectacle."

"He's not my lover!"

"Not yet? He takes the devil of a time coming to the point. He must be a changeling. The Arandalls have quite another reputation."

"Talking of reputations," she said with contempt, "I heard some gossip this morning."

Joss looked at her with narrowed eyes. "Oh?"

Hannah had not wanted to listen but she had not been able to stop herself as she caught the whispered talk of two women at the lane end. Now she looked at Joss with bitter jealousy. "I knew you were without a conscience but how could you cuckold Jabey? After what he's done for her."

"Who says I have?"

"Don't bother to lie to me. Why Nancy? There are plenty of others you could take."

"Including you," Joss said, a hoarse note in his voice suddenly, sending a feverish colour into her cheeks and making her look away with lowered lashes.

"I'd rather cut my throat." She wondered inwardly that it was so easy to lie, knowing her cold voice carried conviction. He would not guess at her feelings when she first heard that he was meeting Nancy on those moonlit nights when Hannah herself lay watching silver stream down the bedroom walls and hungered for him.

"You frigid little bitch," he burst out, temper getting the better of him, those silvery eyes molten.

She stiffened. Joss caught hold of the broken reins of his control, forcing himself under again. Oh, God, he thought, staring at her cold face, one night, Hannah, when you least expect it, I'll sate myself with you, and when I am done you will be broken, finally and for ever mine. He had taken that oath and meant it at the time, his anger with her making it easier, but ever since he had known it meaningless. He had no fear of retribution for breaking the damned empty promise. Joss had regarded the Deity without awe from the day he beat his father with his own belt. The primitive religious codes by which Joe Colby had lived had made Joss detest religion, although he paid lip service to it on a Sunday, since he must to

217

avoid trouble. Hannah had made him swear on the Bible but Joss knew she had as little belief as himself. He stared at her, seeing the tense slender body, the masked face and cold eyes.

Excitement burned in his throat as he watched her. No, he thought, the dream is real enough, but how to capture it? How turn this cold, unresponsive woman into a lover?

He rose. She watched his lithe body saunter to the door. Over his shoulder he said mockingly, "Stock doesn't have the nerve for revenge. Nancy will fall on her back for other men for the rest of their lives and he will blink at it. Do you think he's gulled? He knew what he was getting but he felt he stole something from me when he wed her. He was wrong."

"You are wrong about Jabey," Hannah said. "I warn you, Joss."

He went out laughing.

He laughed a week later when Jabey broke his shift midway to go home after an accident to his arm. Regardless of the pain it caused him he went for Joss with a fierce scream of rage. Naked, Joss closed with him, grunting in amused surprise at Jabey's strength. Nancy drew the grimy sheet around her and watched in silence, a glint of satisfaction in her blue eyes. The baby wailed tinnily in a corner of the room.

A red mist blinded Jabey as he hit his enemy. He was breathing thickly, cursing under his breath in a mindless flood. How long, he thought? Did the whole works know of it? Did Hannah? What sort of blind fool did they think him? How they must have laughed behind his back. He remembered hidden smiles, sidelong looks. He had thought them due to the past but it had not been past. It had been going on behind his back. How many night shifts had he done recently? He had thought Joss was putting him down for them to help his income as they earned more at night. Now he saw other reasons for it. I'll kill him, he thought. Put horns on me, would he? Laughing at me now. He could feel Joss's laughter as his blows began to land. It stopped as Joss fought back, angry now himself. Jabey was fighting like a maniac, beside himself, no longer knowing anything but a desire to kill which ran in his veins like burning metal.

Joss was taken off-guard and flung across the tiny mud-floored room. Irritably he wished they had not chosen to use the cottage. They had been careful in the past but it was cold tonight and Nancy begged him to come indoors where they could stay longer and in more comfort without the fear of being disturbed.

Jabey was after him as he struggled for balance. The door flew open in their struggle and Joss fell out into the dark air. God, he thought. I'm stark naked. Shivering he tried to push his way back into the cottage but Jabey's fist connected suddenly and Joss reeled back, surprised by the power in the blow. Jabey was older than when they last fought, tougher, more fit. Joss landed in the ashes of the path and heard dogs begin to bark along the row of cottages. Lights came up. Faces peered. Voices crossly asked what was afoot.

"For God's sake, Jabey," Joss began, standing. "Let's finish this indoors. D'ye want the whole works knowing?"

"They already know, no doubt," Jabey grunted and drove his fist into Joss's stomach.

"Christ . . ." Joss gasped, folding up in agony. Jabey punched his bent neck and the breath rushed out of Joss's lungs with a fierce wince.

Jabey had hurt his own hand in the blows. He watched Joss go down to his knees and sucked his knuckles, feeling triumph in his veins.

"Hoping to make Hannah a widow, are you?" Joss asked mockingly, lifting his head with an effort.

Jabey's fist flashed at him but Joss rolled aside, ducking, and grabbed his ankles with a jerk that pulled him off his feet. Jabey's head hit the path and Joss lunged forward, smashing a blow deliberately at Jabey's unprotected jaw. Jabey's head rolled sideways and then there was silence. Joss clambered to his feet, shivering in the wind. Jabey did not move. Looking down at him briefly, Joss grimaced. "Poor bastard," he muttered, then walked into the cottage. Nancy looked at him nervously. He ignored her, dressing rapidly.

"You haven't killed him?" she whispered.

"Knocked him out," Joss said drily. "Well, that was the

last time, sweetheart. I've no ambition to feed the worms on your behalf. When Jabey comes to, tell him I leave you to him."

"What about me? He'll kill me. You can't leave me here with him, Joss."

"He's your husband. You wed him."

She sat up, her small white breasts clammy with sweat. "I'm frightened, Joss. Don't leave me here. Take me with you."

He looked askance at her. "Take you where? To my loving wife? You think she'd give you shelter? You knew the risks you ran, Nancy. You must bear them."

He walked out, closing the door, while the baby wailed weakly in her cradle and Nancy stared with stricken eyes at nothing.

Thirteen

TWO DAYS LATER Hannah and Andrew rode into Birmingham together. Hannah had another of her plans for the benefit of the men. It had occurred to her that she could extend her idea of selling them cloth cheaply to other items which they found hard to pay for on their wages. Discussing it with some of the women she discovered that they would be grateful if she carried a range of cheap iron utensils in the stores. Such objects were not made at Shields, of course, although they provided the iron with which craftsmen made them. She suggested to Joss that they start making them and he said irritably that there was not sufficient room to expand into such a trade at present.

"And when I do expand it won't be into iron pots," he muttered. "Wire drawing. That's my aim. I'll build a wire-drawing mill one day. But for that I'll need more land than is available around here." The cold grey eyes glanced at her and away, then he changed the subject to a brisk discussion on the weekly totals in production, which had risen again sharply.

Andrew had offered to escort her to Birmingham when she mentioned the idea of buying utensils cheaply. On the road they passed the tiny hamlet of Timperley and she said, "Isn't this where you have some land?"

"A dozen acres," he shrugged. "Good enough for a small farmer but no great fortune to me in rents."

She glanced around the flat, level landscape. The river wound slowly through the green fields, a silvery bow glinting in the sunlight, with willows and hazels fringing the banks and the air illuminated by that special radiance which comes on days when the sky is faintly misty yet bright, the sun diffused behind cloud.

"Where does your land lie?"

He pointed, halting his horse, leaning forward on the saddle pommel so that it creaked. Giving her a glance he said, "Why don't we go down and look at it? It's a pretty spot."

"Have we time?"

He smiled at her. "We can make time."

They rode down a narrow rutted cart track beside a low hedge and emerged on the river bank where the misty water had a languid brightness to it as it ran between the flat banks. A kingfisher flew across the river in a flash of rainbow colour and her eyes followed it with pleasure. The clean, cool waters lapped the green banks gently. A summer wind moved through the trees, making them sigh and brushing their long green trailing boughs to and fro across the grass. Hannah inhaled the sweet air and gave Andrew a brilliant smile.

"Can we get down and walk by the river?"

They tied their horses to a tree and walked, talking lightly. There was not another human being in sight. No rooftops showed among the level fields. A few cows grazed. There was barley rustling in one field, the whiskered ears rubbing together like dry hands.

She paused and looked around with a poignant feeling. "It is lovely here, Andrew. So tranquil."

"This is where I would build my house," he answered, pointing to a flat expanse of grass stretching away from the river. "What do you think?"

"It would be an idyllic spot," she agreed, imagining it. "A white house with an elegant plain facade. Stucco weathers faster than red brick and looks much better."

"Gardens going down to the river," he said, smiling.

"Walks for the ladies on dry days," Hannah murmured, a faraway look in her eyes. "And this marvellous view for them to see as they sit in the parlour."

"Drawing room," he corrected gently and she grinned at him.

"You'll never quite make me a lady, Andrew."

He touched her cheek with his hand. "You're finer than any lady I ever met."

A flush crept up under her skin and her eyes widened. Andrew moved closer, a strange look in his face, his blue eyes vivid. "Hannah," he muttered and brushed her lips with his mouth so lightly that the kiss had come and gone before she knew it.

She turned away hastily, shaken, and walked on along the river bank. A sleek wet water rat splashed suddenly from the bank to the river and swam away, ripples widening in its wake. Hannah jumped at the sound and laughed nervously. "Why, it is so quiet here after the works. And so fresh and clean. The water is pure as crystal. Look, Andrew, I can see the sand and pebbles at the bottom here, the green weed twisting in the flow, and little tiddlers darting behind stones. Mrs. Poley says it was like that once at Shields before the ore sullied the water."

Andrew stood at her back, listening to the jerky sentences, then said quietly, "I love you, Hannah."

She bit her lip. "When do you plan to build your house, Andrew? Will it have many rooms? It will cost a good deal, won't it?"

"You do not love Colby. You never have. You married him for the works. Hannah, I've a dream I've cherished for a good many years. I want to join the king in exile."

Hannah turned, startled, staring.

"He will come back, I'm sure of that. Ever since I was at Cambridge I've waited for it but lately I sense the tide swinging strongly in his direction. The people are sick of this German intruder. There are a good many wise and responsible men who are secretly against him, Hannah, and although they dare not declare themselves openly they would rise if the true king came back." He looked along the misty bright river with dreaming eyes, their blue glazed bright in the sunlight. "Half the sickness of this country is the perversion of the kingdom by that German butcher. If either James or my brother Tom came back to Arandall, I could go with a clear conscience, join my king, fight to free England from a foreign yoke."

223

Hannah drew in her lower lip with her small white teeth. "Oh, Andrew, don't be such a fool," she said impatiently, and he laughed, looking at her with tenderness.

"I knew you would say that."

"Then why d'you tell me such a wagon-load of nonsense? True king, indeed! A scaly, slippery lot, the Stuarts. German George may be a dull old boor, but at least he has English ministers. Bring back the Stuarts and inside a year we'd have the Pope on our backs."

"True king, true religion," Andrew said with a burning excitement which amazed her. "That is what attracts me, Hannah. The rightness of it. What is the English Church, after all? An arm of the state, founded by a lecherous old king for his own lewd purposes. But the Church of Rome, Hannah, that was founded by Christ himself."

She eyed him drily. "I thought you had grown out of such talk. We'd have martyrs roasting in the streets before we had time to turn round, and Peg one of them, I've no doubt, chanting her Bible as she burned. Is that what you want?"

"Of course not," he said, shaking his head. "You do not understand, Hannah."

"I understand they would clamp our necks in slavery," she retorted. "And I'll not bow my head for that, Andrew. Few Englishmen would. And that means civil war. Would you bring that on us?"

He groaned, gazing at her earnestly. "Of course not. But if we sit still and do nothing, this German dynasty will go on and on for ever. Hannah, if I did go to join the true king would you come?"

She stared incredulously. "Me? Join Jacobites? How can you ask that?"

"It would make it possible for us to be together," he said huskily. "No questions would be asked. You'd get away from Colby and I would always cherish you, Hannah."

She stared at him for a long moment, seeing he was in total earnest. "It might be right for you but not for me, Andrew. I'm no Jacobite. I would not throw in my lot with them for a fortune."

"And me?" he asked slowly. "Would you not throw in your lot with me, either, Hannah?"

Soberly she touched his arm, shaking her head. "It would not do. I'd be your mistress, Andrew, if I ran from Joss, and that's not the life for me." Her mouth moved derisively. "I may be my mother's daughter, but there's little of her in my blood. That's not my road."

"Not my mistress," he said urgently. "My wife. I swear it. In the sight of God you'd be my wife. Your marriage to Colby would not count in the Roman Church. We could be wed over in France by Roman rites and no word raised against you."

She turned and stared along the dreaming, tranquil river. The mist was lifting softly, leaving a bright clear day behind. "No, Andrew," she said. "I'm sorry. It would not do." Turning she walked towards where the horses were tethered and he followed after a moment with a heavy tread.

They returned from Birmingham that night to be met by Joss at the door of Shield House, the light streaming out behind his broad shoulders, his face barbed and cruel. Andrew wheeled away and rode off along the lane without a word and Joss came to lift Hannah from her saddle. She felt his hands on her waist with a shudder, moving away at once, her hand to her aching back. "It is a long ride to the town."

"Arandall looked sick," he said, giving her one of his sharp and penetrating stares. "Quarrelled with him, did you?" His mouth smiled icily. "Or did he try his luck, Hannah, and find as I have, that you're frigid?"

She walked into the house, stripping off her heavy leather gloves, discarding her cloak. "Peg, bring me some meat and bread to the dining room. I'm starved," she said at the kitchen door.

Joss followed her into the bright, polished room and lounged at the door, watching her closely. "What did you find to do in Birmingham all these hours?"

"I ordered the utensils, as I planned."

"And that took all day?"

"We rode slowly." To distract him from his questions she talked of Andrew's land at Timperley. "He wants to build a

225

house there by the river. We planned it, a good-sized, elegant house with a view of that lovely river. It is so peaceful after the stream here. Clean, bright and beautiful. Andrew's house should be perfectly sited there."

Joss came and sat down, one booted thigh swinging while he watched her, the rough shirt he wore open at the neck, his dark hair curling against the grey threads of the material. He breathed an air of raw male dominance, his presence too vibrant for this elegant room, as though he were more at home in the forge, the strident power in him a shock in this atmosphere.

"How much land has he?"

"I am not sure. A dozen acres or so, I think. A drop in the ocean compared to the Arandall holdings around here."

"You liked the idea of the house, Hannah?" he asked, smiling at her, taking her by surprise. "Would you have liked to live there?"

She felt her skin heating and looked away. Did he guess what Andrew had said to her? Joss had an uncanny ability to read her mind.

"It is a lovely place. Anyone would like to live there."

"Along the river, you say?"

"The land borders the river for a while, yes. It runs inland from the bank."

He nodded. "I'd not have thought Arandall had the money to build there. I'd heard he was penny-pinched."

"It can wait," she said, shrugging.

Peg came in with the food and Hannah set to, her head bent over the meal. Joss poured her some wine and set it by her plate and she glanced up to thank him.

"You do not like living so close to the works, do you, Hannah?" he murmured gently. "You've grown so ladylike of late. It has been in my mind to move from here and pull this house down to make room for new buildings for the works."

Hannah's eyes opened. "Pull down Shield House?"

"Why not? It is hardly beautiful. Now, an elegant gentleman's house down by the river at Timperley would alter our status, don't you think? Folk would think more of us if we lived there."

She gave him a quick, sharp look. "What's in your mind, Joss?"

"I was just thinking aloud," he said. "Look out for some good building land, Hannah, with room for a fine house and gardens. There is no hurry."

He leaned across and refilled her glass, poured himself some wine. Hannah watched him suspiciously. Joss had a look which was not unfamiliar to her, a glint in his grey eyes which threatened ill for someone. What was he up to now?

"Aren't you going out tonight?" she asked. Most nights he went off to call at the inn or keep a rendezvous with Nancy, but last night he had stayed at home and it appeared he meant to do so again tonight. The alteration in his habits puzzled her.

He gave her his mocking grin. "Eager to see the back of me, sweet wife?"

"You usually go out." She refused to be put out of countenance by the gleam in his eyes.

"Well, tonight I've a fancy to stay at home and be amused by my wife," he said tauntingly.

"Tired of Nancy, Joss?" she asked directly, her eyes contemptuous.

He leaned back in his chair carelessly, his black polished boot swinging over his knee. "Men do not tire of such as Nancy. She's too inventive in her games. No, I merely have no taste to get my throat cut."

Her quick mind came to it at once. "Jabey's found out?" She lost colour, her eyes anxious. "What happened?"

"He tried to kill me." Joss laughed softly.

Her eyes lashed him bitterly. My poor Jabey, she thought. Oh, God, what must he be going through now? Had he found them together? Oh, Jabey. I warned you. You would not listen.

Joss watched the storm in her face with narrowed eyes. "Stock brought it on himself. He'd no call to wed her. Nancy never was the wedding sort. She's a born whore. One man could never hope to keep her in a cage."

"Whores are made by men," Hannah bit back, hating him. "Was Jabey very angry with her?"

"Enough to kill her," Joss shrugged.

"What did he do?" Hannah put a trembling hand to her breast, feeling the fast beat of her heart under her palm.

"I told you, tried to kill me." Joss laughed again. "He had a good try, too. I was surprised he had so much guts."

"I warned you about Jabey. You underestimated him. But what has Nancy paid for all this? What did he do to her?"

"God knows," Joss said without caring. "I knocked him out and left them to get on with it. He no doubt beat the living daylights out of her. Much good it will do. She'll be on her back for someone else within a week."

She looked at him with furious distaste. "You selfish swine. Didn't you even stay to see she was not badly harmed? It was, after all, your fault.

His mouth contorted, anger in his eyes. "Mine? I took what was offered on a plate. How is it my fault? If it had not been me, it would have been one of the others. Sooner or later he'd have caught her in bed with someone else."

"I wish he had killed you," she flung, getting up and walking out of the room before she lost her temper altogether. Going up to her own room she undressed and put on her cambric nightgown, her fingers shaking as she did up the buttons. Her hair loose, she sat brushing it, the candle flickering beside her head, giving her reflection in the mirror a shimmering softness which put golden lights among her brown hairs.

The door pushed open. She looked into the mirror and met Joss's eyes, feeling her stomach contract. He never came into her room as a rule.

"What do you want?" she demanded tightly.

He did not answer, his eyes brooding on her, and she felt the piercing sweetness of desire thrust through her body, and knew what he was thinking.

"Please leave my room," she said tensely.

He closed the door and leaned against it, arms folded. She stared into the mirror at the tall, broad powerful body, her throat closing. He had a frown between his black brows. Neither spoke. The room was so quiet she could hear the quick rasp of his breathing.

A few paces separated them and Hannah was fiercely aware of the hunger burning between them. She slowly went on brushing her hair, her hand cold and trembling.

"You'll not mention my plan to old Shield," he said at last in a rough, flat tone.

She shrugged. "He would not let you pull this house down, anyway. Not while he is alive."

"That won't be for long," Joss said indifferently. "God alone knows how he has stayed breathing so long. He's so pickled I doubt a snake would bite him."

"Sometimes I hate you," she burst out. "How can you talk of the poor old man like that? You owe him everything."

Joss scowled. "I owe him nothing. I've worked for what I've got. The works does more business under me than it ever did under him. He just ticked along from year to year without a thought of anything but enough money to give him a good life."

"The works was his!" she retorted.

Joss made a violent sound of anger. "The iron trade does not belong to one man. He'd a duty to the workforce as well as to the trade itself. Expand, expand or stand still and then die. That's our choice, and you know it. We have to put back what we take out. Old Shield never did." The grey eyes glowed with a brilliant excitement. "Iron's a cruel mistress. You have to take her by the throat and rape her or you get nothing. The old man saw nothing but the little borders of his own world. He had no vision."

"Oh, is it vision that makes you talk of pulling down the old man's home? I thought it was greed, Joss Colby. Animal greed."

His eyes turned to hot glinting metal. "Call me an animal once more and I'll act like one."

For a moment they stared at each other. Her throat was dry and she pulsed with a hot excitement she could sense in him. Drawing back from the brink of destruction, she turned away. "Oh, I'll not tell him," she said shakily.

229

She could sense the war going on inside Joss, but in the end he, too, drew back, forcing himself under control again. He nodded curtly. "I'm glad to hear it." Then he turned and went, slamming the door, and she walked, shivering, to the bed and fell on it, biting her lip and closing her arms around her body in an effort to stop the violent trembling in her limbs.

One night, she thought, it would go too far, this dangerous game between them, and Joss would take her. She closed her eyes, shuddering. Torn between desire and fear she lay there in the candlelit room for as long as the flame lasted, and when she finally fell asleep the gutted candle smoked in the still air.

It was not long before the whispers running round the works found their way to her ears. Nancy had not been seen for days, she heard. Marion informed her of it, gossiping chattily as she did her work. "They say there was a fight a few nights since." She halted, biting off the sentence and gave Hannah a quick, curious and secret look. Hannah had never given the impression of caring what her husband did but all the servants were aware of his infidelity.

Hannah would normally not have shown interest, but she had to know what was at the root of all the talk. "Quarrelled with each other, you mean?" she asked lightly. "Well, that often happens. No doubt Nancy is staying indoors nursing a black eye."

"'Tis more than that," Marion said eagerly. "He took the baby and the other children along to Mrs. Cregen, and said Nancy was away, staying with relatives, but nobody saw her leave. She's not been seen for days."

Disturbed, Hannah took a walk along the lane to the cottages later that day and knocked at Jabey's door, aware of eyes watching her from other houses as she waited. There was no answer. She pushed up the latch and stepped inside.

He was sitting beside the smoking fire in a hunched position on a low stool. His head turned with sullen animosity as she closed the door. It astonished and distressed her to see that look on his face. He did not look like Jabey. He looked, she thought with a sinking heart, like a morose animal: his cheeks hard-stubbled and grimy, his throat bare in an open shirt

230

which had not been washed for weeks, his hair tousled, an unkempt insolence in his whole appearance.

"What d'you want, Mrs. Colby?" he growled. "Has your bastard of a husband sent you down here to see what I'm up to?"

She walked over to him and put a hand on his shoulder, feeling the muscles contract under her touch. "Jabey, Jabey. What can I say?"

"Say goodbye, Mrs. Colby," he muttered. "And get out of here. I wonder he let you come. Doesn't it occur to him that I might play tit for tat?"

She gave him a puzzled look, and his brown eyes moved over her in a fashion which was unmistakable and made her colour rise.

"Don't, Jabey," she said in a low voice, and lifted her hand to touch his hair, stroking down the rough strands gently.

He hissed through his tight teeth, then his hand came up and pulled her down across his knees, and his mouth sought her lips fiercely.

She made no attempt to struggle but there was no answering hunger in her mouth as it lay under his and gradually he lifted his head, breathing hard.

"You never have wanted me like that, have you, Hannah? Even that slut of a wife of mine gave me more loving than I could get from you." His arm still held her prisoner on his knees and he stared at her fixedly. "I walked in and found them at it. I saw red, Hannah. My eyes were filled with blood. I'd have killed him if I could but he's too strong and too damned sly."

She put a hand to his cheek, stroking it lovingly. "My poor darling Jabey. I wish you had killed him."

His eyes burned. "You lie, Hannah. Don't lie to me. I've seen you look at him when his back was turned. Do you think I don't know that look?"

She looked down, flushing more deeply. "What of Nancy, Jabey? Where is she?"

"Gone," he said. "And good riddance."

"Gone where?" She looked anxiously at him.

He shrugged sullenly. "Who knows? He laid me out and when I came round she'd gone. Maybe he spirited her away. I've no doubt he's got her nicely salted away somewhere. Then he can use her body when he has the fancy and get no husband bursting in to spoil his fun."

She frowned. "No, Jabey. Joss doesn't know where she is."

"So he tells you. He lies."

"Why should he?" she asked.

"To keep it from me," Jabey said. "If I found her, I'd kill her."

Hannah shivered. That was possible, she thought, but Joss had rarely lied to her before. "He said he left her here," she said slowly.

"Well, so he would," Jabey muttered.

She moved to get up and he reluctantly let her go. "You need to wash and comb your hair, Jabey," she told him with gentle teasing. "You look like a bear. That shirt is filthy and you need to shave."

He shrugged, indifferent. She sighed, shaking her head. "Where are your clean shirts?"

"What clean shirts?" he asked derisively. "D'you think she washed my shirts? She never even washed herself."

Hannah sighed. "Take that one off and I'll wash it for you while I'm here." She filled the kettle with clean water from the butt outside in the garden and put it on the fire, then made him take off his shirt and combed his hair for him. While he reluctantly shaved she washed the shirt through and hung it in the garden on the bushes. She knew the neighbours watched and ignored them. Going back into the house she found Jabey looking more himself, his face clean-shaven and his hair damp around his temples.

As he had said, there were no clean shirts. "You'll have to give me these objects," she said, clicking her tongue in disapproval. "I'll have them washed at the house. You must go bare-chested for a while."

There was little food in the house. She found some old bread and mouldy cheese. Scraping the mould off the cheese she mashed it into a saucepan and heated it over the fire while she toasted the bread, then laid the toast and bubbling cheese before Jabey. The odour of the hot cheese made his nostrils quiver. He ate ravenously.

"How long is it since you had food?" she asked scoldingly.

"Can't remember." His face was still sullen but he was looking more normal.

She sighed. "I must go. Are you on shift tonight?"

"Yes," he said. His hand came up and touched her silken skirts. "Don't leave me, Hannah."

She gave a low cry of compassion, bending over him, and his arms came round her waist. He pushed his face into her waistline like an unhappy child, and she stroked his hair, murmuring to him.

She felt the need growing inside him and tried to move away but he gave a strange, thick cry and the next moment he was carrying her to the unmade bed in the room. "No, Jabey," Hannah cried in alarm, struggling, but he was past hearing.

His hands moved over her body hungrily as his mouth found her lips. She felt his weight press her down on the bed and knew she could do nothing to stop him. Torn between pity and alarm she struggled vainly, beating her fists on his back, and he groaned her name, kissing her wildly. Her dress was dragged down over her slender shoulders, his hands moving down as he began covering her collar-bone and breasts with eager kisses, then she felt him dragging her full skirts upwards. His knee began forcing itself between her legs and Hannah sobbed, "Please, Jabey, don't."

The next moment he was pulled away and she stared up, dumbfounded, as Joss's heavy fist smashed again and again into Jabey's face. Blood trickled from Jabey's nose and cuts around his eyes. For a moment he had been too startled to hit back but he staggered away and then came back at Joss with a low animal growl of rage only to be knocked flat by one crushing blow from that hard fist.

He lay still, not moving.

Joss looked round and there was fear in Hannah's face as she saw the glitter in his eyes. He looked down slowly at her from her her naked shoulders to her tumbled skirts. She shivered, pushing them down with a trembling hand.

"You stupid bitch. Couldn't you see what would happen if you came here? Or did you want him?" He took a step nearer, breathing faster. "If I thought that I'd . . ."

"Take me home, Joss," she said quickly, getting off the bed. She swayed, a hand to her pulsing forehead. He moved to her and she deliberately leant on him, closing her eyes. "I feel faint," she breathed.

"So you damned well should," he muttered. "He'd have had you in another five minutes. And then I'd have killed him."

She said faintly, "Water . . . please."

He jerked her gown up around her, tidying it with an angry hand. "No more play acting, Hannah. You're no melting young lady to be frightened to death by a man's hunger. You've fought mine long enough. Stop acting." He pushed her to the door, a hand in her back.

Jabey stirred on the floor. His eyes flicked open and he looked around dazedly, then climbed to his knees and glared at Joss.

"Next time I'll take your head off," Joss told him ruthlessly.

"I nearly had her," Jabey said with an unpleasant grin. "You never have, have you, Colby? I've got closer than you. That surprised me. I'd no notion she was untouched until just now. Maybe next time."

Joss just looked at him and there was murder in his eyes. Jabey laughed hoarsely as they went out of the door.

Joss pushed her down the lane, his arm unkind. The neighbours would all be getting their pennyworth, she thought. The talk would be all round the works tomorrow. And Jabey would be at the works tonight with Joss stalking round him like a hungry animal with prey in its view.

She was thrust up the stairs to her bedroom without a word. Joss closed the door and looked icily at her. "He was right. He nearly had you. Keep away from him. If you take a step in his direction you'll sign his death warrant."

She ignored that. "I'm worried about Nancy. He says she

234

has gone but he does not know where. Where would she go?"

"Hell, I don't care," Joss said. "She's no loss. Are you listening to me, Hannah? Stay away from Stock. He wants vengeance and he knows how to get it, a vengeance which would give him a pleasure he's hungered after for months. He loves you. If you care a penny piece for him you'll stay away."

"No doubt it seems like justice in his eyes, not vengeance. You seem to forget what you and Nancy have done to him."

"What has that to do with it? Stock doesn't give any more for Nancy than I do. Half the men in the works have had what she gave me. Nancy was just the weapon Stock tried to use to beat me with, and it proved a two-edged sword." His eyes were harsh. "You are another matter."

"You shouldn't have let Jabey see you could be reached through me," Hannah said slowly.

Joss's mouth twisted. "I think he has known that for a long time but the soft fool would never use you in the past. Now, I'm not so sure."

She laughed unevenly. "Jabey has changed. He surprised me."

"If he touches you again I'll cut his throat," Joss said thickly. Hannah was so off-balance after the scene with Jabey that her eyes betrayed response and Joss gave a low growl before he pulled her into his arms and kissed her violently, locking his arms around her as though he would never let her go. She struggled to free herself from the wild sensations he was arousing but her heart was thudding against her ribs. At last, terrified of what might follow, she sank her teeth into his lip.

He gave a sharp cry of pain, releasing her, but his first angry look passed into tender amusement. "Wildcat," he muttered, smiling, as though she had given him a caress which delighted him.

There was a cry and a crash outside at that moment. They ran out to find Master Shield lying at the bottom of the stairs, blood on his head.

"Drunken old fool," Joss groaned, running down to lift the old man, shaking his head over him as he inspected his hurts.

The servants ran too, and together they put Master Shield to bed, leaving him breathing stertorously, his gashed head washed but still bloody. Hannah quietly slid off to her own room then and carefully bolted the door, guessing that Joss would try it later. He came with a silent step which she sensed intensely and the latch clicked uselessly. She heard him breathing outside and could feel his frustration. Then he went away and she relaxed, closing her eyes.

The whispers about Nancy's absence grew louder. People speculated more and more wildly about where she was and what had happened to her. It was, all the same, a deep shock to Hannah to hear that Jabey was suspected of doing away with her.

She was angry when she first heard it and spoke sharply to the servants. "What nonsense! I do not want to hear another word of such silly, spiteful talk."

"Where is she, then?" Marion asked, staring at her. "She's not been seen since that night. Her brother has been over asking for her and Jabey Stock put him out of the house."

"That proves nothing. She could be anywhere."

"Nobody saw her go. Why should she just vanish when she could be at her brother's house? Murdered, that's what she is . . . He killed her."

Hannah flared, white-faced. "It's lies. All lies."

"Oh, who can blame him?" Mrs. Poley asked, shaking her head. "Poor man. Distracted, I've no doubt, by her wicked ways. But murder's murder. Someone should do something."

The following day Nancy's brother laid information against Jabey, and the constables came and took him away for questioning. "He'll hang," the gossips said, excitedly shaking their heads. "Poor girl. Well, she was a slut but murder's murder. That poor child, motherless, and the father hanged! It's a shame."

Hannah looked at Joss with a strained white face. "You must stop this. Jabey would not do such a thing. It is lies."

"What can I do? I've not seen or heard of her since that night. Stock was half-demented. Angry enough to snap her neck and then hide the body. Many a man has run mad for

236

less." He looked at her fixedly. "I've been tempted myself."

"It's your fault," she cried bitterly. "You've brought Jabey to this!"

"If Stock goes to the gallows for Nancy it's because he's a fool," Joss said coldly. "He married her. Now he can hang for her." He moved to the door. "I've paid Molly Cregen to take the child. Or did you want her here?" His sarcastic smile made Hannah want to strike him.

"She's your child. Do as you please."

"If I did as I pleased, Hannah, Nancy would have been caught with some other man. Lay the guilt at my door, if you wish, but had you let me into your bed you know I'd never have looked at the little slut."

She had no answer to that. He looked ironically at her as he closed the door, and Hannah felt tears burning behind her eyes.

Fourteen

IT WAS HANNAH, however, who saved Jabey from the threat of the gallows. A stray remark of Joss's gave her the idea. He had called Nancy a born whore. Where, Hannah thought suddenly, would one find a whore in this part of the world but Birmingham? She did not bother to discuss her suspicions with Joss. Andrew had often tried to persuade her to visit the city with him in order to go to the theatre. It would mean that she had to spend the night in Birmingham, however, and Joss would not have that, so she had never even considered the idea before. Now she knew she must go. If Nancy was anywhere, she would be in the dark alleys of Birmingham at night.

"I could stay with your mother for the night," she said and Joss eyed her sharply, the dark-stubbled features weary after a long day.

"How can I be sure of that?" he asked unpleasantly. "Is this a cover for a rather more private meeting with Arandall?"

"I want to go to see a play." Her hazel eyes were clear and direct. He probed them without learning anything. She had long learnt to put up a guard against him. Joss could not pierce the outward calmness of her mask.

When Andrew came to fetch her for the drive into Birmingham, however, Joss was oddly civil. He smiled a good deal and offered Andrew a glass of wine. While Hannah got ready the two men sat in the parlour talking politely. She heard the murmur of their voices and wondered what Joss was thinking as he smiled at Andrew.

She joined them and at once noticed that Andrew looked pale. Joss smiled at her and touched her cheek with one hand, surprising her and arousing her suspicions again. He said nothing, however, that could warn her.

On the ride to Birmingham Andrew was almost silent, a frown between his eyes. Hannah at last asked nervously if something were wrong. He looked at her sideways. "No," he said flatly.

She forgot her concern as they rode into Birmingham. She had told Andrew of her idea of finding Nancy and he had given out little hope. "There are enough whores in the alleys to stock a hundred brothels," he shrugged. "You've little chance of finding her if she is here. It would be like finding a needle in a haystack."

They visited the shops and ate at a quiet inn. When darkness fell Andrew took her arm and guided her through the labyrinth of squalid little alleyways and courts while from the shadows women hissed husky invitations which Andrew ignored. "We cannot walk here all night, Hannah," he said irritably. "Let us visit the theatre and forget this notion of yours."

Her feet hurt and her back ached. She was forced to agree. The idea had been a wild shot at random. She should have known she would not just walk in and find Nancy.

The theatre was packed solidly, an overpowering smell of rank bodies pouring out from the audience. Hannah ate an orange as she listened to the shouted, ranting words. For a while she was disillusioned by what she saw and heard. It was too obviously play acting, the strutted movements, the raised voices dispelling illusion, but then gradually her mind lost that consciousness of pretence. The play sank its claws into her mind and she leant forward, open-mouthed, riveted, impelled by the emotions in the words and now believing as a child.

When they emerged her hands were red from clapping and Andrew smiled at her, the remote chillness gone from his face.

"You enjoyed it."

"Oh, yes," she agreed excitedly . . . "It was not as I'd expected."

"We must go again," he said and then stopped as Hannah's eyes moved past him into a narrow alley. A linkboy's flaming torch showed her some women in the darkness, their faces turned towards the alley opening.

"Nancy," she shouted, and one of the figures stiffened and looked, then turned and began to run. Hannah ran after her with the other whores laughing raucously, shouting obscenities. Andrew followed after a moment, swearing under his breath, feeling a fool as the women cackled at him as he passed them . . .

It was Andrew who caught up with Nancy. He held her squirming, cursing figure until Hannah reached them. Panting, she looked into the white-painted face and saw hatred in Nancy's eyes.

"You have to come back, Nancy," Hannah said quietly.

Nancy used a word that made Andrew flush and Hannah wince.

"You must," Hannah told her. "Jabey has been arrested on suspicion of killing you."

Nancy stared incredulously and then began to laugh. She pushed Andrew away and straightened. "No need for me to come back," she said. Her hand jabbed at Andrew's chest. "He has seen me. He can stand witness that I'm alive."

"Nancy, this life will kill you," Hannah said in a low voice. Even in a short time it had altered Nancy. That much was written in her painted face. The wreck of all hope lay in her bitter eyes. Hannah could smell cheap gin on her breath, could guess dimly at the life she led here. For all Nancy's knowing slyness she was a country girl used to life in a small village among people she knew. The uncaring rush of town life would destroy her. The sale of her body daily would destroy her even faster.

Nancy shrugged. "Let it. Jabey'll be better off without me."

"And your child?"

"Let your husband look after his child," Nancy spat, laughing. "Do you think anyone was fooled by my marrying Jabey? Ruth's Joss Colby's brat and you know it."

"It will kill Jabey to know what you've become," Hannah said angrily.

Nancy stared at her spitefully. "He always knew I was a whore in all but name. I've taken enough of his condescending kindness. I want no more of it or him."

Then she was gone into the dark shadows and Andrew caught Hannah's arm as she would have followed. "No. She is right. Let her go.. She has chosen her life."

"It chose her," Hannah said angrily, but she made no further attempt to stop Nancy.

They rode to Joss's mother's house together and parted. Hannah found it easy to talk to the slight, weary woman who had given Joss life. They both loved him and they both knew him for what he was. They sat by candlelight for an hour talking of him in quiet tones. "He'll never be content," his mother said. "Born hungry, Joss was."

"Why don't you come and live with us?" Hannah suggested. "I should like to have you."

"No, my dear. I love Joss but I see quite enough of him now. At close quarters he's like a lion in a cage that hasn't been fed for a week . . ." His mother laughed wryly. "I'd spend my days jumping whenever I heard his voice."

As I do, Hannah thought.

When she and Andrew returned to the works Joss met them at the door of Shield House and listened as Andrew quietly told him that they had seen Nancy. Joss grimaced ironically.

"Shall you inform the authorities or I? They've dug up Stock's garden today. They didn't find anything, of course, only the white skull of a sheep. For a moment the people watching thought they had found Nancy and I'd swear they were enthralled. They were greedy for proof he'd killed her."

"I'll tell them," Andrew nodded expressionlessly. He paused, looking at his shoes. "Will you come up to Arandall House tomorrow to discuss that other matter?"

"What time?" Joss asked coolly.

"Come at three," Andrew said and turned away.

"What other matter?" Hannah asked, certain that Joss was up to something. Andrew had looked almost ill.

Joss gave her a barbed little smile. "Business," he said and refused to answer any more of her questions.

Andrew found his father sitting in the library with a letter clutched in his hand and tears running down his face. "What is it?" he asked anxiously, bending over the squire.

"James," said his father in a broken voice.

Andrew removed the letter from the tight fingers which held it and hurriedly read it, turning pale. James was dead. Found cold and stiff by his servant in the morning, having died sometime in the night alone.

"Those damned physicians," Andrew said furiously. "They killed him with their mercury and their bottles of poison."

Sir Matthew raised his head, the heavy face wet and drawn. "If Tom doesn't come back from Italy, you'll inherit Arandall," he said. "You're all I have left, boy. Five sons and only one left. It was easier when they died as babies. All these years of watching him grow only to have him die like a poisoned rat."

The poison had been in James's blood for years before that, Andrew thought. He had imbibed it with his mother's milk. The dead woman's defiling fingers still stretched out to destroy her children from the grave. He looked at his father's morose face. Did he realise that? Did he know now what he had done when he brought her to this house as a sixteen-year-old bride? All those years of their childhood when he and his brothers watched their mother and heard the whispered gossip. Poor James, he thought. What chance did he have?

"Tom will come back," he reassured his father. "He's too much an Englishman to stop abroad."

James was already buried. His body had been too far gone in decay to be left above ground. It hurt and yet it was kinder that way. His death and burial had occurred so far away that the sight and sound of it had not touched them until now. The girls cried, of course, and their tears made it easier for Sir Matthew to come to terms with the death. In comforting them he comforted himself.

Andrew sent for the family lawyer the following morning

and was closeted with him for half an hour. Joss arrived that afternoon and spent some time with Andrew and the lawyer in the library, emerging with a smile on his face. He said nothing to Hannah of his motive for the meeting and when she spoke to Andrew he said nothing, either. He seemed changed, though, his face remote. She wondered angrily what Joss had said or done to make Andrew look so pale.

Andrew had been to the constable with news of Nancy's whereabouts that day. Jabey was reluctantly released and returned to the little cottage near the works to find his house in confusion and his garden dug up. The neighbours watched him from a distance, their faces embarrassed. They had believed the tale and now they felt ashamed.

"You are not to see him," Joss warned her. "Keep away."

"He should be told about Nancy," Hannah defied him, lifting her brown head to stare at him.

Joss's mouth hardened. "He knows. The constable will have told him that much and unless he's an even bigger fool than I took him for, Stock will forget her now."

"You've no conscience," Hannah accused. "You made Nancy what she is, Joss."

"She was a whore when I found her," he said impatiently. "I wasn't the first by five years. She had been at it as soon as she was out of childhood. It was in her blood."

"With the others it was just pleasure," Hannah said slowly. "You were different. You forced her to see herself in a light which has made her sick."

Joss stared at her. "Your precious Jabey did that. It was not I who hurt her, Hannah. It was him."

The words were a shock because suddenly she knew it was true. Jabey's chivalry in marrying her, his kindness, had hurt Nancy somehow. It had not been Joss who pushed Nancy over the edge into the dark night that now engulfed her. It had been Jabey.

The realisation sobered her. Joss watched her face and smiled coldly. "Yes," he said. "You see it now."

"Why is life so hard, Joss?" she asked with a wry look.

He shrugged the broad shoulders idly. "Why ask me? Did I

make the world as it is? We have to do what we can with what we find."

"Some of us are better at that than others."

His face had a cold strength as he smiled. "Is that meant for me? I hope I can use what I find, Hannah. I need to."

"Poor Jabey cannot."

His face had that harsh look, his eyes cruel. "Forget him. He was never for you."

She could not. Despite his warning she walked down to the cottage two days later but found it empty. Jabey, she discovered, had gone. "A pack on his back and not a word for any of us," a neighbour informed her excitedly. "God knows where he's off to. Birmingham, maybe, to find her."

No, Hannah thought. That was not Jabey's way. Where would he go? He had never left this little place in his life before. He was as rooted as one of the elms around the fields. Jabey had gone and with him had gone a large part of her childhood.

For a few weeks there was talk of little else but gradually it was all forgotten. People had short memories. They did not really care if Jabey hanged or Nancy whored in a squalid gutter. Either way it made a little gossip for them to exchange, a brief amusement. Once their pleasure in the tale had died they got back to the business of living, fighting for a crust, somehow surviving in the daily grind of the ironworks. Jabey was forgotten as if he had never been.

Hannah had seen little of Andrew of late. At first she had not noticed, occupied with sad memories of Jabey, and then she began to wonder, to worry. Day followed day and he did not come, although she knew he was at home at the great house. It was then she began to sense Joss watching her and to realise that Joss knew why Andrew had not come.

Sitting in her room one night getting ready for bed she heard his tread on the stairs and then his movements as he walked down the corridor. As he passed her door she called him and he stopped dead. After a long moment he opened the door.

She was in her demure white nightgown, her brown hair

loose around her face, her feet bare. Joss flicked a glance over her and then looked into her face.

"You called me?"

"What have you done to Andrew?"

She saw by the expression in his eyes that her suspicions were correct. He smiled. "I?"

"Why does he never come here now?"

"Perhaps he is tired of you." Joss laughed softly. "Hadn't that occurred to you, Hannah?"

She was not distracted. Her face cold she asked again. "What have you done to him, Joss?"

"We did a little business together, that is all," he said lightly.

"What business?"

He grinned. "I bought some land from him."

Her brain flashed at once to the acres by the river. "Timperley?"

He bent his head in agreement, his eyes amused.

"He sold you that land?" She could not believe it. Andrew had loved the dreaming green acres beside that quiet, sunny water. Surely he could not need money so badly that he would sell it?

She stared at the arrogant dark face. "Why have you bought it? To build a house so that you can tear this one down? Master Shield is still alive, remember. He'll never agree to it."

"Oh, I've no intention of pulling this house down," Joss said. "I like it."

"Then why have you bought Andrew's land?"

"I'm building a new mill down there," Joss drawled, smiling, watching her face.

The shock bit into her. "A mill? By that river?" She was white now, shaken, remembering the beauty of the place, the clean river running between its tranquil green fields. "You can't. Joss, you will destroy it. It will be ugly, like Shields. Ore littering the fields. Slagheaps. Dust, Filth. You cannot do that to Andrew's land."

"The builders move in next month," he said. "We'll clear the land now and next spring I'll start to build when the fine

245

weather comes and the roads are clear."

She sat on her bed, her clenched fist at her mouth. "Andrew agreed to this?"

Then Joss laughed softly, eyes burning with triumphant amusement. "Oh, no, Hannah. Andrew knows nothing of it. He sold me the land so that I could build a house for you and my child."

Hannah did not seem able to understand. She frowned, staring, her mind fighting for comprehension. "Child? What child?" Ruth? she thought. Nancy's child? Was that who he meant?

"The child Andrew thinks you carry," he said and watched white flow sharply up her face.

She understood it all at last. She understood why Andrew had kept away from her, why he had sold his acres to Joss without a word to her. Joss had tricked him into selling, lied to him, cheated him.

Anger made her so unstable she could have killed him if she had had a knife to hand. She looked at him with loathing. "You lying, cheating swine. You used me to trap Andrew into selling his lands."

"I thought that apt," Joss said softly, smiling. "Come, Hannah, with all this learning Arandall has taught you, you'll enjoy the irony of that."

"How could you?" she burst out. "Use me like that!"

"Arandall courted you under my very nose." He was not smiling now. His eyes were cold obsidian. "No man does that to me and gets away with it. I stuck the knife into his guts and smiled to see him bleed."

She flinched. "Oh, God, you are a cruel swine."

"I told you, I use any weapon that comes to hand. If Stock had not been such a weak fool he'd have used you against me long before he finally tried to do so. We all use each other, Hannah, if we can – the trick is to escape being used."

"Poor Andrew," she said slowly, remembering his beseeching face as he asked her to come away with him. Turning her cold face to Joss she said: "That is the last time you use me for any purpose. I am leaving you, Joss Colby."

He smiled, almost in physical satisfaction, and her heart missed a beat. She had expected anger but that smile was more terrifying than any words because the intention behind it was a threat she had been fearing for months. He reached round and she saw him bolt the door.

She backed to the other side of the bed, staring at him across it, shivering. "Get out of my room." The words were couched as a command but came out weakly as a plea and Joss smiled, undoing his shirt.

"Lay a finger on me and I'll kill you," she said in a voice that she tried to make strong but which issued from her white lips in a dry whisper.

He walked towards her and she knew there was no escape. She had been living in this house with Joss like a trapped mouse with a cat and now her fate had arrived. Joss had held back for months of his own will but if he chose to take her she would be helpless to stop him.

"You swore an oath," she reminded in a last attempt.

Joss threw back his head and laughed, the strong throat moving with loud amusement.

"Is that all your oaths are worth?" Hannah tried to lash him into anger, hoping to turn him from his purpose.

"Men bind themselves by oaths for their own purposes," Joss said coolly. "You forced me to that one and I hold it worthless. When did you start pleading piety, Hannah? You know as well as I do that the lip service you pay to the church on Sundays is not even skin deep. You have too good a brain to believe that God will strike me down for taking what is mine."

Her breath caught and he looked at her with a crooked smile. "Yes, mine," he repeated. "You've held me off long enough. My patience is not inexhaustible."

"I won't make it easy for you," she warned and his smile was almost grateful.

"Do you think I want you easy, Hannah?" His hand reached out to fondle her shoulder, his thumb moving in a circular caress. She pushed the hand away and Joss laughed. "Fight me, Hannah," he approved.

She flung her hand up and slapped his face hard. His head jerked back with the blow but he went on smiling and before she had recovered her own balance he had her arms in a vice, his fingers digging into her flesh, clamping her against him.

The devouring intensity of the kiss shocked her, bruising her mouth apart, probing intimately, his head forcing hers back until her stretched throat ached.

Hannah felt like a straw sucked helplessly into a whirling vortex but she would not abandon her long struggle against him. She would not meekly submit to whatever he chose to demand of her. As he thrust her down on to the bed she fought him; kicking, scratching, biting, like a maddened animal, her nails scoring dark red lines along his face, her teeth meeting in his flesh.

Joss was breathing thickly, laughing under his breath. He slapped her face so hard her head rolled on the pillow and her ears rang. His hands hurt her as ruthlessly as she hurt him, using the maximum of force, not bothering to try to coax her. Suddenly she realised that her fight was merely exciting him. Joss enjoyed pain, inflicting it and receiving it. The more she hurt him and the more he hurt her, the more he liked it.

The grey eyes glittered eagerly. His heart was pounding above her and his skin was hot as though he had a fever. He had thrust back her nightgown and his hands were fondling the struggling limbs he had uncovered, his breathing shallow and rapid.

"No, Joss!" At the brink of submission she gave a last sharp cry of protest, holding her thighs tightly, twisting to escape.

Brutally he forced her thighs apart. She saw the glazed, hot mask of his face as he penetrated her and her choked scream was cut off.

Joss was shaking, his eyes shut. When his flesh slid into the warm, receptive moistness of her body he felt the hair prickle on the back of his head. He had waited so long that he thought that long-deferred desire would erupt then into instant relief. He lay still, trying to fight it, struggling to hold back.

"Oh, God, Hannah, I have needed you," he whispered.

He raised his head as though his neck could barely carry it

and Hannah slowly lifted her mouth, her arms going round his neck. In that long, consuming kiss they drank from each other, merged at last, all other thoughts forgotten.

For a few moments it was enough, to kiss and be part of each other, then that too changed. Hunger leapt between them. He breathed in short, thick gasps as he moved on her and she writhed in fierce demand, her body inciting his, the driving movements of his loins met by her, arching receptively, engulfing him as he thudded into her. The hammer of his body met no passive metal now. Hannah was fire under him and the flames licked into his blood until Joss moaned aloud in a pleasure close to agony.

Their bodies moved convulsively together, each indifferent to the pain they might inflict, pursuing an elemental need upon each other, like fire tearing through grass, devouring and consuming as it went, because that was its nature.

Joss had always meant to force Hannah to submit to him one day, but he had seen himself using her body violently, crushing her into weak submission. The reality of her response sent him into frenzy.

For the first time in his life Joss Colby lost control of himself. His brain ceased to function. His body moved in its own necessity, his harsh moans of pleasure mere sobbing breaths. He had always used women ruthlessly, his appetite for their bodies deliberately indulged. He had never imagined a woman could wring such piercing, agonising pleasure out of him but now Hannah pulled him into a maelstrom of erotic urgency. He blindly spun round and round in the fierce core and all the cold, clever motions of his brain ceased as he felt himself drown in her.

The stark, driving force fell on her again and again. He hurt her and used her barbarously, piercing her until she knew she could die of him, but that little death no longer frightened her. She invited it with hot, silent ferocity and Joss shuddered and groaned at her response.

"I love you," he cried hoarsely and for a moment they both lay still in incredulity. Joss had never known until then that the emotion he felt whenever he thought of her was love. He

249

had thought of love as a weak sentiment, the vapid emotion of fools. Women had called him love and Joss had secretly despised them. He had known he hungered for Hannah with a harsh, physical need which ate at his vitals but he had not recognised that need as love. The word still seemed to him tepid, a frail and inadequate name for what he felt, but it served to tell her what Joss had to say. She was necessary to him; not merely her daily presence in his home, but this physical joining which she had resisted for so long.

It was not only Joss who suffered blinding revelation. Hannah discovered what she should have known from the first day she set eyes on him.

She was Joss Colby's woman. That was why she had always been able to read his mind, why she had fought him for so long. Other women might submit tamely to Joss's enforcing body, but Hannah had known herself his equal, his mate, and she would not have him use her as he had used others.

Theirs was a relationship fashioned in the blood, beyond the comprehension of the brain. Her mind had warned her that Joss would crush her as he had others, but her mind had not recognised what her blood had known – her own capacity to meet Joss Colby on an equal footing.

She had met pain with pain, her body hurting and exalting him, melting him as he melted her. The marks of her passion were visible on him, and each one inflicted had wrung a shuddering cry of pleasure from him.

Andrew had taught her to act like a lady, but it was the raw animal in Hannah which Joss had invoked. And as Joss cried out his love for her, she knew that she need never have feared him. His eyes told her that he was as helpless as herself in the grip of the extremity driving them both. When he made love to Nancy under her eyes she had seen him in complete control of himself, aware of everything he did. Now he was blind with passion, trembling.

"Joss," she whispered. "I love you," and gave him back the answer she sensed he needed.

He closed his eyes and sighed.

Locked together, they swept into the rushing waters of

oblivion, and fell, moaning, their bodies clamped together in mutual heat.

Neither spoke afterwards. They had exhausted all words. They fell into a deep, drained sleep, still locked together, and woke to find the room filled with daylight.

Hannah lay, eyes closed, listening to the muffled thud of his heart, that tilthammer which had pounded her into a wild malleability last night and which now kept up its regular pace beneath her cheek. Her lashes flickered against the warm, bare chest as she opened her eyes to look at him.

Joss looked at her, his eyes brilliant. She felt her face burn and he laughed. "Hannah, Hannah, is it wanton to lie with your husband?" His hand stroked her cheek. "Will you always be so hot in my bed? My God, Hannah, I thought I would burst into flames. I never guessed so much fire smouldered under your sullen little face or I'd have blown you into flame a long while since."

She wound her fingers into the short black hair on his chest, tugging it cruelly, feeling his intake of pleasurable breath. "You are still a conscienceless swine. You cheated Andrew out of his land."

"I paid him a good price."

"Joss, you'll destroy those lovely meadows if you build a mill!"

"I need a mill, woman. We shall make a fortune with a wire-drawing mill down there. I rode to look at it and it was exactly the site I wanted. A perfect site for a mill. Water at hand, flat land, good access from the road. It could not have been better."

"Give Andrew his land back, Joss," she said quietly.

He looked at her in silence for a moment. "No," he said in the end.

"If you want me, you will." Her gaze was steady.

"Are you threatening me, Hannah?"

"Yes. Either me or the mill, Joss."

He touched her cheek with one finger. "I'll have both."

"No."

Her cool voice and level gaze did not disturb him. He

smiled slowly. "I would not be the man I am if I listened to you. I am sorry, Hannah. Arandall does not need that land. What would he do with it if he had it? Leave it lying fallow for another fifty years, feeding a few skinny cows. No, I can make use of it. I need it. Our future depends upon it." The long fingers stroked her skin. "Yours and mine, Hannah, and our children's future too. It begins now, Hannah. The future is opening for us. Iron will be king in a few years and we must have that mill."

"How many mills do you want, Joss Colby?"

"As many as I can get. I told you, I'm not content with standing where I am. I mean to be as powerful as the Arandalls have been. They had the means to dictate all our lives once. The future passed out of their hands a while since. I have grabbed it into mine. Do you think I'll let your softness for Andrew Arandall alter my plans?"

She moved her hand slowly over his body and heard him gasping with pleasure in the caress. "Please, Joss."

"You think you have me in a noose, don't you, Hannah?" he murmured thickly, his face flushed. "You're wrong. Yes, in some ways I'm at your mercy now that you know I love you, but do you really think I'll do as you bid like some tame lapdog? I will not return the land to Arandall. In the spring my new mill shall rise up on his fields."

"You'll destroy that land."

He looked contemptuous, his hard bones taut. "I'll give work to hungry men. I'll feed children. I'll have iron pouring out of my works in wagon-loads. What do I care about a piece of land, a few green fields and a river?"

"Or me?" she asked stiffly.

Joss looked at her directly. "You would not use blackmail if you did not know I care. You call me a cheat, Hannah? What are you doing? Trying to make me do as you wish by threats? Would you sell yourself to me? How is that better than Nancy?"

She flushed. "You twist what I mean. You always do."

"Arandall is likely to have more land than any man has a right to want," Joss said.

"What land?" she frowned.

"James Arandall is dead and the elder stays on in Italy and shows no sign of coming home. They think he has become a monk. It begins to look as if Andrew Arandall will be master at the house before too long."

Hannah lay back, thinking. "He will make a fine squire. He has more conscience and more kindness than any of his forebears."

"And he'll not miss a few green acres," Joss murmured, watching her face.

"He will be very angry when he knows you lied about building me a house."

"My shoulders are broad enough to bear his anger," Joss told her with mocking indifference.

"And when he knows you lied when you said I was bearing your child he will hate you," she said with her eyes on his face.

Joss looked at her through half lowered lids. "That, at least, is likely to prove true. If I haven't made a son on you within a year I shall be disappointed."

"I hope you will be then!"

He laughed, pulling her down into the bed. "Oh, God, Hannah, I shall enjoy making my boast come true."

She relinquished the struggle after a moment, admitting angrily to herself that their lovemaking the night before had bred in her an irresistible need for him that even her anger with him could not fight. Damn him. He was so sure of his own power, so sure of his future, but he underestimated others from time to time, as he had dismissed Jabey until forced to recognise that passion and rage could change men's natures. He had underestimated Andrew, Hannah thought, and one day she suspected Andrew would surprise Joss, but for the moment there was nothing Andrew could do. Joss held the deeds of that land now. He would have his second mill. Andrew could not stop him. It would take a strong man to stop Joss Colby's headlong climb to power.

She remembered his mother's wry words. "Joss was born hungry." He was hungry for power, hungry for life, allowing nothing to stop him or get in his way. She realised now that she had been the only obstacle which had ever slowed Joss Colby's race to the future, and now he had her and she would never be a threat to him again.

We'll see, Joss, she thought. You may have got away with using underhand methods against Andrew this time but in future I'll have my eyes open and if you try such tricks again I'll surprise you. Loving you does not mean I will stand by and watch you cheat, lie, manipulate to get whatever you want. You are one of the strong and you know it. Few could ever trip you up. But I am one who could and we shall see.

Joss was angry. He sensed that she was not more than half aware of the caresses he was giving her and he needed her as she had been last night, that slight little body turning his blood to fire.

"What are you thinking?" he asked angrily. "Hannah?"

She lifted her lids and the hazel eyes shone bright as green glass. Joss gasped as she kissed him. "Oh, my love," he groaned and then all thought in either of them dissolved into the molten element of mutual need.